Rough Love

LM MORGAN

Copyright © 2022 LM Morgan
All rights reserved.
ISBN: 9798805490553

DEDICATION

For Ethan and Liz. I literally couldn't do any of this without you.
Thank you so much for your amazing support.

This is a work of fiction. Names, characters, places, and incidents are the products of the author's imagination or are used fictitiously. Any resemblance to actual events, locales, or persons, living or dead, is entirely coincidental.

PLEASE NOTE
This story depicts explicit sexual relationships between adults. It is absolutely not suitable for those under the age of 18.
Trigger warning – this story involves graphic sexual scenes, dark elements which some people may find upsetting.

Chapter One

"Ashes to ashes, dust to dust..." The coffin holding my sister's body was scattered with dirt by her nearest and dearest before being lowered into the ground. My heart broke watching her leave us. I hated being powerless against fate or whatever divine overseer decided it was time for her to go. I cursed everyone and everything, while not speaking a word the entire time.

Afterwards, everyone who had come to pay their respects left in search of a stiff drink and the promise of a buffet dinner. Everyone except my family and me. As we stood watch, my father held me tightly in his arms. His embrace was strong and supportive, yet I couldn't help but feel as though I was the one holding him upright, rather than the other way around.

It suddenly dawned on me how my only sister lay dead in the ground. I wish I could write about the fun times we'd shared, or reminisce over our lives together, but I couldn't. The truth is, she'd been a stranger to me most of my life, but I still felt the loss like a gaping hole in my heart. In a family of five children and a long-gone mother, the sad fact was that us girls hadn't stuck together. I wished it wasn't so, that we could go back and change things, but time doesn't work that way. Things done cannot simply be undone. She and I weren't a united front, staying strong in the face of all the men who guarded us and kept us safe, while they also controlled every aspect of our lives. I'd always wondered if it was perhaps our ten-year age gap, or because of how our personalities had seemed the polar opposite of each other's. I could never be sure.

Unlike me, Dita had a loud mouth and a temper on her to rival any of our three brothers. She was headstrong and independent until the very end, and while our father doted on her regardless, he and I had always been a closer and more natural team thanks to my quieter nature and easy-going attitude.

I knew I'd spent my twenty years alive on the planet wrapped in cotton wool. I was no fool. But part of me liked it. I enjoyed being a daddy's girl, and I didn't mind when he treated me like his baby, because that was how my entire life had always been. Now it was just my three brothers and me: Nico, Thomas, and Bradley. Dita was born between Nico and Thomas, and then Brad had quickly followed. Eight years later, I'd then been conceived out of the blue and had reportedly been utterly unplanned for my dear parents. Since the day I became more than just a rapidly growing bunch of cells they had doted on me, though. Twenty years later I knew my father saw in me a combination of the wife he'd lost to breast cancer when I was three years old, and the baby girl of the family who had never given him lip or caused trouble.

Dita, on the other hand, was a wild child. She was always out drinking and taking drugs, being brought home by the police, or by her latest squeeze. I'd often found her sneaking her boyfriends into our large house in the centre of Birmingham, England, in the middle of the night, much to our dad's dismay. There was only so much of that he could put up with before laying down the law, and it was something that always had me cowering in my boots, while Dita always acted as if she couldn't have cared less what he thought or the way he expected her to act.

To me, he was an intimidating man who I loved and respected more than anyone, but also feared in equal measure. Our dad had been a member of a local motorcycle club, the Black Knights, since long before any of us were born, and while the closeness of the club and security therein was all we'd ever known, the life could also make those affiliated with the club a little bit fearless. As though they thought they were untouchable. Dita was exactly that. It seemed to me as though nothing and no one could harm her without the weight of the club coming down on them hard, and while it was probably true, even I saw how she'd pushed her luck on a far too regular basis.

It wasn't until she started seeing my father's second-in-command and the club's Vice President, Tobin Stone, two years before that she finally calmed down. Her skirts were no longer the size of a belt, her language became less vulgar, and Dita had rarely gone out and come home drunk after that. She'd happily played the role of the powerful VP's doting fiancée, or so it'd appeared. Dad's right-hand-man had seemingly come through for my sister exactly when she'd needed it most. And yet, in the end, none of that had mattered. Nobody had been able to stop the inevitable from happening. A drunk driver had still run Dita over at a zebra crossing on her thirtieth birthday. I was told she'd been killed instantly. I guess you could call that a blessing, but I'm still not sure.

At the funeral, my dad, brothers, and I had stood

huddled together. We hadn't broken apart until the very end, when Nico led the other two away and left me to tend to our father. They also saw to the guests during the wake after the service was over, while I remained by Dad's side. He was void of not just emotion but also words, thoughts, and I think if I had left him alone long enough—breath. He seemed to have ceased everything to mourn her silently, yet somehow also so loudly it consumed me. I spent the entire afternoon with my hand in his, refusing to let go even when family members and friends tried to come and take him away for their obligatory, 'I'm sorry for your loss,' discussions. I didn't say a word either, I just watched him. My father looked older suddenly. The lines on his face were somehow deeper. The grey flecks in his hair more distinguished. He'd had dark brown hair once, but now it was like a mixture of what seemed to be a hundred different shades ranging from brown and grey to white. He hadn't lost any though and had barely receded, his hair still thick and full. I peered into his eyes, seeing sadness behind the dark brown hue of them, and I leaned into him a little more, offering as much comfort as I could.

When he later took his seat in the huge armchair that'd been his spot for as long as I could remember, I climbed into his lap as though I were still five years old and curled myself into his embrace. No one even batted an eye. We all knew I was too old for this, but he'd brought me up never to care what anyone thought of me. I might've been a mollycoddled Daddy's girl, but that suited me because people just left me alone rather than try to pull me into their drama. They knew I wasn't interested, and that I wasn't going to defy my father's order, that I remain well behaved.

Yes, he'd even gone as far as to dictate so much as

that over the years.

I never argued with it, though, or tried to resist him. An introvert at heart, I'd always loved the peace that being left to do my own thing and being locked away in self-imposed solitude brought. I loved nothing better than to curl up with a book and be alone. At only twenty years old, I'd already completed two master's degrees, and I had learned to speak three languages fluently. I'd never been drunk, had sex, or taken drugs, and hardly had any friends. I wanted and needed for nothing, and my father always saw to everything when it came to taking care of me. He controlled every aspect of my life, and I never once complained. I knew Dita hated him for controlling her in the same way as he did me and had lashed out because of it, but I couldn't be like that. She'd never understood how I could be okay with this life. But there we have it, just another example of how very different my sister and I were.

I guess in the end; I fell asleep in my father's arms, because the next thing I remember is him carrying me to my room. My brother Thomas woke me just long enough to tell me to get changed and go to bed, and after he left, I did just that. When I was finally alone, wearing nothing but the bare body I was born in, I slid under the covers and nestled myself within my thick duvet and soft sheets, fiddling with the corner of my pillow between my fingers—something I'd done since I was a little girl. I'd always slept naked, unable to sleep if I had any clothing on, or I'd always wake up dripping with sweat in the middle of the night. I was safe, though. My room was kept locked from the inside, and of course because my brothers were so protective no one would ever dare slip inside my ivory tower in our dad's house.

You see, my father, Garret Proctor, is an exceptionally powerful man. As far as I've always been aware, he's no drug-lord or gangster, but still feared and respected by all those who frequented our home to talk business with him. No one messes with him and gets away with it. Put it that way. My brothers are intimidating guys, too. They've all been highly trained in martial arts and other such skills from a young age, each of them huge, burly, and scary to almost anyone whose paths cross theirs. Even I know the stories of how nobody who ever got in their way seemed to stick around long enough to tell the tale.

The other thing that's made our family so powerful yet complete at the same time is that our father's not only a member of the Black Knights, but also the President of the motorbike club. My whole life, they've passed themselves off as just another group of motorcycle enthusiasts, but even I can tell that they're much more than that. They conduct secret dealings and have meetings all hours of the day and night. We've never wanted for anything yet no one in my family seems to work a nine-to-five to earn their wage. Their jobs are within the club. Their lives tied to it for seemingly ever, and I guess I figured mine was too, only I'd yet to find out in what capacity.

I loved it, though, the life I was born into. I've grown up listening to the purr of engines at any time, day or night. The roar of men's laughter and the backdrop of rock ballads were the background sounds of my youth. I always knew I was safe with them. Home.

But there were still the scary times, and I can be honest and say I've been sent off to safe houses far too many times for me to count. We have the highest spec security system I've ever known and I'm clever enough to know you only need that sort of protection when you have enemies who can penetrate the sort of security most homeowners invest in. I may've been protected, even from the truths, but I was never a fool. Well, I always thought I wasn't…

***

About a week after the funeral, I was sat lengthways on one of the large leather sofas in the living room of our home that doubled as the clubhouse. Things had gone back to relative normality, and the club was back to business as usual. Listening to music on my laptop, I was finally making time to check my emails and social media websites. There were so many people who'd commented to say they were sorry and offered their condolences to my family, but as far as I knew, hardly any of them had even been close to my sister, or me. It was all a farce. One ignorant bimbo after another wishing us well and saying they were sorry for our loss. I ignored more than half, while writing quick thank you notes back to the others.

A short while later, our housekeeper Sue brought me over a pot of tea. I hadn't asked for one, but it was just another typical British thing to do in times of grief, so I couldn't be surprised at her for having taken it upon herself to bring me a cup. I thanked her anyway and carried on with surfing the Internet and busying myself watching crappy videos and reading threads on my favourite blogs. I commented back and forth with a few of the regulars, as well as adding my own reviews for the movies, books, and new music releases they were debating about. This was my usual routine. My head in either a book or my laptop, and I was happy there. Content.

After another half an hour, the door opened and in walked the hardest looking group of men I'd ever seen. Anyone else might have wilted at seeing them, but these were my family, some by blood and others by service to my father and their club.

My sister's ex-fiancé, Tobin, stood at the head of the group. He was leading the way and looked intense, focussed, and full of purpose. I hadn't seen him since the funeral, so guessed that he'd taken a few days out to mourn Dita. We'd never spoken much, so I couldn't know for sure, but figured it had to have been hard losing the woman he was planning on marrying. Now, he was back, and his 'Vice President' badge on his cut was clear even from across the room. He caught me watching and stared back at me as he led the group over towards the huge meeting room where they were about to get together for church—their version of a business meeting.

After a couple seconds of our gazes locking, I thought I'd best look away, but Tobin then put me at ease by giving me a half smile. He also raised his hand in a polite wave, which I returned, and then he ducked inside the doorway to greet my father while the rest of their band of bikers milled around in the suddenly incredibly full living room of our home. My three brothers each grinned over at me, as did the other men, but everyone was quiet and ready for their summons, so didn't stop for chitchat, which was fine by me.

Looking around at the thirty or so men, all of them menacing and brutish, I knew they should scare me. That I ought to be wary of them. Any friends I'd ever made during my school years were all far too terrified of the club and its members' reputations to ever come over to my house, but I'd never seen them that way. They'd each taken care of me over the years, many of the older members having babysat me as a child or having given me lifts to school and back when my brothers were unavailable.

None of them ever looked at me or treated me the same way as they did the girls who draped themselves on their arms every weekend when they were looking for some fun. I think that to many of them I was like their own little sister, the protected one, and they knew how much my father doted on me so followed his lead without question. Neither my father nor I hid our closeness, so I always liked to think that as part of the newest members' initiation into the club they had to swear to never touch me or try anything, otherwise my dad or brothers would have their balls on a plate.

My father, Garret, was no idiot and didn't suffer fools gladly. Anyone who'd ever stepped on his toes usually ended up with a broken nose as their first warning and shattered kneecaps as their second. I never saw anyone after their third, but never dared to ask what the outcome would be those times. Part of me didn't want to know.

After the meeting was over, my father left the room first, wandering straight over to me and planting a kiss on my head before retiring to his study for some peace and quiet. I didn't follow him. He knew where I was if he wanted me, and we'd spent a lot of time together over the previous few days, so I decided to leave him to it. Even though he'd not necessarily asked me to stay with him while he mourned Dita, he hadn't asked me to leave either, so I had just sat and soundlessly provided him with the comfort and companionship I had somehow known he needed but would never ask for.

My eldest brother, Nico, then came and plonked down beside me. He gathered my legs up onto his lap and almost knocked my precious laptop on the floor as he did so.

"Hey!" I cried, gripping it like a baby, holding the computer to my chest when I had finally closed the screen. "This thing has my entire life on it," I added, smirking over at him. Nico had never been the computer geek type of guy. In fact, he barely knew how to use his smart phone, and didn't own a computer. Whereas I had two laptops plus tablets, e-readers, and mobile phones. Technology had always been a big thing for me. I loved working at computers. The logicality of it all and the intricate elements of web design and formatting were a big pull for me career wise, and I hoped to put that love and skill to good use one day.

My middle brother, Thomas, then sauntered over and took the seat to my left and grinned broadly, his dark brown eyes alight with mischief.

"No point trying, sis. He probably has no clue what that even is," he teased, giving Nico the finger when he gave him the hand gesture that indicated Thomas might be a habitual masturbator. I simply laughed and slid the computer under the sofa and out of the way as I pulled my feet up and grabbed my drink.

I then watched as the boys then resumed their usual night-time behaviour and each drank beers and shots, while I happily sipped on my tea or pushed the boat out with a cola here and there. Nico and Thomas could almost be twins. They looked so alike—both the double of our father with their dark brown hair and eyes. Nico was taller, though, and broader. He'd spent his entire life looking up to our dad and idolising him, and thanks to that he'd almost become a carbon copy of our patriarch—whether he'd done it on purpose or not.

They chatted loudly all around me while I sat quietly and went largely unnoticed as always, but one thing I did keep spotting out the corner of my eye was Tobin. He was playing pool with some of the other club members, winning as usual, and I kept catching his eyes on me. I was hardly part of the conversation around me, consisting mostly of my brothers throwing insults at one another or talking about their girlfriends, or lack of one in my closest brother, Brad's case. As the banter spilled out of them, I did as I always did. I smiled and listened, nodding, and laughing along with them, but not offering up my own part of the conversation. I wasn't confident enough to join in on the banter.

After a few more shots had been downed and the last cigarette of Nico's packet was finished, I finally stood and made my excuses. I always chose to leave before the group got too rowdy, and certainly before the half-dressed women arrived to fawn over and flirt with their biker boyfriends or desired conquests.

They understood and thankfully never pushed for me to stay longer than I felt comfortable. Nico decided it was his turn to see me upstairs, and he walked me to my room, where I hugged him goodbye, hating the pain that was still in his eyes. But I guess I must've had the same look in mine too, because he hugged me back just as tight, and I realised then how much I needed it.

He then turned and left without another word. So, in I went for my usual bedtime routine of relaxing with a movie or falling asleep listening to music, yanking off my thick cardigan as I went. When a knock at my door came just a few minutes later, I was sure it must be him again, so didn't hesitate to answer it. I flung open the door with a grin, but then stopped in my tracks when I found Tobin standing on the other side of my doorway. He was smiling down at me, his pale blue eyes bright with jollity, and he had my laptop in his hands.

"You forgot this," he murmured, handing it to me. I took it and thanked him and was then suddenly aware of how I was only wearing a revealing strappy vest top, but Tobin was being the perfect gentleman and so far, I hadn't noticed his eyes wander down to my very on-show cleavage even once.

We stood there for a moment, neither one of us saying a word, but I didn't mind. Whether it was the smell of his leather cut or the smoky remnants of the clubhouse bar on him, I simply had to take a deep breath of it and inhaled. That smell was home to me, more so than any air freshener or flowery linen. He grinned when he saw me relax and finally seemed to decide to say what was on his mind. "Urm... There's something I've been working on. It's out of town. Your father and I are taking your brothers to go and see it in about half an hour. Would you like to come?" he asked and began rubbing his stubbly chin with his fingertips.

I found myself staring at the tattoos on his hands. They were a strikingly colourful contrast to his olive skin and black clothes, looking almost delicate against his manly dress sense. But I'd always liked them. I'd wondered before how many other tattoos he had but had never even dared to ask Dita in case she got jealous. I didn't know why it intrigued me either, but for some reason I'd often thought about his ink and enjoyed looking at the designs he'd decided on.

"Sure, let me grab my jumper," I replied, in a bid to tear myself away from my staring. I then turned and wandered back into my room. I knew I'd need to cover-up before daring to head back out amongst the throb of men below. It wasn't a lesson I'd had to learn, but one that had been ingrained in me since childhood. If you didn't dress like a slut, they didn't treat you like one. As awful as it sounds, I had seen it for myself and knew it's true. My own brothers developed a harsher tongue when it came to dealing with a skimpily clothed girl than they did a well-dressed professional woman in a suit. I had adopted the same judgements thanks to their influence, so couldn't deny it affected my choice of wardrobe as well.

"Take an overnight bag, we're staying until at least tomorrow," Tobin informed me, breaking my thoughtfulness, so I quickly set about grabbing some toiletries and a change of clothes while he stood watch from the open doorway. I didn't complain about the intrusion or ask any questions about where we were going. I just did as he asked, and I could tell he seemed to like my compliance.

I began thinking about Tobin's history and wondered how he'd managed to become Vice President of the club after just a few years of membership. My father had chosen Tobin to replace his old VP when he had died suddenly, and I often considered whether Tobin had perhaps saved his life or something as remarkable as that, because Garret Proctor was nothing if not loyal to those who were true to him and served him well. He rewarded only those in the club who'd proven themselves trustworthy time and time again but had never put much stock in the new members until Tobin. Really, my brother Nico should've been awarded the badge, but not this time. The vote between club members had deemed Tobin the rightful taker of the VP title, and I'd noted at the time how Nico hadn't seemed surprised. As if he'd known it wasn't his time.

"Do you wanna ride with me?" Tobin asked when my cardigan and soft leather coat were both on and my backpack hung from my shoulders. His request took me by surprise. I only ever rode with my brothers because the back of the bike was usually where the wives and girlfriends sat, and Dita had always ridden with Tobin. I wanted to ask questions like why he wanted me to or where we were headed, but as always, I couldn't bring myself to cause a fuss.

"Sure," was all I could manage in response, before following the grinning man downstairs, out the side door and down to the car park, where my father and brothers were already waiting for us. Nico tossed me my helmet, and I slid it on in silence as they discussed the plan, which was when Tobin informed them I was riding with him. I half expected a groan from Nico, or at least a look from my father granting his permission, but when nothing else was said about it I figured it'd already been pre-arranged, so waited patiently for Tobin beside his sleek black bike.

I climbed on behind him a few minutes later, saying nothing as I slid my hands around his waist and held on tight. I then heard as he snapped his visor closed and before I could take my next breath, we were off.

Tobin rode way faster than my dad and brothers on their huge choppers. He ducked in and out of the heavy traffic with ease and soon had us breaking off ahead of the others without a care. I shrieked and buried my face in his back, gripping him harder as he weaved. Having never ridden that way before. My brothers always rode carefully with me on the back, but I couldn't deny that it was a thrill to break the rules and speed through the city and out onto the motorway.

While I couldn't hear him speak over the roar of the engine and the sounds of the traffic around us, I was sure I could feel Tobin's chest constricting and vibrating as he laughed at me and cringed. I felt so foolish squealing, like a silly little girl, but I just couldn't help it. Tobin was so dangerous. Sliding between gaps in the traffic, Nico would've never risked with me on the back. While I trusted him to keep us both safe, I couldn't help but react to the first thrill ride I'd ever had and held onto his leathers so tight I thought my hands might seize up.

When we then left the motorway and began speeding down some of the country roads, I finally relaxed. There was no more traffic around us to zoom through, just rural Britain and its hedge-lined roads to ride down. I loosened my grip and peered up over Tobin's shoulder, letting the rush of cool air hit me through my visor. Even behind my helmet the autumn breeze felt nice, and when he began to slow, I felt disappointed.

We'd been riding for around half an hour when Tobin pulled up outside a tall dark building on the roadside. It had gravel all around and a huge doorway to one side but was otherwise too dark for me to see properly. I could tell right away, though, that this had once been a country pub. There were huge windows on the ground floor and an archway entrance that I guessed would've previously been used to welcome visitors and entice people driving by to stop for a drink, but now the place was empty and had clearly been closed for a while. I could tell it hadn't been abandoned, though. There were security lights that came to life with our presence, and the gravel beneath our feet had clearly been freshly laid. The exterior of the building had recently been cleaned up, too.

Tobin unlocked the door and led me inside, flicking on lights as he went, and I gasped as the interior of the pub came into focus. The old bar was now decorated in black and blue—the club colours—with the logos and Dark Knights patches painted on the walls in murals dedicated to my father's club. Hard wood floors stretched over the vast ground floor and the windows were each covered in thick black curtains rather than be open to prying eyes.

"What is this place?" I finally asked him, walking over to the huge bar.

"It's mine. I bought the old pub at auction about a year ago and I've been fixing it up ever since. I've been here the last few days doing the finishing touches. I guess I needed some time alone, and this place was perfect because it helped me to clear my head," Tobin answered, joining me at the bar and staring down into my eyes intensely. "Dita and I were going to move in at some point and this was going to be the new clubhouse. The main house is getting a little small for all the new members and at least here we have plenty of room to socialise and have our meetings without feeling cramped. Being out in the middle of nowhere helps too," he told me with a small laugh.

"It's amazing. You should be proud of yourself," I answered, smiling warmly, but Tobin just shrugged my compliment off.

"There's so much I want for our club. Changes that

need to come about and it's time to make it happen. We could have an amazing future if we put our minds to it and this is just the first step. Your father and I have many plans that are yet to be put into place, but we'll get underway soon and I just hope it'll go to plan…" Tobin tailed off, but I didn't push him to say the rest of what was on his mind. We didn't know each other well enough for a start.

"Well, this is a good place to begin," I replied with a genuine smile. The new clubhouse truly was amazingly warm and inviting while still cool and manly. Perfect for the club. I slid off my coat and placed it on one of the stools before turning back to Tobin, finding him standing so close to me I gasped.

"You and Dita are so very different, you know? She would've spouted off a load of things that weren't to her liking, or additions that needed to be made by now. And yet you're so reserved, so quiet. How did the two of you become so different women?" Tobin asked, and I struggled to know how to handle the way he'd spoken, almost as if it were a compliment. His voice was so hoarse and masculine, his gaze intense. I felt vulnerable beneath that stare but didn't pull away from him. In fact, I savoured it. I didn't understand the heat roaring to life in my belly, but I knew he had put it there. I knew it was because my mind was wandering. Considering things it shouldn't. Scenarios I wanted to have happen yet had no idea whether they could be real or fantasy. Like, what if he kissed me? What if he told me he wanted me? Was it wrong to want him?

I forced myself back to reality. He was a friend. The man mourning a loss I couldn't fathom. The woman he was going to marry and probably have a family with. He couldn't possibly be thinking of me when he'd just spent the last few days in solitude to help him grieve.

"The men I love are flawed and controlling, but I would never change them. Dita always wanted more than this life of bikers and bars. She wanted to put her mark on everything and never let anyone tell her what to do. I like to think I understood her reasons why, but don't want the same things. I've never felt the need and, in all honesty, I often think I'm not like that because I'm lazy." I laughed at my nonchalant response. "I just want a quiet life, really. To sit and do my thing. Interact when I'm ready."

"I've noticed," Tobin said, laughing too as the rumble of bikes outside halted our conversation. He stepped back just as my father entered, his three sons filing in behind.

Tobin watched them the same way as I was, and he had a broad grin on his handsome face as he regarded the four men. I could tell without having to ask that he truly respected each one of them. That he considered them his family, too.

***

Dad seemed delighted with Tobin's efforts at renovating the new clubhouse. So much so, he insisted we all stay for drinks and get a takeaway so he could enjoy the place and spend some time there, just the few of us before opening it up to the other club members.

Together, we chatted long into the small hours. I even had a couple of glasses of wine that I am positive my father watered down with lemonade, but I was happy to just feel wanted and included in something that was club business. Normally, I was sent silently to my room at whatever point he decided was enough for me. That, or the club members near me, would walk away to talk in private, but not that night. My father and Tobin talked at great lengths about the plan to have the old clubhouse as their meeting spot in Birmingham, while this would become the main house. They discussed how they would need someone to take over the running of it, but then stopped talking at that point, as though undecided who would be given the honour of taking charge.

When I was literally dropping off while resting my head back on the sofa, my father roused me and led me up to a large bedroom on the second floor that had been fully kitted out with new furniture and smelled of fresh linen and plug-in air freshener. When I was alone, I stripped off and slid under the duvet, snuggling into the cold sheets with a smile before dropping off to sleep almost instantly.

I was fast off when the door opened a short while later, and only stirred when I became aware of the covers dipping ever so slightly, realising someone was sitting beside me on the bed. I completely freaked out, ready to scream at the top of my lungs, but when I looked up, it was Nico.

Even though I was shattered, I rubbed my eyes and peered up at him in the dim light being cast in from the hall, wondering what was going on.

"What are you doing?" I asked as I pulled the covers up to make sure my naked body was covered. I had no reason not to trust him, but still, you always had to be careful.

"I'm here to make sure you're safe, Dahlia. To be sure you do as you're told," was all he whispered in response, and before I could ask him anything else, Thomas joined us. Each of them then stood on either side of the room but stayed silent. When a third shape came inside, I assumed it must be my other brother Brad. That there was perhaps an issue with security and how my father and Tobin must be dealing with it downstairs while my brothers stood guard over me, but no.

The third intruder on my otherwise peaceful slumber was Tobin. Without a word, he closed the door and came inside, moving slowly and softly across the soft carpet, while my heart began thumping hard in my ears. I had no words, no breath, and barely any brain function in that moment. I think the word is dumfounded. I was in shock. I waited for the next comment to be made as to what the hell was going on, but none of them said a damn word. It was so dark that I could barely make out Tobin's tall form at the end of the bed, but I could see that he was undressing, and I gathered the duvet around myself even more.

"I've come to be with you, Dahlia. I won't hurt you," his voice came from the shadows, deep and haughty.

"What are you doing?" I asked again, although I somehow knew exactly what he was up to. It didn't matter that I was inexperienced. I knew what happened between a man and a woman in bed. Tobin seemed to be expecting me to give him everything that lay beneath those lovely sheets of his, and I shook my head. This wasn't how it was meant to go. It was meant to be perfect. Not rushed and with an audience.

"I'd like you to give yourself to me," he replied, climbing up onto the bed. I could see his hard length sticking out from his waist, ready and waiting to take my innocence, and paled. I looked to my two brothers who were stood silently beside me, each one looking away from the bed, yet keeping guard, and I wanted to scream.

Tobin pulled back the duvet and slid it over my legs so I was only covered with the thin sheet and climbed up over me. He then put his hands on my face, kissing my lips softly, and I could feel his stubbly chin grazing against my soft skin. I shook my head and pulled away. It just didn't feel right. I tried to slide off the bed, but he caught me by the hand and leaned in again, intent on kissing me. With my free hand, I then slapped his face. Not all that hard because I think I was still in shock, but with as much force as I could muster.

Tobin laughed. He actually laughed at me, and in a second, I had gone from shocked to furious.

He wrenched the thin sheet away from my body and gasped as he took in the sight of my full breasts and curved waist. I'd had an hourglass figure since I was thirteen and always hated the fact that I was never going to be one of those skinny girls I saw on TV, but Tobin seemed enamoured by my shape. As if he liked what he saw. I began to tremble. No one had seen me naked in years, not since I was a little girl getting changed on the beach without a care, or in the swimming pool changing rooms.

"Please don't do this, Tobin. I don't want to," I whispered as I tried to cover myself, and could hear the pleading sound in my tone.

"But you're such a good girl, Dahlia. You always do as you're told. I know we can be amazing together, just let me show you."

"Nico, Thomas," I pleaded, looking up at my so-called protectors. "Tell me this isn't happening? You can't be okay with this?"

Nothing. Not a single goddam word. They might as well have been statues.

Tobin pulled me down onto the bed by my wrists, lying beside my still trembling body while planting delicate kisses to my face and neck. There was no hurting or forcing me, so I had to assume that was what Nico had meant with his earlier explanation. I realised they were there to make sure it all went to plan, and that I was not hurt in the process of Tobin getting what he so forcefully desired. The very idea turned my stomach.

I struggled against his hold, and Tobin eventually loosened his grip. "Can I just have a minute alone in the bathroom?" I asked, nodding over to the en-suite, and he agreed.

I then stood and wrapped the thin sheet around myself and ran for the door as fast as my scared legs could carry me. I heard Nico and Tobin shout from behind me but didn't look back as I flung open the door and shoved myself into Brad's back. He'd seemingly been keeping guard from the other side and hadn't been prepared for an escapee. In his shock, he fell forward onto the hallway floor and I jumped over him, running towards the landing and down the stairs. I almost made it to the doorway when my father stepped in front of me and gathered me up in his arms.

"What are you doing?" he asked, shushing me, and smoothing my hair. "Who are you running from?"

"Daddy," I cried, nestling into his embrace. "Tobin, he..." I couldn't finish. Tears were falling from my eyes in waves and going down onto his blue shirt as I even thought about what had just gone on in that bedroom.

"It's okay, I've got you now." He hugged me tighter. "Did you do it?" he asked and was so cool and calm I would've thought he was talking about something as everyday as making a phone call.

I went cold, staring up at him in shock, but he kept his arms tightly around my shoulders. I tried to fight him, to push him away, and in that moment, I think my heart actually broke.

Chapter Two

"You knew what he was doing?" I demanded.

"Yes, of course I knew. Tobin's my VP, Dahlia. I promised him my daughter's hand in marriage when I gave him the badge. You've had time to mourn your sister, but now you need to take her place," my dad replied, and I had to wonder what on earth was going on in his club. That was not the way the world worked. We were not in those times anymore where fathers just gave their daughters away to a man of their choosing, like a bonus package attached to a business deal. How could he expect me to go along with it? Just because Dita was dead did not mean I had to take her place.

As far as I'd been aware, she and Tobin had gotten together without any say-so from our father, and they'd been genuinely happy together. I was not some second-best consolation prize that Tobin would have to accept now that she was gone.

"You don't own me, Dad. Please. You can't decide this for me," I implored him, but my father remained closed-off. "Maybe in time I might choose Tobin, but why must I be forced? I've never let you down. I've always been here to do whatever you wanted of me, whatever the club expected, and now you're just throwing me away?" I cried, feeling hurt and betrayed.

"Don't you see, Dahlia? That's exactly where you're wrong. It's because you are the most perfect, wonderful thing in my life that the gesture means so much. Tobin and I have been through more than you'll ever know. He's given the club everything over the years and has earned the right to ask me for any reward he wants. The only way I can repay my debt is with my most precious jewel—you."

He turned me around, and I saw my three brothers standing at the top of the stairs, watching us intently. "They're your protectors and will watch over you forever, just like I will. The four of us will always be here to make sure you're safe. But I cannot keep you locked away any longer. I wanted to, believe me, I did, but it's time to let you go. Your life has been put on hold for far too long and Tobin will give you an amazing future. Trust me."

I panted, feeling under so much pressure I was in turmoil. What would happen if I refused? Would he kick me out and take away everything I'd taken for granted all my life? Would I be allowed to stay, but be shunned by the club for refusing to follow my sister's lead? Every possibility I could imagine seemed a worse fate than going through with it, and I crumbled. I begged him one last time.

"I do trust you. But I need more time. I don't want our first night to be like this. Please ask him to wait until I'm ready?" I had to ask. My determination was softening thanks to my father's kind and loving words, but I was still terrified of handing over my virginity like a mail-order bride. I wanted to feel safe with Tobin, to love him and want him inside of me, but then and there, the sheer thought of him taking his prize this way made me want to vomit.

"No, it has to be now. The two of you must go back

home tomorrow having fallen madly in love and we can then begin preparations for your future together. I need to know for sure that you belong to each other properly, and other than the pair of you finding a priest and getting married first thing in the morning, this is the only way."

I couldn't understand it. My father had never been so old-fashioned about this kind of thing before. He was staring at me like he had countless times when he was lost or scared but couldn't talk about it. I knew that look. He was doing what he had to, not what he wanted to, and I got the feeling he didn't really want me to go and complete the act either but was too proud to call it off.

It seemed as if he needed closure, an incentive of sorts, before he could properly let me go. I wondered if perhaps Tobin taking my virtue was the only way he could think to force himself to consider me a woman at last, however I wasn't about to let him off easily.

So, against my wishes, I stepped forward, walking slowly towards my brothers. I got halfway up the stairs in stunned silence, before finally gathering the courage to turn and speak my mind to the man who'd always taken such good care of me. The man I'd never had to raise my voice to or be angry with. I'd never spoken out of turn to him my entire life, and yet in those last few minutes he'd become a stranger who I felt deserved my contempt. Before I knew it, my words were flying.

"I'll do this for you, Dad. But know this. I will hate you from now until the day I die for making me an object you've traded, rather than a human being you love and respect. No matter whether Tobin and I fall madly in love and live happily ever after, I will always hate you for this." His face fell, and I knew the look he was giving me probably mirrored my own. It was a look full of pain and internal suffering. I wondered if I'd broken his heart, just as he had mine, and hoped I had. He deserved to be hurting over this.

I climbed the last few steps and stared into the forlorn faces of my brothers when I reached the landing. They were the few people I'd trusted with my life countless times, and yet in that instant they seemed like nothing more than extensions of our father's puppetry, not their own men. I eyeballed each in turn before uttering a venomous promise. "Which one of you is gonna hold me down, then? I'm telling you now, I am not going to go quietly, or without a fight." None of them said a word, so I stalked back into the bedroom with them, watching my every move.

Inside the room, Tobin was laid on the bed in wait, but had at least covered himself up. He seemed to have been waiting patiently for me to return, as though he knew my father would get me to change my mind, and I hated to be back there, proving him right. The evening before had been lovely, and I'd felt a real connection between us. Something that could've been cultivated in time.

Now I knew that it'd all been a sneaky scheme to get me there and into his bed. I hated him, too. "How long have you been planning this?" I asked coldly. I was hovering at the end of the bed with the sheet still wrapped around my naked body tightly, trembling despite not being cold.

"A while. Dita and I grew apart the last few months. It wasn't natural between us and never had been, so I started pulling away from her. We were too alike—fiery and strong-willed. I knew I needed someone calm and quiet, which was when I found myself watching you."

God, he was gorgeous. His olive skin was flawless, and his pale blue eyes shone at me from across the room. I hated how drawn to Tobin I was, even after everything that'd gone on, and forced myself to remain indignant. Not letting his flattery sway me as he carried on. "Even when she died, I still watched you. My eyes never left your face at the funeral and at the wake your father caught me. I came here to clear my head, but the silence only made me worse, and before I knew it, I became obsessed with you, Dahlia. So, as soon as I stepped foot in the clubhouse today, I told him I wanted you."

Something inside me raged, something primal and instinctive. I was suddenly hot. I wanted him to say more, to tell me again how much he wanted me and all the ways he'd become obsessed by me. In a perfect world, I'd be so ready to let him woo me relentlessly, but this wasn't perfect. So, I forced myself to remain calm, remembering our audience and the situation at hand.

"So why can't we just go out for a while and see where things take us? Surely that's better than you forcing your way into bed with me?" I asked and could hear the pleading tone of my voice again. Tobin shook his head.

"No, your father needs to know he doesn't own you anymore. The 'Daddy's Girl' routine needs to stop, and this time I won't let anything get in the way of what I want."

"Oh, so this is just you laying claim over your consolation prize?" I spat with as much venom as I could. And I think it genuinely shocked him.

Tobin flicked on the lamp beside him and was instantly bathed in yellow light. He looked angry, downright infuriated that I'd dared say anything so harsh to him, and I was glad. I hoped he'd realise how angry I was about the whole situation and how ridiculous it all was.

Before I knew what had hit me, he dived forward

and wrapped his arms around my waist, pulling me forward onto the bed. I fell on top of him, our bodies colliding, and in less than a second, he'd flipped us over and was on top of me, nestled between my legs.

Tears welled in my eyes as he pressed himself against me, while heat bloomed for him atop my thighs in striking contrast. My body was defying every order I was trying to give it, and while I was glad for my layers of wrapped cotton between us, I knew it wouldn't be long until he had taken control of them, just like he had my body.

"Don't you see?" he whispered, stroking my face gently, but I shook my head. "You just brought your father and brothers to their knees. And here I am, ready and waiting to give you everything you desire to make you mine. We're all victims of you, Dahlia. I'm your consolation prize, not the other way around."

In that moment, there was a huge part of me that wanted to believe him. I'd never been called a strong and desirable woman in all my life but liked the feeling his words gave me. I desperately wanted to be seen as decisive, independent, and powerful, but I knew Tobin was wrong about me. I wasn't any of those things because I'd been taught not to be.

I'd seen for myself how Dita had needed to fight her way through her entire life because of her sharp tongue and quick temper. I hadn't wanted to be like her, so had gone in the other direction and was now a ghost. I realised I'd become a shell of a young woman, rather than a whole person. I hadn't lived. I hadn't loved or made mistakes. How could I suddenly have the strength to take on my family or the club?

I stared back at Tobin, struck dumb and afraid. He

truly was a gorgeous man and was everything I was attracted to with his slim, toned body and ruggedly handsome face. He was every woman's fantasy, surely, and I let my eyes rove over him, drinking in the sight of the man towering over me. I was right when I'd wondered about the number of tattoos he had, too. Now that he was naked atop me, I could see that his ink continued from his hands up his arms in impressive sleeves of vibrant colour and emotive art. The tattoos climbed up over both shoulders and headed up to his ears on each side. He caught me staring at them and smiled knowingly. I was putty in his hands already, and we both knew it.

I thought back to the feel of my arms wrapped around his waist when we were riding together and the few minutes of closeness we'd had when we were alone after arriving at the new clubhouse. I wanted that feeling back. I could work with that and could see us going somewhere, but this forced, arranged affair? No chance.

Tobin was going to ruin it if he pushed me, and I knew things would never be what they could've if I'd let him. Yes, I would no-doubt become the dutiful 'old lady' if I lay back and let him have me. I'd probably live out my days as a kept woman who continued to sit silently beside her powerful, overbearing husband and never rocked the boat, but I didn't want that. I wanted love and lust, mutual respect, and excitement. I was not ready to lose my virginity while my brothers watched over us, and my dad waited for confirmation outside.

"This isn't happening, Tobin. Not tonight. Say whatever you want, but I'm not going to fuck you," I murmured. My heart was pounding so hard in my chest I thought I might pass out, but I had to try.

Tobin laughed. Again! He laughed out loud, and kneeled up between my knees, giving me a full view of his impressive body and the hard-on he'd just been pressing into my thigh.

"One sister who couldn't get enough, and another who doesn't want it at all?" he pondered aloud, clearly growing impatient with my stalling, but for some reason, he listened to me. Tobin slid backwards off the end of the bed and pulled on his clothes while I watched him, wide-eyed.

"I'm not my sister. The sooner you realise that the better," I called as he and my brothers left me alone again.

"Don't I bloody know it," was all I heard in response as he slammed the door closed behind him.

Chapter Three

Early the next morning, after probably just an hour or so of fretful sleep, I decided to get up. Being in that bed was no use. It just brought back the memories of the night before, and I wanted to scream. I was disgusted that things had gone so far. It shouldn't have even been allowed to happen, let alone Dad and Tobin's plan, almost having worked. And what was with my brothers watching over us like that? Yuk. It seemed I needed to remind them we weren't living in medieval times.

Annoyingly, though, there was another set of memories that were haunting me, and certainly not bad ones. The memories of Tobin grabbing me, kissing me, and telling me he wanted me were playing on repeat in my head. The image of him kneeling naked at the end of my bed the night before had me buzzing with my own need. His amazing body had been completely on show, his huge erection ready and poised to be inside of me, desperate for me to accept. He'd become the man of my every fantasy in that moment. The man who then told me how he'd obsessed over me. Me! The girl who sat quietly through life, always on the periphery, and yet had also become the poster child for having delusions she could remain incognito while growing from a girl to a woman.

It had also been the first time I'd ever even seen a man naked, let alone been close to doing anything sexual with one, and what an experience it was. Although the circumstances of it all made me want to punch him, and the others, in the face, I also found myself throbbing somewhere inside that had been long since ignored.

As I flushed red-hot for the umpteenth time, I knew enough was enough. I slipped into the en-suite and quickly got washed and dressed before sneaking out past my three brothers, who'd evidently camped out in the hallway. I made my way down to the ground floor and opened the curtains in the landing, then stared out at the gravelly expanse that led to the road.

I knew I could just run away while they were all still sleeping, but where would I go? What would I do for money? No-doubt I'd end up having to give away that part of myself I'd fought so desperately to keep hold of the night before if I ran off, which was a much worse fate in my albeit naïve opinion. I was no idiot, but also not savvy enough to understand the world outside of my father's MC. He'd made sure of that my entire adult life.

Even with my studies and endless supply of books to keep me occupied, I'd never moved out when I went to university, or travelled the world with my friends. I had never learned to take care of myself or handle my own finances. I didn't know how to cook or clean, or anything like that. Self-sufficiency was a lesson I hadn't been allowed to learn, and now I understood why.

I wandered through the bar and instead of finding comfort in it, the smell of leather, whiskey, and smoke that was permeating from within was making me nauseous. So instead, I found my way to the kitchen. I put on a percolator of coffee and hunted down some bacon, eggs, black pudding, and tomatoes in the fridge, so decided to give cooking a full breakfast a try. As I began putting together the ingredients, I had an epiphany.

I'd found many times over my lifetime that one of the advantages of being an introvert was that you could step out of your own skin and look at the world from other angles more easily. My quiet nature had often led me to end up sitting, watching the people around me, and taking in far more than my father had ever realised, and when I stopped to think about it, I knew a lot of sensitive information about his club, and the people in it.

Yes, we'd all seen the outside façade, but I knew the members' roots and their personalities. I knew many of my father's secrets and lies because either he or one of his members had let things slip without realising I was listening in. This knowledge was valuable, which made me valuable too, and I endeavoured to make sure I stayed the same way. I'd been respected and even feared by them because of my position beside the President. I was never one of the girls they ogled at and degraded. The guys wouldn't dare, but as I began thinking about it more, I realised that in many ways he'd turned me into my mother. I had become a matriarch of sorts. The woman that was to be always protected and cared for by her band of brutes, but never used and abused, disrespected, or put in harm's way.

Tobin had been right, and that was why everything had fallen to pieces the night before. If I'd laid back and let him have me, we still would've ended up where we were that next morning. Things were awkward and uncomfortable, and I knew that it would have been the same, no matter the outcome. My dad said he would let me go at last, but what

I'd taken as him being old-fashioned gave his real reasons away.

The only way Tobin and I could truly move forward would be for him to take Dad's place as my guardian, and I wasn't about to let that happen without it being on my terms. I knew that without my father's detachment from me we were stuck in limbo, but I didn't care. I would've happily kept us there for as long as it took for me to feel ready to give myself to Tobin naturally, and without an audience. I vowed then and there to make sure that my father, brothers, and would-be-lover, all realised at long last that despite my quieter nature, I was not one to be messed with, nor would I wilt under the pressure they'd decided to collectively put me under.

I realised I was still standing at the fridge, staring into it in a daze, so grabbed the whole packs of the breakfast ingredients, not just one portion's worth I'd taken before, and set about making them a feast. Those five men whom I loved and hated in equal parts that fine autumn morning would have a full breakfast ready for them when they awoke. I was going to do what the respected woman did. I was going to turn the other cheek and crack on. I knew they'd be surprised, and that was exactly what I was going for.

"What are you doing?" Tobin's voice came from the doorway, and I turned from the stove to look at him. He was at the kitchen door, leaning against the jamb groggily, as though he'd just woken up. My eyes widened as I took him in. He was wearing nothing but grey tracksuit trousers and a pair of socks, showing off his inked-up arms and toned body again. There was no looking away from every curve of muscle and line of art that looked almost radiant in the bright morning light.

That aching throb came back from deep inside of me, and I mentally shushed the purr that was rising in my throat. It was not the time to get all girly and let him have that which I'd clung onto for dear life the night before.

"I'm making you all breakfast. Are the others awake yet?" I asked, pouring him a mug of coffee, and he stepped closer.

"No, just me."

I turned back to flip the popping bacon and stirred the pan of baked beans, before moving sideways and buttering the toast, while he sauntered forwards. I assumed he would take a seat at the huge table, but instead Tobin shocked me by pinning me to the counter from behind. His powerful body was pressed against mine, and regardless of anything I'd tried to tell myself, I knew I wanted him.

I jumped and dropped the butter knife onto the breadboard with a yelp of surprise. Tobin laughed. This one was far from the cruel laugh he'd given me the night before though. This was a deep, gravelly sound, and I imagined it being the same laugh he'd given me as we rode to the new clubhouse together.

He planted soft kisses on my neck and collar, pulling the top of my cardigan away so he could get to the soft flesh beneath, and I found myself panting. "I still want you, Dahlia. As much as ever. In fact, maybe more," he murmured, mesmerising me with each syllable. "I'll give you some time to come around, and I want you to know I'm sorry for how things happened last night. It was too fast, too forceful, and I'll never do it again. You can trust me."

His hands reached down and skimmed my breasts before cupping me between the thighs. I froze in shock but wasn't scared that time. His hard-on pressed into my back, and I found myself closing my eyes. I remembered exactly what it looked like and wondered how it would feel to touch and even how it might taste. "You're very hot down here. I hope that's all for me?" he groaned. Tobin then rubbed his fingers across the seam of my jeans, and I bucked as he pressed against my swollen clit. I wanted to believe him. To trust him like he'd told me to.

"If what you're saying is true and you really do want me, I'll never let another man touch me as long as I live, Tobin. All of this is yours, just as long as you care for me the way you've promised," I replied, grinding against him, and I swear he actually growled in response to my prowess. "This won't be an arranged marriage, or me being coerced into your bed because my father made you promises. I want romance and passion, excitement, and love. Can you give me those things?" I asked, turning to face him, and Tobin's stunning blue eyes peered down into mine. They seemed full of all those things, and I couldn't help but swoon.

"Yeah, baby. I sure can," he replied with a stunning smile.

His kisses then overwhelmed every one of my senses. Bringing my hands to his still stubbly face, I kissed him back, my body curling into his. My hips then ignored my inner commands to distance themselves from that hard probe between Tobin's thighs and pushed against him, despite knowing that it was still in search of a place to bury itself.

I knew I was far from ready. Images of him pressing himself into me so forcefully the night before sprang into my mind and had me backing off in an instant.

"Don't ever try and force me again, promise me," I

said, stepping to the side and away from his hot body. I focussed on the food, finishing off frying the last of the eggs, before sliding them into the dish, keeping them all warm in the oven alongside the other ready items, while Tobin watched me with a scowl.

When I finally turned to look at him properly again, he stepped forward, but instead of kissing me, he just wrapped me in his arms and held on so tightly that I could barely breathe.

"That was never what I wanted, or how I expected it to go down. In all honesty, I thought that you'd just go for it. I'm not used to rejection, and I guess I was arrogant enough to assume you would feel honoured that I had chosen to come and have my wicked way with you." He laughed, seeming embarrassed, and I appreciated his honesty.

I went to respond, but he shushed me, seemingly needing to say his bit before he'd let me speak. "Your father insisted your brothers be there to make sure it went smoothly, but I think it was more than that. I think he needed to control the situation, but neither of us thought for an instant that you'd say no. I was so very wrong, and all that bravado was a front, Dahlia. That's why I walked away in the end. I couldn't force you, not when what I really want is for us to be real and happy together. Last night isn't the way to begin something this special," he told me with a shy smile.

It felt as though he was ranting, but I was so glad to hear every word of it, and I believed him.

"Real, happy, special?" I murmured, repeating his words to ensure they sunk in.

"Yes. I promise not to try and force you ever again.

Please let me do this properly?" he stroked my dark auburn hair away from my face, peering down at me solemnly.

"I guess I can do that," I conceded. My voice was quiet against him, and I felt him relax as my understanding of his actions from the night before registered.

We then held onto each other for a long time. Just listening to his heart beating and his lungs filling with air brought me comfort, and in that moment, I realised that the only person who'd ever held me that way before was my father.

The transition was so clear I felt as though I could document every second of it. I finally understood what Tobin had meant by needing to have that moment of impact to signify my release from my father's protective bubble and the switch into his. I knew my dad would always be there for me, that he would love me and take care of whatever I needed, but the torch for my safety and care had already been passed. Whether I was on board yet or not.

Regardless of us not having sealed the deal the night before, I guessed my words to my father had probably been enough to sever the once so strong ties we had to each other, and I couldn't help but feel sad. I had to trust that Tobin would fill those boots, though. I believed he would guide me through the next chapter in my life and take care of me, just like my father once had, only different. Perhaps even better.

An awkward cough then broke through the silence, and I jumped. Tobin didn't release me right away, though. He waited a few heartbeats, which I suspected was a show of dominance, but was glad that he was ready to show my family he was now the one holding me close and comforting me when I'd needed it.

When I looked across at the four men hovering by the door, there was no hiding my red eyes and puffy cheeks. I hadn't cried, but I had buried myself in Tobin's embrace and had let myself get lost there. I was feeling emotional, and I guess it showed.

Nico, Thomas, and Brad could only look down at the floor, seemingly embarrassed. But not my father. He stared me right in the eye and smiled that same smile he'd always worn with me. I sighed in relief at his warm gaze but didn't step forward to embrace him like I would've done every day of life leading up until the night before. For starters, Tobin still had his hands on my waist and didn't seem ready to let me go. Second, it no longer felt right. The cord had evidently already been cut.

Instead, I ushered for them to take a seat while I grabbed the coffee jug and poured them their much-needed caffeine fixes, along with cups of juice and water. It wasn't long before Tobin took his seat at my father's side, and I began plating up their surprise breakfast. My brothers thanked me and tucked in, while my father watched me serve Tobin, a smile on his somehow older-looking face.

When I took a seat next to my new beau, my father finally began eating, as though he'd been waiting out of respect for me, but I couldn't be sure. He'd never done anything of the sort before. After his first bite, he groaned in delight, and then gave me a thumbs up, seconded by each of the other men at the table.

"She cooks. Who knew?" Brad asked, pouring himself more juice, and I grinned. I was glad the banter was on its way back, and before long all five of my favourite men were laughing and shouting, throwing insults at one another from across the table.

I replenished their plates until everything was gone, and then each of them sat back with seemingly full bellies and contented smiles. I hadn't asked them for their verdicts. In fact, while we'd sat there, I'd gone back to my old, quiet self. After serving them with a smile and a sense of purpose, I watched them as I slowly made my way through the small mound of food in front of me. It wasn't the olden days where women were submissive servants of their husbands and family, but I sure as hell was enjoying having those five men all to myself. I liked taking care of them and had to admit, being responsible for their happy faces gave me a kick I couldn't ever describe.

I understood then how things had been changed between us, but knew we'd probably never speak of the night before ever again, and that was fine by me. As long as there wasn't a repeat of that demeaning treatment, I was happy to carry on, regardless. And, even if I wasn't, what other choice did I have?

"I'm really proud of you, Dahlia," my dad said, breaking my reverie and catching me completely off guard. His words silenced the chatter around us in a heartbeat. "You've become the woman I always dreamed you'd be. The woman your mum once was. You'll make a wonderful wife and mother, but most important of all, you make us better men for knowing and loving you."

I wanted to cry. His words were so unexpected and powerful that despite the wedge that had been driven between us, I knew I would remember them until the day I died. I swallowed the lump in my throat and stood. Climbing into his lap was oddly so foreign and immature to me after everything that'd happened, so instead I went to my father's side, kissed his cheek lightly, and thanked him.

I knew in that moment that the little girl I once was had well and truly gone forever but didn't care. I'd finally become a woman, and it felt good to have matured in their eyes at last.

Things would undoubtedly be different back home for me from that moment on too, but I knew I'd still be worth far more than any other wife or girlfriend of the club. I would be the respected and privileged old lady at the top. I knew I'd most likely end up feared and even hated by some of the other girls who hung on the arms of the club members because of it but couldn't care any less. They'd all been fine with me when I was the shy, quiet, President's daughter sitting in the corner with a book. I hadn't been a threat. Going forward though, I would be Tobin's girlfriend, and I knew it would change my entire life.

I was grateful when Tobin later suggested to my dad and brothers that they head back home without us. He and I needed some time alone to figure things out, and while I was scared, he might try and push things between us again, I had to trust he'd been telling me the truth about taking things slower.

"Garret knows nothing happened last night, but he's promised to let you go anyway, and that's a big step for him," Tobin told me once my family had left and we were alone. I had to agree. After all our years of closeness, I thought he would've had a harder time letting go, too. "He's very set in his ways, but at least he saw for himself how our connection is there, and that he needn't force anything between us. He couldn't let you go without knowing someone else was there to take care of you. But I promised them all that I'd be the perfect gentleman and step up to the plate, and I meant it. We'll get there in our own time." He looked so genuine and relaxed, not fidgeting, or avoiding my gaze like I'd expect if he were lying, so I trusted him.

"It feels so strange being let out of the almighty grip he's always had on me. I guess I should feel glad and free, but I don't. I miss it," I admitted as we set about clearing up the kitchen. He nodded. Tobin seemed to understand exactly how torn up I was without me having to really say much more, and I appreciated he didn't try to make me explain myself to him.

We soon got stuck in with the cleaning, neither of us saying anything more, and I was surprised to find him doing more than his fair share of the housework and tidying. I'd never taken him for the tidy sort, but then again, I had to remind myself that he and I barely knew each other, really.

We spent the next few hours straightening the huge bar area and clearing the bedrooms, stripping the beds, and cleaning up after my brothers. Tobin only sat down once the house and bar were all in order again, and I had to laugh. I even wondered if perhaps he had OCD when it came to keeping things clean but didn't dare ask him in case he took offence.

"Can I cook for you this time?" he asked when I'd finished wiping down the windowsills and had closed the windows and curtains. A chill had crept in with the twilight, so I wanted to allow some warmth to spread back through the vast and incredibly clean house. I nodded, smiling broadly, and Tobin seemed delighted.

After a wonderful dinner of pasta carbonara that he'd made from scratch, we relaxed in front of the television and chatted quietly while watching some awful reality TV show he seemed to be a fan of.

Our conversation was light, and although I felt more relaxed with him, I was glad when bedtime came around. The lack of sleep from the night before caught up on me, and after saying goodnight, I headed up to bed for some much needed rest.

At first, I was worried, listening for the door to creak open again, but there was nothing. I eventually fell asleep and slept surprisingly soundly.

In what felt like the blink of an eye, I then awoke to find bright sunlight streaming in late the next morning. There hadn't been so much as a peep from my intended, and I hated that I was a little disappointed. There was a part of me that'd wanted him to come to my room, as silly as that sounds. I wanted him to still want me, like he had the night before.

I got dressed and went downstairs, where I found him sat cross-legged on the floor of the bar. Tobin was building some shelving units and looked good in his black tracksuit bottoms and white sleeveless vest. I offered to help, not thinking he'd accept my proposal, but he slid me the instructions.

"Can you read Swedish?" he joked, and I shook my head, laughing.

We then spent the next few hours getting to grips with the flat-packed units and after a while we'd perfected our technique. As a couple, we put together numerous bookshelves and a coffee table, and it felt good to focus on something. We made a good team, and I was surprised to feel utterly at ease with that realisation.

Chapter Four

"How about we get ready, and I'll take you into town for dinner?" Tobin asked me later that afternoon. We'd just finished putting away the new furniture and had binned the boxes and plastic wrap. The bar was spotless again and looked great with the new additions, plus I was ready for something to eat after just snacking all day while we'd been working. I wanted to see what lay beyond the new clubhouse's walls.

I also had the exciting realisation that Tobin had just asked me out on a date.

"I'd like that very much," I replied with a smile. I could feel myself blushing at the very idea of going out with the gorgeous man, but I was also glad he hadn't planned on keeping us holed up day and night while waiting for me to calm down enough to let him woo me. There was an exhilarating level of freedom being at the new clubhouse, and I was starting to like it more and more. The trip was the first time I'd ever been alone with someone other than a member of my family and while it still felt strange and scary without at least one of my brothers watching over me, being there with Tobin was also turning out to be exciting and enjoyable.

We headed out around seven o'clock that evening.

I had no choice other than to wear the jeans and t-shirt I'd brought with me two nights before as I hadn't packed anything else, so just had to go with what I had to hand. I'd had no idea at the time that we would be staying longer than one night, or that I might need a nicer outfit. However, Tobin didn't seem bothered by my skinny jeans and boots combo in the slightest. If anything, I caught him eyeing me up when I came downstairs to meet him by the doorway. His expression made me wonder if he liked my slim legs being kept hidden in their black denim rather than on show underneath a skimpy skirt. I began to hope he preferred the natural look to the dolled-up style most of the girls who visited the club seemed to think was necessary to hook themselves a biker boyfriend. It wasn't that I minded that look. In fact, there were times when I'd envied those women for rocking it with such confidence. Don't get me wrong, I'd tried, but had failed miserably. Whenever I'd sneaked into Dita's closet when I was younger and tried on her clothes, I'd look awkward and about as sexy as a seal in a tutu.

After locking up behind us, I caught Tobin watching me again as I slid my leg over his bike and nestled in behind him for the short ride to the closest town. His wry smile made me swoon and when I wrapped my arms around his waist again, heat bloomed inside of me, and I had to calm my panting breath. He was getting to me. Breaking through the walls I'd built up the night we'd arrived at the new clubhouse, but I was letting him. I wanted him inside those walls with me. I needed him to break them down. To come charging through them like some knight in shining armour. Such a romantic notion, but I was genuinely enjoying having this gentler, more natural Tobin around. He wasn't the same arrogant guy who had come into my room two nights before, expecting me to give myself to him, and I wanted it to stay that way.

Within seconds we were off, speeding down the winding roads, and I gripped Tobin tightly, stifling my squeals this time. When we slowed, I took in the scenery and watched as we approached a small town. Tobin then stopped outside an Indian restaurant and led the way inside, where we were welcomed by the waiter instantly with a warm smile and a handshake. I could tell they were already well acquainted before the man even opened his mouth.

"Tobin, great to see you again. Are you coming to eat with us today, or just here for another takeaway?" he asked, looking across at me with a warm look in welcome. I just smiled. Being out and about suddenly felt strange for some reason. I wondered if it was thanks to me being on Tobin's arm in public, clearly out on a date. I'd never been on a date before, so wasn't sure how to act or what to say.

"Yes, we're staying. A table for two please, Ashan," Tobin replied, so I knew for sure then that they knew each other well. I guessed he must've already been going around the local businesses to figure out if our club would have any trouble moving there before doing the work on the old pub. Our guys would stick out like a sore thumb but more than that, bikers also had a bad rep no matter their club history or allegiances to causes or foundations. The Black Knights worked hard to develop a good reputation, and I knew we had connections with big charities across the UK, and yet still my father was often treated like an outlaw. It was just the way of things, so even I knew we had to have good relationships with the locals wherever we went—especially places we frequented. They needed to know we didn't shit where we ate, as it were. The way Tobin and our server chatted away like old friends told me he had indeed gone above being just courteous to our nearby business owners. I also knew that whatever deals he'd struck with that restaurant, or the promises he'd made regarding preferential treatment and perhaps a regular 'donation' by our club, they were fundamental in creating such strong relationships with the locals.

We then followed Ashan to a table and took our seats. The place was small but brightly decorated in the typical Indian style. I could smell the spices in the air, fragrant and inviting, and my tummy rumbled. I was more than ready to get something in front of me. Ashan handed us our menus as soon as we were settled, and Tobin set his straight down while I took a good look at the variety of curries and other dishes available.

"I know you'll want the strong Asian beer, my friend, but how about your lovely companion?" Ashan asked, looking down at me with a kind smile.

"Lemonade please," I replied, but then felt silly. I wasn't driving, and I wasn't a child, so I quickly added on a glass of rosé wine to my order. Ashan bowed and left us to decide on our food order, so I took a good look and then peeked across the top of my menu, finding Tobin watching me. "So, you've been getting to know the locals?" I asked, having decided on some small talk.

"Yeah, I needed to make sure we weren't gonna get any grief off them once the new clubhouse is up and running. This place is good, but rarely very busy. The club will change that for Ashan and his family who own it." I nodded in understanding. Quid pro quo was always a good thing where our guys were concerned, and a boost in income for the restaurant would clearly not go amiss. "I've been getting the chefs to make me takeaway dishes while I've been working at the house. They make the best chicken tikka masala I've ever tasted," Tobin added, just as Ashan came over with our drinks.

"Too kind, my man," he said, clapping him on the shoulder. "So, is this the fiancée I've heard all about?" he asked, and it quickly became obvious that Tobin must've told him about Dita. Talk about cringe worthy. I blushed, feeling awkward, but Tobin didn't seem fazed in the slightest.

"Yeah, this is Dahlia," he introduced us, and I shook Ashan's hand awkwardly before burying my face in my glass of wine. When he left us again, I stared over at Tobin, unsure what to talk about after that bombshell. I also realised just how little I knew about the man my father had pretty much arranged my relationship with. I knew that I'd been kept out of their world as much as Dad could, but it made me sad to think it'd meant I'd never gotten to know Tobin better when he was with Dita. I hated how my sister had been engaged to this man, and yet I hadn't even asked her about him or his past. Unease hovered over us, but he seemed to sense it, and quickly explained Ashan's comment.

"Don't worry. I told him when we first met that I was engaged, nothing more. He was just being friendly." I hoped that really was the extent to Ashan's knowledge about our history.

"Good, 'cos that was embarrassing," I replied, and Tobin seemed hurt. I hated upsetting him, so tried a different tactic. "Just because it was a shock, not because I wouldn't want people thinking we weren't together. I guessed he must've thought I was Dita and didn't fancy explaining how she'd died and I'm her sister but am out on a date with you..." I wanted to curl up and die. My explanation wasn't sounding anything like I'd wanted it to, so I stopped digging myself further into that hole and took a deep breath. "What I mean is, I think it's about time you and I got to know one another properly, don't you?" I asked, and Tobin nodded. I was glad he seemed happy with my eventual explanation.

"Good plan," he agreed, taking a long swig of his Asian beer.

"Why don't you do the talking? Tell me about yourself. You already know all about me and my life, and I'm not really one for saying a lot anyway, so there's not much I can tell you that you don't already know," I said with a shrug.

"That's true," Tobin conceded, and he reached across and took my hand in his on the table. I didn't pull back. In fact, I quite enjoyed the feel of our hands as they entwined in the soft tablecloth, so left it right where it was, watching the artwork on the back of his hand dance as he moved. So dark, the black roses and skulls were shadows with just a hint of colour, but they were mesmerising, as was his voice when he finally began to talk. "Well, I guess I should start by telling you how it is that I joined the club. You see, I never knew my father. I grew up near London and it was just my mum and me. We never struggled for money, thanks to her working as the manager of a group of bars owned by my uncle, so it wasn't a hard upbringing. I'm not looking to tell you a sob story or anything." He laughed gruffly, and I peered up at him, basking in his wide, almost awkward smile. "When I turned eighteen, I joined the Army and spent the next few years going through basic training, before I eventually trained to become a pilot."

"Whoa, I had no idea," I replied, and my voice came out a quiet sigh. It hit me how I really had spent my life in my bubble, so wrapped up in my own world, I guessed.

Ashan came back and took our order. Two lots of chicken tikka masala, of course. He also deposited some poppadum's and dips for us to tuck into while we waited, and we both thanked him. I watched Tobin's hands as he snapped the large cracker into pieces and began scooping up mango chutney and some kind of salsa. I was utterly fixated on the tattoos on those hard-worn hands again and wondered when he'd gotten them done. Surely, they hadn't been allowed while he was still serving? Before I could ask, he began telling me more of his story, and I continued to watch him in awe.

"I loved it in the Army. I was made for that life of hard work, and flying was like a dream come true. When things first kicked off in the Middle East, I was still in pilot training, but when I qualified, I went straight out to Afghanistan for my first tour. A few months in, an RPG hit our helicopter, and we went down. My co-pilot was my friend. Probably my best friend. We'd met in training for the Air Corps and had been inseparable since day one." He took a deep breath, as though readying himself for the next part, his eyes on the poppadum in his hands. "We crash landed, and he died in my arms after I managed to pull us both clear of the wreckage. The whole thing fucked me up. Even though I wasn't wounded, I suffered with posttraumatic stress disorder badly and was sent home on leave for a few months. I signed off then. I knew I couldn't fly again and wasn't into transferring over to another Corps."

We sat in silence for a few moments, me watching him, Tobin staring behind me without focussing his eyes on anything in particular. I knew he was remembering those dreadful days, and I felt awful for asking. All I'd wanted was to get to know him better, but my heart was suddenly aching for him. I wanted to kiss and hold him. To take him in my arms and tell him I cared that he'd made it through, because I did.

He took a deep breath, shook away his far-off look, and fixed those pale blues of his on me again, bringing back his cocky smile and playful demeanour. "While I was at home, my mum finally told me the truth about my dad. She'd stayed quiet on the subject for years, and I finally found out why. He was married, no other kids as far as she was aware, but he was part of a motorbike club and she had just been a hook-up, not a proper old lady. It turned out he was your dad's best friend, Chuck."

I was in shock. I'd known Chuck and his wife, May, my entire life. I'd heard she couldn't have children, so Tobin was right that they'd had no kids, but I never took him for a cheater. The pair of them had always seemed so in love, even after years and years of marriage. When he'd died two years before from a brain aneurism, it'd hit us all hard. I remember Tobin stepping into his position of Vice President after Chuck was gone, but never even considered that the reason why was because he was his son.

"Tobin, I'm so sorry. I had no idea," I murmured, but he shrugged it off.

"When I came to the club to find him, Chuck was already having headaches. No one had any idea what was coming, but how could they? He helped me get through the PTSD though, and even May opened her heart to me. I think she saw how much I needed some guidance and structure. A father to lead and care for me through my dark days. It was only a matter of weeks until I became a prospect. The rest is history, as they say. Your dad took me under his wing when he gave me this badge," he said, pointing to the label on his chest that showed off his title.

"My father is a good man. I hated speaking to him the way I did, but I won't apologise. I can't," I replied, staring up into Tobin's face.

"He wouldn't want you to, either. You meant what you said and were right to feel that way, so don't ever take it back. You're usually so quiet and you've gone along with everything he and the club have wanted for you since the day you were born. When you finally spoke up and said your piece, especially something so forceful and poignant as you did the other night, everyone stopped to listen. The entire club respects the shit out of you, Dahlia."

"I wish," I mumbled, unable to accept his words, and unwilling to let myself hope they might be true.

"The shock of you finally sticking up for yourself will give you their attention every time. What you said to Garret was exactly what he needed to hear. You cut yourself off from being his little girl and started being a woman in his eyes. All without the need for evidence that you've outgrown the cotton wool he'd wrapped you in, or become a woman in the traditional sense. That's why he agreed to leave us alone yesterday," Tobin told me, and he seemed so sincere I believed him.

I then watched in contemplative silence as he licked a dab of chutney from his finger and found myself thinking naughty things again. I grabbed a piece of poppadum and dipped it in the sweet sauce, more for a distraction than anything else.

"I've never opened up to anyone before. Nor have I spoken up about anything to do with my father or the club. But I guess the fear and shock over what was happening got to me, so I let him have it. Even my brothers seemed surprised to hear it." I laughed, thinking how odd it had all been, but that I was strangely glad it had happened. I was a woman now, with a voice to be heard and a life before me that was mine to lead.

Plus, there was Tobin. He really seemed to want to be with me, and I felt as though he was going to do right by me. I knew in that moment things were really going to happen between us, but that he seemed happy for me to fall in love with him on my own terms. It felt good finally being given the lead. My own time to decide and act on my feelings as I saw fit.

"I'm glad that in my own fucked up kinda way I helped you get there," he replied with a shrug. Tobin sat back in his seat and watched me while our friendly waiter brought over two large dishes piled high with chicken, onion, and peppers, all coated in thick red sauce. The rice soon followed, along with naan bread and bhaji's, and we both inhaled deeply with appreciative sighs before laughing at one another.

As I watched Tobin pile up his plate, I smiled widely, feeling close to him, which was something I hadn't thought I would be doing with the guy quite so much, or so soon. And yet, I felt completely at ease with him. I blushed when he caught me staring, but he just offered me a dazzling smile and handed over the plate with the naan on it.

"You were watching me after the meeting the other day," I told him, more of a statement than a question. "Had everything already been decided?" I'd been wondering how the decision had been made to hand my virginity over like some kind of business transaction and figured it was time to hash it out, even if I didn't like what I heard.

"Yeah, we put it to a vote," Tobin answered, and my mouth dropped open in shock. I cringed and buried my face in my hands.

"Oh God, how embarrassing!" I cried, but he just laughed.

"Not like that," he answered, and rolled his eyes. "I'd been here doing up the new clubhouse and had decided once and for all that I wanted to pursue you. I wasn't lying when I told you how much I'd been obsessing about you, Dahlia. I've been watching you for a long time, not just the last few days."

"Jesus, Tobin. You can't say things like that. No one has ever said so much as 'hi, you're cute,' to me before. I'm not equipped to deal with it," I replied as I looked back up at him, laughing timidly. But it was true. His words sent my body into chaos, responding to him in a way I'd never known before, and I didn't know how to handle it.

"Get used to it, babe. I'll always tell you," he told me with a wink. "When I got back to Birmingham, I went to your dad and asked his permission to take you out. He wasn't pleased. You were always the little lamb he'd refused to let any of his wolves have a nibble of, so to speak, and he took some convincing."

I had to laugh at his terminology, but it was pretty apt.

"How did you do it?"

"Well, I politely reminded him of his promises when I became VP. He told me I could have his daughter's hand in marriage, and I insisted he still honour it. I know it's old fashioned, but I figured I'd use his own words against him to get what I wanted. He caved, but said I had to put it to the club first. The rest of your extended family had to agree. In church, I told the other guys how I'd decided to woo the crap out of you and asked if anybody had any objections." He took a large bite of the mountainous plate of food before him and watched me, letting what he'd said sink in. When I showed no reaction other than a shy smile, he carried on. "The first to give his blessing was your father, and then everyone else followed his lead. They wanted this for us, too. So, with the club's go-ahead, I brought you here. It was your dad who was then pushing me to seal the deal quickly, hence the other night." He fixed me with a serious stare, and while I was desperate not to come undone in front of him, I couldn't hide my distaste.

I shuddered, remembering the blank look on Nico's face when he'd come in to wake me. He'd been so distant, but I'd assumed there was trouble going on downstairs or something, not that he was there to watch over us at my father's behest. Gross. Why on earth would he need that kind of confirmation that the deed had been done? Wouldn't Tobin's word have been enough?

"But we didn't do it, and yet he's gone home without us. Let me guess, we aren't to go back until I'm a proper woman, so to speak?" I asked, catching Tobin off guard with my candid question, and he nearly choked on his mouthful of chicken.

"God, I love it when you do that. I told you what happens when you finally open that pretty little mouth of yours," he said, taking a long swig of his beer and then indicating to Ashan that he wanted another. "But you're right. There's no rush, we're officially here to get the new place in order so no one is missing us. Your dad doesn't want us back there until you and I are together properly, though."

I took my first bite of curry and nodded in agreement to Tobin's earlier comment about it being good. The food really was amazing. I said nothing more about me, my virginity, or the man sitting opposite me to whom it'd been promised. I chose to let those things remain unspoken, at least for the time being.

Tobin and I were a good match. I felt it in my bones. He was fiery and wild, while I was cool and calm. He would bring me up while I would keep him grounded and, if we could get past this first bump in the road, I really believed we could become a great couple.

Images of his naked body flashed through my mind again as I thought about us being together, and I guess he must have noticed the flush of my cheeks because he gave me another dazzling grin. I think it must've been obvious that my decision not to hand myself over too easily was already dissipating, but I didn't mind. As long as he kept on being the guy he'd shown me, I was ready to keep letting my guard drop.

If I was his, then it meant that he was mine, and I was going to make sure he knew not to mess me around or cheat on me like he had with Dita.

Chapter Five

After our lovely meal, Tobin and I went across the street to a welcoming looking country pub. Inside, the décor and feel of the place was warm and neutral, far from the black covered walls and its leather-clad punters I was used to, but I liked it. Although we were new faces, the locals seemed okay with us intruding on their late-night pints, so I even felt comfortable enough to lean into Tobin's hold and let him slide an arm around my waist, finally settling into the idea of being his girlfriend.

After buying our drinks, we took a seat on a huge sofa near a softly burning fireplace. The warmth was lovely, and it wasn't long before I found myself snuggling into Tobin's arms. We chatted about everything and nothing, laughing together so effortlessly that I forgot all about the other people around us. It felt good. Amazing, actually.

When he later headed off to the bathroom, I checked my phone for any texts or calls from my father or brothers. There was nothing, which was highly unusual, but I was glad that they weren't pestering us.

"Hey, excuse me," a voice then said from over my shoulder, and I looked back to find two women around my age standing staring at me with girly grins on their overly made-up faces. "Erm, are you going out with that biker guy?" the same one asked, twirling her fake-blonde hair in her fingers. I smiled and nodded, taking a good look at the girl and her friend, and I couldn't help but cringe when they decided to take a seat on the sofa beside ours. They were the sort of girls I'd endured my entire life. Promiscuous and dressed in a way that screamed 'daddy issues', and with all the personality of a cocker spaniel—bouncy and so eager for attention, they'll do whatever tricks you want. I know I was being judgemental, but I'd seen these girls by hundreds, and none were any different from the last.

"Yeah," I replied.

"Cool. Does he know any single biker blokes?" she asked with a sultry smile. I knew my guys would eat those girls for breakfast, but I maintained my cool and nodded again.

"Yeah." I was really pushing the boat out with the responses, but I wasn't sure how much interest Tobin wanted in the club from the locals, so was glad when he came back over and hovered behind me. I looked up and caught him watching the two new arrivals with intrigue.

"Hello ladies, what can I do you for?" he asked politely, offering them one of his trademark grins, and they both giggled overdramatically.

"We were just wondering if you guys were passing through, or if you were staying in the town? We heard a bike club was gonna be moving in and we're regulars here so wondered if it was true," the blonde replied, lifting her chest in a clear attempt to get Tobin's eyes off me and down to her clearly stuffed cleavage. It didn't work.

"Yeah, we've got a new place not far from here. How about next time my boys come up we give you a text with the time and place? You can bring along any friends you think might like to come and give us a warm welcome," Tobin replied, and she positively jumped for joy in her seat. I handed Miss Giggly Blonde my phone to put in her number and smirked when I saw the name she had typed in.

"Sunny Skye?" I asked, trying not to roll my eyes at her porn-star pseudonym.

"That's right, and tell your friends I'm a model," Sunny answered and I just nodded, stashing my phone back in my pocket. We then quickly said our goodbyes to her and her friend, and Tobin tucked me under his arm. He waved to the bartender on the way out—another of his new contacts in the village, I had no doubt—and then led me from the pub.

Outside, I climbed onto the bike behind him, loving how I felt so used to riding with him already. I then slid my hands into the front pockets of his jacket and held them tightly in readiness for heading back to the new clubhouse. Tobin turned back before sliding on his helmet, peering over his shoulder at me with a wicked grin.

"Hold on tighter, babe. I wanna go fast," he told me, and laughed when I then yanked my hands from his pockets and linked them closed around his stomach. "In fact, just to be safe," he added, pulling my legs up off the pegs and around the front of his hips so that I was completely wrapped around him. Before I could say or do anything in response to his move, he roared the bike to life, and we were off.

Tobin wasn't joking when he'd said to hold on. The town whizzed away in a heartbeat and before I could even think straight, we were amidst the darkness of the country roads. I don't even know how fast we went, but my insides felt as though I was on a rollercoaster going upside-down.

When we then came to a stop outside the dark clubhouse, it took me a few moments to catch my breath, but Tobin didn't seem to mind sitting with me a little longer. In fact, he spun me around him so that we were then facing each other. I ended up perched in front of the handles of his bike, my back arched by the gas tank so that I was uncontrollably pressing against him.

My cold fingers clung to the lapels of his cut, curling around the rough edges of the leather. My legs were still wrapped around his waist and when he pulled off his helmet and then mine and peered down at me, I was speechless.

His kiss was sudden and fierce. I'd seen those sorts of kisses on TV and read about them in books for years but had never experienced anything like it in real life before. It was what some might call a kiss full of want, need, desperation, and lust. There was no denying how much he wanted me, and while I was excited, flattered, and even turned on by it, I was still scared.

I knew what would happen if we kept it up. We would end up climbing into bed together when we got inside. There would be no stopping us a second time, no backing out, and anxiety speared in my gut. I wasn't ready. Not quite yet. I trembled, whether from the cold or my fear I couldn't be sure, but Tobin felt it and lifted us both off the bike effortlessly. Leaving our kiss on pause, he settled me down on the gravelly floor, and I followed him over to the door. I then peered up into his dark face when he hesitated, his hands twirling his keyring in circles around his finger.

"What's up?" I asked.

"You know how the clubhouse back home is just called 'the clubhouse'?" he asked, and I nodded. "Well, I figured this place needs its own name, so that everyone knows where we are talking about, or which clubhouse we are meeting at." He stepped forward and peeled the plastic coating from a sign on the door I hadn't even noticed was there. I tried to think back to whether it had been there when we'd arrived a couple of nights before, but I had no idea.

As the printed image beneath the wrapping became clear, I gasped and let out a girly sigh I wanted to kick myself for. On a black background sat a reddy-orange flower that looked almost like a daisy, but I knew right away that it wasn't.

"It's a dahlia," I said, staring up at Tobin wide-eyed.

It made sense to have the sign there on the door rather than out front where our club's presence could be understated and almost invisible from the road. Tobin couldn't have put a marker up on the old hanging post where the pub sign would've gone back when it was a normal pub, as people would see it so might wander in thinking we were just another bar, and even I knew we simply couldn't have that.

"Yep, I've named this clubhouse after you. I want us to live here and oversee the running of it together. I might own the house, but everything inside—what it means and the purpose it serves—is for the club, and for you," he told me, grinning broadly. "I meant everything I said before about respecting you and wanting this to be right between us. Together we can do amazing things, Dahlia. I just know it. We can live here and go back to your dad's whenever we're needed but can have meetings here and the prospects can run the bar while your father and I deal with business. You will be free to live your life by my side rather than under your dad's thumb. What do you say?"

Every ounce of fear left me in that moment, and it suddenly dawned on me how Tobin was so much more than I'd ever thought he was before. He'd done all of this for the club, but also for me. He wanted to give me a good life with him. For me to love him and be happy by his side. I trusted he didn't want me to end up just another old lady, sat at home while he went about club business and told me nothing. From what he'd said, I'd have direct involvement in taking care of the club members. My club. My family. It would be like the morning before, with my brothers and father. Something real and an opportunity to care for them all because I wanted to, not because I was expected to.

I didn't answer him. I couldn't find the words to describe how he'd made me feel over the last two days. His words had been the icing on the cake, and I knew what I wanted. Who I wanted. I climbed up onto my tiptoes and pinned Tobin to the wall behind him, kissing him with such intense passion that my head spun. I then giggled when he pulled my legs up and around that waist of his again. Our lips locked as he finally got the door open and carried us inside. He slammed it shut behind us and locked it again, all the while kissing and holding me tight. Our bodies were so close the heat coming off us was overwhelming, so I soon longed to shed our clothes and let my body follow his heat's lead. I wanted what I knew he could give me in abundance.

Anxiety bloomed inside of me again, but I didn't stop my kisses, and was grateful when Tobin took the hint. He carried me upstairs without putting on any of the lights, knowing his way even in the dark, and then set me down at the top of the stairs.

The bedroom was pitch black as we clambered

inside, stripping off our coats and jumpers as we went, our lips never far from one another's. Before I knew it, we were standing there in just our underwear, lips still locked and hands going everywhere, but I wasn't afraid anymore. I wanted it to be right and to feel good, how I had always dreamed, and so far, Tobin was hitting every mark perfectly. There was just one thing I needed first.

"Can I just have a minute?" I murmured, stepping back, and peering up into the darkness in search of his pale blue eyes.

"As long as your minute doesn't turn into you trying to run off again?" he replied, his tone sincere even behind the jokiness, and I was glad. He wasn't pressuring me or making fun of my fight-or-flight response from the last time we'd been together naked.

"I promise. I just want a quick shower. I feel yucky," I told him, and then felt my way over to the en-suite in the dark. Tobin said nothing more. Nor did he follow me inside, and I was grateful for the moment to reconnect with my thoughts.

Running the hot water, I climbed in and made quick work of washing my hair. As I lathered up and washed my body from head to toe, I'm sure I took somewhere close to one hundred deep breaths to calm myself down. I'd always known that my first time would be scary though, so put my anxiety down to just nerves rather than anything else.

I wanted Tobin. I was absolutely sure of it, and as I washed between my thighs, I could feel my body's readiness to carry on where we'd left off. I was tender and sensitive, wetter than I'd ever been before. Every one of my senses was heightened. My skin was tingling and desperate to be touched, and when I shut off the shower, I dried myself with an awkward smile. I was ready.

Tobin wandered in just as I was finishing drying off, making me jump, but he simply grinned and kissed my shoulder with a gentle, appreciative touch. His loving gesture sent my body reeling with fresh hormones, and I accidentally dropped one side of the towel I was using to the floor. As I stood naked before him, I didn't shy away, though. I dropped the other edge of the towel and Tobin watched me, biting his lip as he saw my body react to the sudden chill. My nipples hardened, and I could see his eyes on them. He seemed to enjoy having caught sight of my bare body in the bright light of the bathroom, but I suddenly felt embarrassed. It was a stark contrast to the dark bedroom, and I cringed.

"You're so beautiful," he groaned, slipping off his boxers to reveal his very ready hard-on, and I blushed. Tobin said nothing else, though. He didn't bring any attention to my reaction, nor did he come closer. He simply climbed into the shower and re-started the jets, watching me through the glass door as he washed himself, and I knew he was making sure he was prepped for me too. While he washed, I plaited and tied up my auburn hair, still naked. I could feel his eyes on me the entire time I fiddled with my long braid and brushed my teeth, and the entire experience provoked reactions in me I'd never had before. I felt powerful, sexy, and beautiful. Tobin was the one making me feel that way, and I wanted him to know I felt the same about him too.

When he finally climbed out of the shower, dripping wet and sexy as hell, I threw him a towel and then wandered back into the bedroom while he dried himself off.

There, I flicked on the bedside lamp and then lay down under the covers in wait. My entire body was buzzing, full of every emotion imaginable, but I knew I was finally prepared for what was about to happen.

Tobin climbed into bed beside me and he leaned up on one elbow, watching my reaction as he ran his free hand over my face, neck, and then down to my stomach. He leaned in and kissed me hard, just like before, and I swooned. When he pushed me back against the pillow and climbed over me between my legs, I couldn't help from trembling, but he kept his hardness away and continued to just kiss me. When his hand found my nipple, I moaned loudly in response, unable to help it, and Tobin laughed against my mouth.

"You like that?" he asked, pinching the delicate bud gently and rolling the flesh between his fingers in a move that had me arching my back in response. I was shocked how a pinch there could cause a wave of pleasure to surge through my belly. I'd never imagined anything like it, and I moaned loudly again as he ducked beneath the covers and his mouth moved downwards. He then pressed it against my other nipple, licking and sucking it into his mouth while his fingers continued working at the other side. I was in heaven. My breathing ragged. Never in my life had I felt the way Tobin was making me feel. Never before had I explored my body or discovered the carnal pleasure that awaited me in private. I hadn't thought it was appropriate, but my only fully lucid thought was how foolish I'd been not to experiment and explore my own body for all those years. How many times had I felt the heat burning between my thighs and ignored it? Too many. Far too many...

After a few minutes of that amazing attention to my

nipples, Tobin then slid his hand down between my thighs and it was his turn to moan as he discovered just how ready I was for him. Even I could tell how hot and wet it'd become down there as his fingertips glided across my untouched skin, stroking his way against my folds without any resistance from my body. Before I knew it, he had one inside of me. It caressed me gently, tenderly seeking unchartered realms just an inch at first, then deeper. When he began sliding it in and out, again and again, I opened my legs wider. I needed it. Wanted it. All thought left me as Tobin took my body and made it his. When he then disappeared beneath the covers and his mouth suddenly joined his hand between the apex of my thighs, I cried out. Tobin sucked and tickled the swollen bead there while a second finger joined in the fun inside of me, and I writhed wildly on the bed. I moaned, shocking myself with how loud I called his name as I came for him, hard. It was my very first orgasm, but it was absolutely the most amazing experience I'd ever had and was quickly followed by a second when Tobin refused to release my body from his grip. He continued regardless of my release and quickly had me seeing stars.

"Shit, oh my God!" was all I could manage as I came undone at his command. When I was breathless and spent, Tobin kissed my stomach and breasts in a wordless meander back up towards my face.

"I've never tasted something so sweet, nor have I felt perfection like this. I've never seen a woman so flawless as you, Dahlia," he groaned against me, while I laughed shyly and snuggled into him. "We don't have to do anything else, you know? I just want to lie by your side and watch you sleep. I want to keep you safe and be with you. I made you a promise, and I'm sticking to it," he said, staring down at me.

I knew with absolute certainty that he would back off if I said so and felt empowered by his promise. I appreciated his effort, but it was no use. No matter that he'd already given me one of my many firsts, I wanted more. I had to have him.

"After what you just did, you're not going anywhere," I whispered, curling my body so that I pressed my still trembling core against him invitingly and Tobin inhaled sharply. His body responded in an instant, telling me he wanted more of me, too.

"I'm clean, and I know you're on the injection. But I need to know you're sure, though?" he checked, looking into my eyes as though he had to be absolutely certain, so I decided to be brave and show him I meant every word. I reached down and took his hard-on in my hand. At first, I wasn't all that sure what to do with it, so I fondled his heavy shaft with a clueless grip, and guessed how to administer the right strokes, but he seemed to enjoy it, so I carried on.

"Absolutely sure," I whispered after a few minutes. I then kissed his lips and guided him towards my still soaked and sensitive opening, leaning back so he could climb over me on the bed again. Tobin was trembling as he lifted himself up, waiting as though forcing himself to take it slow, but once he seemed sure there were no doubts to come from me, he let his body fit itself against mine.

After dipping the tip in and out a few times, he then properly let himself go. He pushed inside with one final, deep plunge, and although pain seared through my core at the intrusion, I didn't stop him. Tobin's eyes never left mine as he moved slowly inside of me. He even kissed away the one stray tear that fell onto my temple after the initial shock of pain had hit.

"I'll never hurt you again," he whispered as he swayed back and forth inside me, going slow and gentle, and I kissed his soft lips in response. I then wrapped my legs around his waist to welcome him deeper when the pain began to subside, which was when Tobin took the hint and let himself speed up. He was still being careful not to go too fast or too deep, but I was happy and relaxed regardless of the ache.

He seemed to sense it and he found his rhythm, making love to me for a while before he then released inside of me. When he bucked and stilled, he remained pressed against me, our bodies sticky with sweat, each of us trembling. I was still aching from my releases and the twinge that still throbbed deep within after my first time, but the wonderful intensity of it was amazing. I was smiling so wide that Tobin couldn't seem to help but grin back when he caught me.

"You okay?" he asked, sliding back and out of me. He gently wiped me clean with a towel he must've had at the ready and cleaned himself up, all the while watching me intently. He then lay down beside me and wrapped me in his arms.

"More than okay," I replied, snuggling into his embrace. I could've sworn I heard a sigh of relief come from him, but I didn't want to check to make sure. Our first time together was exactly what we'd both wanted all along. The previous attempt was just a bump in the road caused by my dad getting far too involved in my personal life than he ought to have, and I was truly glad I'd spoken up that night.

After a few minutes, the slickness between my legs

started to irk me, so I slid out of Tobin's hold and scurried off to the bathroom. I took another shower and washed away the small smear of blood left between my thighs after our lovemaking with a gentle swish of my hand against my tender folds but was glad I wasn't overly sore. I felt tired, though. Aching from the inside out, but overall, I was good. More than good, I felt incredible.

Tobin had a quick shower after me again too, while I climbed back into bed and pulled the covers up around my neck, waiting patiently for him to finish and come back to me. He did, and together we then slept so soundly it was as though I'd blinked and it was morning again.

My body was achy and still a little tender as I came out of my drowsiness, but the soreness was a welcome reminder of Tobin's gorgeous body, his amazing touch, and of how I had finally become a woman thanks to him. Despite everything, it had happened, and I felt wonderful.

Chapter Six

"Does this mean we have to go home now?" I asked Tobin when we were sat opposite one another at the kitchen table later that morning, drinking coffee and eating cereal together. He was sitting opposite me and had his hands on my ankles, which he'd pulled up and placed either side of him on the bench so that he effectively sat between my legs. His hands caressed my calves and feet in hard, yet carefully pressured sweeps to help massage them, and it felt amazing. I had the notion he wanted his hands on me at all times because he'd been the same all morning, and I relished in his attentiveness.

"What Garret doesn't know won't hurt him," he replied, grinning roguishly at me from over his cookie cereal. "I'm not quite ready to give you up yet, babe." I couldn't help but beam in response. I was glad to hear he was in no rush to get back to the crazy normality that was still technically home. Back there, we would be surrounded by the club members, and it would be back to business as usual for Tobin. I wouldn't have his undivided attention like I had at the new clubhouse and wasn't ready to give him up yet either.

"I like your thinking," I replied, watching him with a smile.

"I say we stay for as long as we can get away with it. This is gonna be your home, after all, so we'll just call this your settling-in period. We do need to go and buy you some new clothes for the time being, though," he added with a smirk. I nodded in agreement, but then fixed him with the hardest, most stern stare I could manage. Forcing my good mood aside to play the part of the angry girl.

"Now then, Tobin Stone. You haven't actually asked me if I would like to move in with you, or if I would like to marry you. No more calling me your fiancée and less of the expectations about me moving in, okay. I think we both know I deserve a lot more wooing, thank you very much," I teased, my eyes alight. I then revelled in his surprised look.

"Shit, you're right!" he conceded, placing one hand on his heart, and bowing his head. "Please accept my sincerest apologies, my lady."

"You're forgiven," I replied with an air of grace to my tone, playing along. "And I suppose that seeing as you have named this place after me, I should at least consider your offer to live here, but don't take it for granted that I'm staying," I warned. I needed to keep my little bit of power where I could, and Tobin seemed to pick up on it right away. He shook his head profusely.

"Absolutely not. But I must insist that we get you some new clothes. I'm so sick of that god awful cardigan now," he joked, leaping back as I swiped at him with a pretend slap. He did have a point, though. It was time I ditched the frumpy old lady clothes I'd always used to hide in and tried dressing like the twenty-year-old I was.

Within an hour, we were back in the nearby town.

Even though I could tell he hated shopping, Tobin stayed with me while I wandered the small precinct and picked up a few new outfits. When I was finally finished, he pulled me into the nearest coffee shop and breathed a sigh of relief that it was over.

"Come on, I didn't take that long!" I insisted, but then took in the number of bags we were carrying between us and quickly changed the subject rather than admit I'd indulged. Tobin was a perfect gentleman, though, so apart from a little teasing, he left the subject alone. I loved laughing and talking with him so easily and was glad things hadn't become awkward after our night of passion. I wasn't sure what else I'd expected, though. A huge sign over my head? For someone to turn up and hand me a certificate stating my acceptance into womanhood? For him to be congratulated by every other man we passed on the street?

I was getting lost in my head again, so the conversation ran dry, but it wasn't an uncomfortable silence. Far from it. For a while, we just sat back and watched the world go by as we ate our cakes and drank coffee. We chatted a little more here and there, but we were both simply content to enjoy our moment and I loved watching Tobin as he people watched. He took in everything and everyone around him. Not missing a beat.

Tobin was a confident and powerful man. He was as intimidating as any of the other club members, despite him not being as tall or muscly as some of the others. Everyone noticed him and not just because of the cut or the tattoos. The girls in the town had all watched him as they passed us. I'd caught many of them whispering to one another or giggling like idiots, but he seemed so used to the attention he either didn't notice or had learned to ignore them.

Part of me wanted to snuggle into him tighter just to rub it in that he was with me, but for one, I wasn't that cocky, and two, I knew those girls didn't stand a chance with someone like Tobin. Any of his club brothers would've gone over and asked for phone numbers if they were being ogled at like that, and I knew how when we'd be sat in the same coffee shop a few months later with them, they'd be doing just that. Not Tobin. Whoever those women were that he'd cheated on Dita with, I figured they must've been special. I also knew they couldn't have been club regulars, otherwise there would've been trouble. Part of me wondered if he'd gone to a prostitute or had one-night-stands while away on club business, just like his own father had seemingly done all those years ago with his mother, and I hated the idea.

"What are you thinking about?" I asked, basking in his gaze when he turned those amazing blue eyes of his on me. Excitement swelled within me, the memory of the previous night coming back in full force, and I loved that we'd shared so much in just the short time we'd grown closer.

"I was remembering what we were doing twelve hours ago," he teased, seeming to have been thinking about it too, and I grinned. "And how I want to do it again. Can we head back to Dahlia's now?" Tobin then asked with a wink. He leaned closer and tucked my hair behind my ear before whispering into it seductively. "I'd quite like to get you naked."

"One last stop and I'm all yours," I replied, grinning widely when he shook his head and gave me a pleading look. "No more clothes shops, I promise. I just figured out what the new clubhouse, I mean Dahlia's, is missing," I told him. I smiled when I corrected myself, because it sounded so big-headed calling the new place after me, but just hoped in time that I'd get used to it.

We left the café and headed towards where his bike was parked, but on the way, I pulled Tobin into our last shop. It was an electronic place, so full of tech and gadgets that my inner geek purred. I found my desired item with ease and paid the cashier, shaking my head when Tobin asked to see what I'd bought. "It's a surprise."

When we got back, I quickly put my new clothes away in a ready and waiting chest of drawers and wardrobe while Tobin took a shower. I knew for sure then how the room I'd slept in those first three nights was from then onwards going to be mine and Tobin's room. Ours. I smiled to myself, still shocked at how everything had panned out, but I wouldn't have changed it for the world.

I grabbed the last of my shopping bags and opened my newest gadget. After playing with it for a few minutes, it was ready, so I ran downstairs excitedly. I then ducked behind the wooden bar and began fiddling with the cables before Tobin had even finished his wash.

"Where are you, babe?" he called from the bedroom a few minutes later, and I could hear him opening and closing his drawers, looking for some clothes, before padding downstairs to find me. As his foot hit the bottom step, I hit play on the new MP3 player I'd bought for Dahlia's while we were in town. One of the rock albums I'd just purchased online and synced to the device, then filled the entire downstairs floor. I could hear Tobin laughing as he neared me, and by the time I clambered to my feet again, he was standing on the other side of the bar in wait. He stared at me with those baby blues I was rapidly falling in love with. "God, you're such a geek," he said, but I simply shrugged.

I then handed him a beer from the under-counter fridge and grabbed a can of cola for myself. I was glad when he didn't make a comment about my choice of soft drink. I'd had quite a few glasses of wine over the previous three nights. Well, a few for me, and wasn't all that bothered about drinking any more.

Next, I headed around the bar, but didn't go to him. Instead, I went to the couch, where I relaxed into it and let the sounds of my favourite band wash over me with a smile. Tobin joined me, which was exactly what I'd wanted, and as soon as he sat down beside me, I climbed into his lap, straddling him with a nerve I didn't know I had. We kissed fervently, so deep and passionate that I could feel my body aching for him again but ignored it and focussed on him instead. Tobin's erection was pressing into my thigh with such tenacity that I knew he needed seeing to. When I released him and began stroking, he inhaled sharply, letting me know he was on board with my plan.

"Show me how you like it," I said, cupping and pulling in the way he directed while he groaned in response. He was huge, something I was still getting used to, but I loved the softness of it. I hadn't expected the skin to be smooth. I'm not sure what I had expected, but I wrapped my hands in a tight grip and moved them up and down like he directed, finding myself getting off on watching him come undone because of me and my actions. His hands were inside my knickers before I could even take them off, and the next thing I knew they were gliding in and out of me like they had the night before.

"Fuck," he cried as he came all over my jeans, while I laughed awkwardly at the mess he'd made. This was another thing I hadn't been prepared for. However, Tobin was too distracted to notice my surprise. He pulled out his delving fingers so I could peel off my dirty trousers and then had me back in his lap so fast I shrieked in surprise. "Lay down," he ordered, turning us so I lay lengthways along the soft leather on my stomach. He then nestled himself behind me.

I felt embarrassed when Tobin slid my knickers down, knowing he was getting an eyeful of not just the front but the back too. However, he didn't seem to care at all. He slipped his hand between my thighs and rubbed my tender clit, causing my hips to move with him instinctively. And together we then moved to a delicious rhythm. When he slid backwards and two fingers crept inside my wet opening, I kept up the movement. I'd found my flow, and it wasn't long before I was panting and bucking, my release imminent. I came hard when his other hand began strumming at my swollen clit again and screamed his name when he withdrew and his somehow hard and ready to be satisfied again cock filled the space where his fingers had been.

Tobin took me effortlessly from behind in hard thrusts, and he didn't hold back this time. I cried out at the fullness but didn't stop him. It was a pleasurable invasion I was still growing accustomed to, and I didn't want it to end. My body clenched around him tightly and even though the tender muscles still resisted his presence, it didn't hurt anything like it had the night before. When he picked up speed and began pummelling me harder, I suddenly climaxed around him and he stilled, which was when I felt the throb of his release inside of me.

"You drive me crazy, Dahlia. So, fucking crazy," he mumbled, laying kisses across my back as he pulled away. I couldn't respond. I was an elated mess, downright exhausted and unable to utter a single syllable in response yet thrilled beyond words.

After a quick clean up, we lay down together on the sofa and listened quietly to the thrum of music still blaring out all around us. Tobin had me wrapped up so tightly that I felt safe and protected, more so than ever before, and I had to agree that he'd been right all along. We were perfect together, exactly the right fit and balance that it was already impossible to imagine my life without him.

"Ask me and I'll say yes," I murmured, feeling sleepy, and I felt Tobin lean down and kiss my forehead gently.

"Will you be my girlfriend?" he asked, laughing at how ridiculous it sounded, but he also seemed to know I needed him to say it and for me to say yes off my own back. Something inside of me still felt as though I was a gift my dad had given to his right-hand-man, and I wanted to at least feel as though some of it had been my idea.

"Yes," I replied, looking up at him with a smile.

"And will you move in with me? I couldn't bear living here without you. This place won't mean a thing without you in it," he then added, his voice so soft and full of emotion that I twisted around so that I could kneel between his legs.

"Well, dur! Of course, I will. I thought that was obvious," I replied, grinning and planting deep kisses on his full lips. Tobin pulled me into him, pinning me to his chest and hips, while his hands ran down every inch of me. I knew

I was being a tease, but I meant what I'd told him before. I needed to maintain a little bit of control, otherwise something deep inside of me knew I would eventually explode.

***

We spent the next five days in our amazing bubble. We made love in every room of the house and sometimes for hours on end. Tobin taught me how to express myself without any words as we explored one another's bodies and learned how each other ticked. I soon came to realise, thanks to our privacy, that I happened to be rather vocal when it came to our bedroom antics. I blushed and cringed inwardly every time I screamed Tobin's name or begged him for more in the throes of passion, but he never seemed to care. In fact, he kept telling me off for holding back or being embarrassed about it.

"It's always the quiet ones, don't worry," he told me, running his hand up over my stomach. He caressed each of my breasts while kissing the inside of my thighs, watching as I came down from another of my glorious highs.

We were in the kitchen and I was sat on the table before him, my legs wide open and I was stark naked, but I had completely stopped worrying about showing off my body to my lovely new man. It felt as though Tobin had made it his mission to make me feel good about myself. He'd never pushed me further than I was ready, nor did he ever tease me harshly about my shyness or timid ways. He was leading me into womanhood, and I gladly followed, feeling on top of the world.

I truly believed he'd enjoyed having me to himself

that week and was pleased to see that when his phone finally rang, he seemed in no rush to head back to the club. Reality kicked back in as soon as he answered, though, and my heart sank.

"Yeah, okay. We'll be there," was all I could hear of his side of the conversation. I pouted and climbed down from the table, grabbing my dress from the counter as I went. I started clearing up, guessing that the call meant we'd have to leave our little fortress soon, and I knew he'd like everything to be clean and tidy before we set off back home.

"What time?" I asked when he'd ended the call, running the hot tap to wash the dishes.

"It's Thomas's birthday celebration, plus your dad's called a meeting at eight o'clock. We need to set off in about an hour, babe," Tobin replied. He wrapped his arms around me from behind and nestled himself into my back, kissing my neck softly. I could tell he was just as disappointed as I was and that we'd both need a push to get us back home before my father came down on us both for taking the piss.

I forced myself to step away from his hold and set about the house, picking up discarded clothing and carrying it over to the hamper. I wiped down the bar tables and chairs while he grabbed the hoover and took my unspoken hint. We moved silently and so in sync, but I even enjoyed those moments and it wasn't long before we'd finished. I then showered and climbed into my skinny jeans and pulled on a blue shirt, the colour of which was the perfect match for Tobin's eyes. So was the sole reason I'd bought it.

After checking and double-checking the locks, we then climbed onto his bike and sped off. I gripped Tobin tightly as he rode back into town and buried my head in his back, feeling sad that our time of solace was over. He didn't seem to mind one little bit. When the roads were clear, instead of speeding away like when we'd ridden out, he meandered down the straights and slid one hand down to his hip so he could grip mine tenderly. He was in no rush, either.

When we arrived and walked into the building that was still both my home and the clubhouse, it should've felt normal, yet it was far from it. I felt like a completely different person than the girl who'd left a week before, and when we ducked inside the club, members treated me differently too. Tobin draped his arm over my shoulder and led me inside to a roar of cheers and calls from his fellow bikers. He grinned broadly, soaking up their approval at us being a couple, while I followed my old habits and retreated into myself, blushing as I kept my eyes on the floor.

My brothers greeted me awkwardly, our night the week before still evidently fresh in all our minds, but they seemed to be trying their hardest to forget it, and I gratefully did the same. I hugged Nico, accepting a kiss on my cheek that was a rare show of emotion from the huge man before doing the same with my other, more relaxed brothers. Nico and Tobin then sloped off to one side, talking quietly with one another, so I focussed on my closest brother to my age, Brad.

I failed to hide my surprise when he told me about a new girlfriend he wanted me to meet, however I nodded and immediately agreed. He wasn't the sort to have real relationships, so it had to be someone special for him to want me to meet her. Brad seemed overjoyed by my reaction, and I was glad that my approval seemed to mean so much to him. The other club members stayed away so we could greet each other in relative privacy—a sign of respect—and I appreciated the effort.

My brothers all seemed pleased with how things had ended up between Tobin and me. They were calm and relaxed with us, but I got the feeling Nico was grilling him, regardless of Tobin technically outranking my brother within the club. While I couldn't help but wonder what was being said between the two best friends, I kept my prying eyes and ears away. I'd never wanted to be that girl. The one who demanded to know everything that was going on in her boyfriend's life. So, I quickly made my excuses and headed to my room to deposit my bag.

Tobin caught my eye but didn't stop me from going. I knew he more than likely had a lot of club business to catch up on, and I wasn't about to get in the middle of it. I knew how things would work now that we were back there. The boys would have their meeting and then we would all get together afterwards for drinks and the chance to catch up properly. But, in the meantime, he needed his VP persona back, and I found myself wanting some peace and quiet.

A couple of hours passed and, while I enjoyed the silence of my room, I couldn't help but miss the man who'd been with me day and night during the week before. I began packing up some of my things, thinking about our plans to move into Dahlia's together, and I smiled to myself as I contemplated our new life there. When a knock at the door finally broke the silence, I assumed it must've been him and flung it open, only to find my father standing on the other side with a kind smile. I instinctively stepped forward and wrapped myself in his arms, holding on for just a few seconds before stepping back and ushering him inside.

"How are you?" he asked, leaning against my chest of drawers, and I smiled up at him from where I perched on the edge of my huge bed.

"I'm great, did Tobin talk to you?" I asked, tailing off before I accidentally hinted at something gross about me and my lack of virginal repose. He was clearly unnerved by the elephant in the room as well and shuffled on his feet, evidently not wanting to bring it up either.

"Yeah, we're all very happy for you both. How do you like the new clubhouse?" he eventually asked, looking uncomfortable.

"I love it. Tobin wants me to move there with him and he's named the bar after me," I replied, fiddling with my hands. It all felt incredibly awkward, and I hated it, but had to believe that we could get back to our old way once the unease dissipated.

"I know. I designed the new sign and gave him my blessing to ask you. I want you two to be happy, Dahlia, but I don't think you should rush into anything. I know some things were said and lots of truths came to light last weekend, but I want you to know that you don't need to run off with Tobin because you think I want rid of you. You're together now, but there's no need to go too fast. Sometimes I wonder if that was part of the problem between him and Dita," he replied, fixing me with a sad stare and I knew right away he was feeling a little lost. No matter having pushed me and Tobin together, he still seemed sad at having had to give me up after all our years of me doting on him as the most important man in my life.

"I'm not rushing anything, Dad. I will always be here for you and the boys, and I'll be a part of this club for the rest of my life," I promised, and he seemed to relax. "I guess I'm just finally becoming that woman you wanted me to be, and with that comes some independence. Tobin will take really good care of me, I trust him."

"As do I," he said, stepping forward to gather me up in his arms again, and I let him. "I just need some time to let you go. I never dreamed it would be this hard." I wanted to comfort him more, to take back the harsh words I'd uttered to him the first night we'd spent at Dahlia's, but I couldn't do it. I'd meant those words and vowed to myself I wouldn't ever take them back just to make him feel better.

A knock at the door halted any reply from me and Tobin walked in a split-second later. He had a hard stare, dark and brooding for some reason. When he saw me and my father holding onto one another tightly, he pursed his lips together, seemingly to stop his reaction from coming out. I noticed the malicious look he gave my dad though; a look he quickly hid again behind a half-smile. When we parted, Tobin didn't say a word, he just nodded in respect to his club President, who kissed my cheek and left us to it.

"Are you okay?" I asked but could tell without him even saying a word that Tobin was on edge.

"Yeah, I guess it's just weird being back here." He tried to bat his mood off with a cloak excuse, but I wasn't buying it.

"My father will always be involved in my life, Tobin. I don't want it to be him or you."

"I know that. I would never expect you to push him away. It's just that, shit, you might as well know. He's put our move to Dahlia's on hold until things settle down here. He doesn't want us there on our own 'cos there's been trouble with the Red Reapers again. One of their guys got into a fight with one of our prospects last night. The guy broke his cheekbone and wants revenge, but your dad has said no. There's been issues with their guys getting pushy for months and Garret thinks we should all stay here until he can have a sit down with their President."

My mind raced. I'd heard how another local bike club, the Red Reapers, had been growing in numbers, but didn't know things had turned violent again. Their President had a good relationship with my father, but it seemed their younger members weren't so keen on sharing turf with our club. I wasn't completely sure what pies my dad's club had their fingers in, but from what I could gather, my brothers Nico and Thomas ran a lucrative drug business in and around our part of the city. They frequented the nightclubs and bars, university campuses, and even restaurants with their goods, which were snapped up in no time by the addicts and habitual users aplenty.

They had no idea I knew all about it, though. Dita had told me a long time before. She'd gotten into using cocaine to keep herself alert and awake enough to party all night during her early twenties. When I found her stash, I demanded to know where she'd gotten it, and she burst out laughing, telling me to go and check Nico's bag. I didn't do it; I was too scared, but after that I watched them all silently, as usual. I was the unsuspected spy—part of the furniture, as it were. Eventually, I did start to notice bags of money and backpacks full of product changing hands, along with the sly looks and whispered conversations. And knew she was right.

I could tell there was more to the problem with the Reapers that Tobin wasn't telling me. His expression was almost pained, and about more than just small-time fights with other clubs. He seemed to have shut down that conversation, though, and I wasn't about to push him.

"We'll stay then, but I hope you're sleeping in here with me?" I asked, gazing up into his eyes with a sly grin, and he nodded.

"Where else could I ever sleep but in your bed, babe?" he answered, pulling me in for a kiss. I let myself enjoy being wrapped up in him and smiled to myself at his attempts at giving me a pet name, but I liked when he'd called me babe. "I have to admit, even though he's your father I hated seeing you in another man's arms," Tobin added, and he stroked my cheek with his thumb while I laughed shyly. I liked that he was jealous of other men getting close to me, even if it was my dad. I would never kick that hornet's nest for the fun of it or to get a reaction from him, but I also wouldn't ever hold back from showing my affection to my father or brothers, so hoped he would get used to it.

Before I knew what was happening, Tobin lifted me up and carried me to the huge bed, lying me down beside him. His lips caressed mine with his practised skill, knowing now exactly how I liked to be kissed. His mouth commanded mine and was so powerful and wanting that no part of me ever wanted him to stop. In that moment, I would've let him have whatever he wanted of me, and it just so happened that right then, he wanted me. It was a gift I was all too ready to give him, and when Tobin unbuttoned my fly and slid his hand between my legs, I didn't even flinch. I opened myself up and welcomed his long fingers inside of me, arching up on the duvet to allow him even deeper access, and he accepted.

A soft knock at the door a few minutes later made me jump, and I grabbed Tobin's hand, ready to wrench it away from inside my trousers. But he shook his head. He covered me with his powerful body, hiding what we were doing from whoever was on the other side of the door.

"What?" he called, giving me a wink as it opened, and Nico's head appeared around the small crack.

"Hey, sorry to intrude. Dad wants you guys' downstairs. They're giving Thomas his birthday present tonight and he wants everyone there," he informed us. Tobin nodded in understanding while I buried my face in his shoulder in embarrassment.

Not only had he not pulled his hand away, but he hadn't stopped his wonderful strokes. And almost as soon as the door shut behind my brother, I exploded in orgasm. I bit down on Tobin's shoulder in an attempt to quieten my pleasure-fuelled cries, as well as punishment for his cheekiness. I then heard a deep growl come up from his chest, as though the pain stirred something within him, something primal.

I was barely lucid again when he flipped me over and pulled my jeans down to my knees. As I felt Tobin lift my hips upwards to meet him, his fly fell open, and he pressed his raging hard-on inside my already flooded core. With no regard for being overheard, he pounded me into the mattress, making it creak and bang against the wall as he drove us to a shared orgasm. I got the feeling he wanted to claim me there at Dad's, just like he'd claimed me over and over again at the new clubhouse but didn't mind one little bit.

After cleaning ourselves up, I used the bathroom and re-applied my makeup. I was still flushed and knew I reeked of him, all male and sex, but there was nothing I could do. We needed to get downstairs.

Eyes roved over us both as we strolled into the clubhouse bar, as though nothing had happened. I felt the club members' gazes over every inch of me and wondered if everyone there knew exactly what we'd just been up to. Tobin didn't care, of course. His cocky nature probably made him want to give every guy in the room a nod and a wink, but I was too busy staring at the ground to watch him or see his friends' faces.

We then sat down and had a few drinks with the guys, celebrating my brother's birthday together as a group, before the women were eventually ushered away so that he could be given his present—a stripper named Cherry.

I led the handful of girlfriends into the smaller living room towards the back of the house, listening to them drone on about their day or how much they hated their bosses. Blah, blah, blah.

I couldn't have been less interested, but for some strange reason those women who had never been bothered about me before were unexpectedly looking at me for input. It was as though suddenly, I mattered, and they were hoping I might pipe up and join in on their conversation. I had nothing to say, though. With no job of my own and nothing exciting going on in my life other than my relationship with Tobin, there was nothing for me to chat about. I wasn't prepared for the change in them either, and thanks to my quieter nature I didn't know how to make small talk.

All I had in common with those women was the club and I knew for dammed sure that as the VP's girlfriend I wasn't going to pander to them and act as if I was grateful to be included in their conversations at last. I decided instead to see what I could get away with. Tobin's words were ringing in my ears from those first couple of days we spent at Dahlia's. He'd told me I had the full respect of the club, whether I knew it or not, and how when I spoke up, everyone stopped and listened. So, I decided to give it a try.

"Girls, do you wanna grab the plates and stuff from the kitchen? I'll start getting set up for the cake," I said, my head high and I watched them all jump to action with a grin. They quickly got to it and headed off into the huge kitchen in search of the housekeeper. She had made cakes and snacks for the club members and guests to enjoy after the boys' tantalising treat in the bar, and I smiled at the delicious array. Not quite knowing what to do with myself, I shuffled with the dinner set in an attempt to look as though I was helping before I nestled into my usual spot on the sofa. There, I watched as the women all clucked around and put together a spread worthy of a full banquet, rather than just a few dozen bikers and their old lady's. There was a sense of community there I hadn't noticed before. A life those women were leading that they found meaning in, and I was glad to have them around me. I hoped I'd learn to fit in with them, eventually.

Jodie, Nico's long-term girlfriend, sat down beside me after a few minutes, and I smiled across at her. I'd always liked Jodie. She'd always been kind to me and never condescending. She seemed to understand that while I hardly spoke or participated; I wasn't stupid or a fool to what was going on around me. In her hand was a small glass of wine for me, which I took with a murmur of thanks.

"No problem," she replied, her smile seemingly genuine. "It's good that you're finally taking part in the proper club stuff. We're a really nice group of women here. Each of us are strong and we support one another one hundred per-cent, so don't ever worry about trusting us.

You've always been around on the outside, quiet and in your little bubble. I have to say, it's lovely to have a chance to get to know you properly at last." I was shocked, appalled by my snotty behaviour, and I understood exactly where she was coming from. When I was just the little sister, protected and loved by the club but still not actually a part of it, I was an outsider there, but from the moment I'd become Tobin's girlfriend I was one of them. Just another old lady and I needed to earn their respect, like I had with the bikers who had raised me.

"I guess I figured we never had anything to talk about before. All I know is this life my father has kept me in all if these years. You girls go off and work, socialise with people outside of the club, and have a life away from this place. My only escape is in my studies and online, how sad is that?" I replied, and Jodie seemed happy to hear that I wasn't looking down my nose at them, rather that I wasn't sure where I would fit in.

"Nico is my entire world, Dahlia, just like Thomas is for Letitia, and Calvin is for Shannon over there," she said, talking about Tobin's cousin. Jodie looked over at the others, and I followed her gaze, smiling at them. They seemed to know that we were talking about them but didn't mind. I wondered if perhaps it was part of my initiation or something. Whether Jodie had been sent to talk with me. To make me see they were more than just a group of biker chicks. "My life outside of here means nothing without Nico. I hope you understand that?" Jodie added, smiling in a way I'd only just learned about. A loving, respectful way. She truly did care for my brother, and it was lovely to finally see for myself how relationships weren't quite as black and white as I'd once thought.

"I do now. This past week with Tobin has shown me what I was missing out on. He and I seemed to click even after all this time of knowing each other, but there it was and now I cannot imagine things any other way," I replied, surprised by my honesty. "It's an odd feeling, especially after his history with my sister."

Jodie nodded.

"I was good friends with Dita. I miss her terribly, but I do want you to know that she and Tobin were together for appearance's sake only, especially in the last few months. I think she knew early on that things were just a bit of fiery fun between them rather than anything serious, but it was your father who wanted Tobin to marry into the family. You two are much better suited," Jodie said, looking down as though feeling guilty for saying something. I had to agree, but in honour of my sister's memory, I didn't say it aloud.

Before long, everything was ready, and the women all sat down and chatted around me. I tried to jump in here and there, aiming for at least some input in the conversation, but it was hard thanks to the few loud ones in the crowd, Brad's new girlfriend, Tammy, being one of them.

"Is it true Tobin named the new bar after you when you'd only been together one day?" she asked me outright and I was stunned, as were the rest of the women it seemed. However, they all looked at me, clearly hoping that I might give them the details, as they too were desperate to know the truth, but hadn't wanted to ask.

"I think it's safer to say my father had a hand in naming the new clubhouse too, but yes. It's called Dahlia's."

"Tell us everything. How did you two get together in the end?" Tammy pressed, and I sighed, trying to hide my annoyance, but couldn't help my lovesick grin taking over my blushing face.

"We all went to visit it and ended up staying the night," I missed out the part about my midnight caller, choosing to elaborate slightly on the facts instead because the very thought of those women knowing the truth would have killed me. "The next morning, we were both up early and got talking. He told me he liked me and wanted me to stay behind to help him get things ready there. I was sure Dad would say no, but he agreed. The rest is obvious really."

"The way he looks at you is intense, have you noticed?" Letitia, Thomas's fiancée, asked and I nodded. "So hot, like he wants to jump your bones then and there. I bet you two were barely dressed this week?" she asked, and I buried my face in my hands, laughing uncontrollably at her too open question.

"Okay, okay. I think that's enough. Dahlia is not ready to talk about this stuff, and we shouldn't push her. Let's just talk about something else," Jodie chimed in, and I was glad. Following her lead, the others soon began talking about their own sex-lives instead and while I was grossed out to hear about what they were getting up to with my brothers and close friends in the club, I was glad that the limelight was off me.

After a little while, I excused myself and headed to the bathroom, ready for a breather from all the girly nonsense. On my way, I heard wolf whistles coming from the bar. I couldn't resist a peek at the performance, and I gasped when I slipped my head around the doorway. The stripper was truly putting on a good show. Her long black hair swung in a ponytail to her waist and her clothes were now long gone. She was bent over in front of Thomas with what I could only assume was a banana inside her lady-parts.

All the guys were egging him on to take a bite and, through the sea of leather-clad burly men, I saw my brother bend down and take not one bite, but three, finishing off the entire thing while the woman wriggled herself in front of him.

She was brazen, confident, and beautiful. When she moved it was elegant, like a dancer, and she had every guy in the room eating out of the palm of her hand. Even I had to admit she was hot and seemed to be in the right profession.

I slunk away after that, not needing to see any more, but as I did, I caught Tobin's eyes on me. No one else seemed to have noticed my tiny presence, but he had, and he gave me one of those sexy as hell winks of his before turning back to the show.

Chapter Seven

I climbed the stairs, feeling hot. I wanted to take off my sweater but wasn't ready to wander the busy house in just a camisole, so headed back to my room to dig out a shirt to wear instead. As I passed Dita's old room, I noticed the door was ajar, and I poked my head inside. Nothing had been touched since before she had died and I wondered when my father might get around to going through her things, or whether it would be left for me to eventually take care of it all.

It was odd. As if she were due back at any moment. Not gone forever, like I had to keep reminding myself. The smell of her perfume still lingered, and her dirty clothes were still in the hamper as though they might be washed and worn again, when I knew they would probably just get thrown away. I ran my hands over her dresser that was covered in various makeup items, along with hooks that had jewellery hanging from them and the lotions and potions she'd used daily to keep her skin soft and youthful looking. I had hardly ever been in her room before. We were never really close, and I had always put it down to our age gap but thinking about it we just never really connected. It was such a damn shame we hadn't had the time to try and change things between us.

I took one of her bracelets and put it on, deciding that I would keep it in her memory and in my moment of sorrow I decided to grab a few small bits and pieces to hold on to as well. I took her small bottle of expensive perfume, a scarf that she had worn when we had all gone out on my twentieth birthday earlier that year, and a small trinket box that held my mum's wedding ring inside. I hadn't even known she had it, and as I climbed up and turned to leave, I thought about our mother. I wondered what it would've been like to grow up with her around, and I missed the idea of who I thought she would have been to me. The lessons I might've learned for having had her around. The woman I might have become, thanks to her example.

I sat on Dita's bed, sniffing the scarf like some lunatic, and I felt something hard resist the pressure from beneath the sheets. Lifting back the duvet, I found Dita's laptop just sitting there. It matched my own, but I had hardly ever seen her use it. The standby light was on though, and I wondered how long it could have been there, waiting for her to return and use it again. The battery had lasted well, but it wouldn't have carried on for more than a couple of weeks and so I grabbed that too, interested to see what might be on it. Perhaps some photos or her favourite music.

Back in my room, I deposited the bits I had taken in my bedside drawer and slid the laptop under my bed, needing to wait for the right time and some privacy before I could even think about looking inside. Shaking off my sadness, I then grabbed a shirt, slipped it on, and climbed back downstairs just as the stripper was being seen out of the back by Thomas, their lips locked and their hips gyrating against one another's open fly's in motions Tobin had recently taught me. While I was annoyed at him for straying while his fiancée was just a few feet away, I said nothing, as always, and didn't bother to stop them.

"Did you like the banana trick?" Tobin's voice then whispered in my ear from out of nowhere and in a sudden move, I was yanked into a dark corner and pinned to the wall from behind. His hard length pressed into my back, and I pushed against it, making my man groan with satisfaction.

"Very imaginative, but I doubt I'll be trying it anytime soon though," I whispered, spinning myself around to face him, and Tobin took the opportunity to kiss me deeply. I could tell that the stunning stripper had worked her magic on him too; he was on fire and clearly needed to release some of that tension soon. So, I dropped to my knees and unzipped his fly, looking around to make sure that no one would catch us before I sucked that tension right out of him with a satisfied smirk.

Before too long, everyone was gathered, having sung Thomas a happy birthday song. We then began tucking into the cake and other tasty treats and I enjoyed the fun atmosphere. Tobin kept me close the entire time, his arm either around my waist or shoulders, and I noticed when we moved into the bar that many of the regular girls who came to have fun with the single guys at the club were giving me evils. They were dressed in skimpy skirts and tops that barely covered their arse or cleavage, all just there for fun and fucking. Many had seemingly had their sights set on my new beau for a while, so were disappointed to see that Tobin had moved on from Dita without their help.

"Sweet and innocent, my arse. I bet she's had her eye on him for years," one girl, Hadley, said to her friend as I passed on my way back from the bar. I knew she was just jealous, but still, she was in my house and if she thought she could get away with that, she sure had another think coming. I'd never liked that girl. She was one of the easy lays the guys allowed back time and time again because she was so starved for attention she welcomed any she could get. Everything about her offended me and I remembered how she and Dita had some run-ins over the years, too. And now she dared to start on me? With two bottles of beer in one hand, I wandered straight up to her and put my face right in hers.

"What did you say?" I demanded, and Hadley's mouth dropped open in shock that I had dared confront her.

"Nothing," she stuttered.

"Damn fucking right. I catch you saying 'nothing' about me again and I'll make sure you're never invited back here again. Got it?" She nodded and tried to look away, but I caught her chin in my free hand, leaning in closer. "Don't you ever talk about me or my family, Hadley. I would hate to have to show you just what I'm capable of," I added, not even sure what I was threatening her with, but it seemed to work and both she and her friend stood in silent shock as I barged past them. Without so much as a backwards glance, I sauntered away and sat down on Tobin's lap, handing him his beer while I took a long swig of mine, and he gave me a wink.

In front of everyone, I then let him stroke those gorgeous hands of his over my legs, arse, and back. I let him stake his claim on me and enjoyed it. I felt powerful and more in control thanks to his touch and craved more of the confidence he was giving me.

"How soon can we get outta here?" he asked, kissing my neck gently, and I giggled. So, he wanted more, too.

I looked up and caught my brother Brad watching us with an odd expression, almost as if he was angered by our public display of affection. There was none of his usual soft, playful look there and it suddenly made me feel uncomfortable. As if I was playing it up too much. Like I was embarrassing him, and myself, by allowing Tobin to paw over me.

As I stood and straightened my clothes, feeling a little flustered, I caught my dad watching Brad. He was nestled within the usual crowd of his loyal men who were chatting to him, but he was seemingly ignoring them, choosing instead to watch my brother as he watched me.

"I'll be back in a minute," I told Tobin, who clearly wanted to ask me what was up, sensing my sudden iciness. I was glad when he thought better of it and let me go, watching my every step until I was out of sight and in the hall.

I used the bathroom, taking my time while I tried to shake off the image of Brad's face from my mind. Part of me didn't want to go back to the bar, feeling awkward and uncomfortable that he seemed so disgusted with mine and Tobin's affection for one another. I knew I had to, though. I couldn't just up and leave anymore.

My dad was waiting for me out in the hall and his scowl was gone as he took me in and smiled.

"Got a minute?" he asked, and I nodded. I followed him into his office, taking a seat opposite him at the huge desk. He poured himself a glass of whiskey but didn't offer me one. I guessed I was still that little girl in his eyes regardless of him having passed the proverbial torch to his VP. "Your brother doesn't agree with you and Tobin being together. I can see it on his face. I think that perhaps you draping yourself all over him should be kept for private times," he said, taking a long swig of his drink. I wanted to scream at him and argue that this was what their collective vote had pushed on me, but once again I stayed quiet, nodding like the doting daughter I knew I was expected to be. "Oh, and if anyone tries to challenge you again like that slut out there, you take her outside and beat the shit out of her. Don't let anyone belittle you, Dahlia, especially not the likes of her. Teach those wannabes a lesson. Use the next one who talks to you that way to set an example to the others that you aren't to be fucked with."

"Shit, Dad, that's not who I am. I crapped myself just getting in her face like that. You know I'm not one for fighting or even having a row," I replied, a smile on my lips, but I understood what he was saying and promised myself that next time I would do exactly what he had told me to.

"I know, but if you're going to be the queen of this castle, you need to demand the other's respect. You know me and the guys all love you, but the women only know you as the quiet girl you once were, so they probably think you're weak. Together we are going to change that perception though and before long everyone will know you are number one around here," he replied, twisting the half full glass in his fingers. "Part of that responsibility is taking charge when I need you to, but also not asking questions or getting too involved in club business if I make it clear you're to back off. You're going to be more than the namesake of the new clubhouse or just the VP's girl. Things are kicking off and I want you to take the women and kids to Dahlia's and keep them there until I give the all clear. The guys and me need to go on a run and we'll be back in a few days, maybe a week.

Some of them will stay with you though, and your brothers will stay here to hold down the fort." He said nothing more, and I knew not to question him any further. I'd been issued my orders and knew my dad expected me to follow them to the letter. It felt odd to be leading the women away to the safety of another house for a while, just like I had needed to do so many times before, and yet I would have to be the one to take charge. I knew from the recent talks that there was a problem with the Reapers, but it seemed odd that most club members would head off on a run in one go if that were what was kicking off. I never knew what that term really meant, just that a few guys would go away to conduct business and it was only ever discussed at their closed-door club meetings. Still, I agreed to do as he had asked, unsure how to take care of mums, children, or even myself away from his house, but I was sure going to give it my best shot.

Tobin was waiting for me outside Dad's office and together we headed straight upstairs to my room. I flopped down on the bed, suddenly exhausted, but as he began peeling away my clothes, I squirmed in excitement. It didn't matter that we had already had our fun earlier that afternoon. I was ready for him again and Tobin knew it.

He pinned me to the bed from behind and grabbed my hands. He slid his fingers between mine so that we were locked, entwined and so very much one as his hard length found my slick opening. Tobin pushed my thighs open using his knees, stretching my own knees up and wide as he pressed inside and began pounding me hard. I groaned and buried my face in the duvet as I screamed his name, unable to control my uncharacteristically loud moment and Tobin let go of my hand so that he could grab my chin and turn my head to the side.

"Don't you dare hold back. I don't care if everyone in this entire house has to hear you scream my name," he whispered in my ear, moaning as I clenched around him uncontrollably and I nodded, letting him elicit another scream from me.

***

The next day, we got everybody ready, and I started packing some things to take with me to Dahlia's. As I was slipping my laptop into my backpack, I quickly grabbed Dita's one out from under the bed and put that inside too, figuring I might try and boot it back up while I had some time alone at the new clubhouse. I then donned my jeans and leather jacket and pulled my bag onto both shoulders, before enjoying the show as Tobin then wandered in from the en-suite. He began drying himself and then dressing in front of me. I watched his slim body move with power that had nothing to do with muscles. His ink, as well as that dark olive skin and short dark-blond hair, was mesmerising, but when he shot me a look with those pale blues, I could've melted on the spot.

"You're riding with me, by the way," he told me, and I shot him a cute smile.

"Where else would I be than with you, baby?" I replied, taking his offered hand when he was ready before following him down to the bikes. Brad was at the foot of the stairs, his expression much the same as the night before, and I immediately let go of Tobin's hand. I still couldn't get over the weird vibe he was giving off and was finding it a little upsetting. He and I had always gotten on well and I just had to hope that he was doing it either out of his care for me, or his loyalty to Dad. There was no confronting him. I wasn't that girl, but I hoped to God that by the time we returned from Dahlia's, he had sorted whatever problem he had out.

We arrived at the new clubhouse way ahead of all the others, thanks to Tobin's speed. We'd also travelled by bike, rather than us going with the convoy of cars driving up with the families of the club members all piled inside.

Tobin unlocked the door and together we quickly set about opening the curtains and cracking the windows open a little to air the house out. Luckily, everything was still spotless from when we had left it and so we had nothing to do as we waited for the rest of the club but wrap our arms around one another and hold on tight.

"I'm going to miss you, Dahlia," he whispered into my hair, smoothing it gently down around my face and shoulders.

"Me too," I replied, holding him tighter. "I can't believe it's been such a short amount of time, but I can't bear the thought of being without you," I added, surprising even myself.

"I want you to know that there's only you for me now, no one else," Tobin said, making my heart leap in my chest. I knew he was talking about the times he had cheated on Dita and had to admit, I was relieved to hear it. The sheer thought of him in someone else's bed made me want to cry.

"Same here. I'll never be with anyone else as long as I live," I replied, staring up at him with wide eyes. "And I think I'd kill any other woman who so much as even tries it on with you, Tobin." We both laughed, knowing that it was an empty threat coming from his timid girl, but I really hoped he understood what I had meant by it. That he meant that much to me.

"My heart stays here with you, Dahl, don't even worry," he replied. The sound of my shortened name came out like he was also calling me 'darl' and I liked it. My sister had called me her little darling when I was younger. I hadn't been called that in a long time, but it reminded me of her once loving way with me and I liked Tobin was giving me an affectionate nickname too.

The others soon arrived, and we set about showing them to their rooms and settling everybody in. After a short while, my father ushered me to one side, and I then followed him into Tobin's office towards the back of the bar. Inside were filing cabinets and a huge desk in the centre with a PC on it, and I noticed right away how there were no windows for prying eyes. Once we were both inside and the door had closed behind us, Dad lifted a duffle bag up from the floor and put it on the desk, opening the zip to reveal stacks of cash inside. There must have been thirty thousand pounds in there and I guess my face said it all, because he then started to laugh at me.

"There's a safe behind that painting," he said, pointing to the wall behind me. I turned and grabbed the bottom of the frame, pulling it towards me. And what do you know, there it was. The small alcove was currently unlocked, and a modern locking mechanism sat on the front while a huge metal lever opened its airtight void.

Dad started handing me piles of the cash and I knew to place them inside. When he reached the bottom of the bag, he pulled out a wallet and handed it to me, and I cocked one eyebrow. "Legal documents. The deeds to this place. Important stuff that I'm entrusting to you to keep safe. A copy of my will is in there, plus the details of the bank accounts for the club and my personal ones. You and Tobin are in charge if the worst ever happens to me," he said, reaching down again into the duffle. While he remained focussed on the task at hand, I shrunk. The very idea of potentially having to get his affairs in order someday made the colour drain from my face. I wasn't prepared to lose another member of my family.

"Dad, I don't know how to lead. Perhaps Nico should hold on to these?" I asked, my voice a harsh whisper. Dad looked up at me, giving me that hard Proctor stare that both he and my brothers had, the one that made you wish the ground would swallow you up so that you could escape it.

"You are the one and only person I trust with my legacy, Dahlia. There is no one else in this world that I would entrust my life, my belongings, my wealth, or my estate to. As for being a good leader, you just do whatever it takes to look after these people and the rest will come easily. As long as they know who you are underneath that timid exterior, they will trust you to lead them, and you'll show them that person in time just as you have shown me and Tobin." A tear fell from my eye, one treacherous drop of weakness that I had been trying so hard to hide the last few days and I hated showing him just how overwhelmed I was and how much I had clearly needed his encouraging words.

"I love you, Daddy," I said, wiping my cheek and reaching out for whatever was left in the duffle. "I'll always do right by you and the club, I promise."

"I know you will, and we'll do right by you as well,

just like always," he replied, his expression much softer. He then handed me two guns from the bag. They looked like pistols and were surprisingly heavy when I took them into my palms. I wasn't surprised to find weaponry in the club, as I knew most of the guys packed some kind of protection but was still stunned that he was expecting me to have some as well. After sliding them inside the safe with their ammo, I nodded to my father and swung the door closed.

"You choose the code now and only yourself and Tobin can know it. You must never leave the safe unlocked. Even if you're alone in the house. This door," he pointed to the office door behind him. "You lock it every time you leave. Security is incredibly important, but we also need to make sure that no one gets their hands on that cash or those weapons." I understood. There were children here as well as teenagers, and if they had the opportunity to fool around with a gun, they would no doubt take it and could do something awful.

"I'll never leave it unsecured, Dad. I promise," I told him, staring at the keypad as I wondered which code to use.

"Good," his voice chimed from over my shoulder. "This model also has a camera built into the keypad and will send you an email with the photograph of the person who unlocks it every time it is used. As long as all you're getting are photos of you or Tobin, it's all good. Oh, and don't choose dates or names for the code—too easy to guess," he said, leaving me alone then, and I heard the door close behind him.

I put my computer geekiness to good use and decided upon a code made from mixing Tobin's name and mine. I added random numbers and was sure no one would ever just guess to take each letter from our names in turn to create my otherwise jumbled array to make the password. It might take a bit of working out the first few times I did it, but I was sure that before long we would both have it sussed and after punching in the code three times to program it in, I was all set.

Closing the painting behind me, I then grabbed my bag and pulled out Dita's laptop. It looked no different to mine, except a small dent on the side that I would easily identify and so I didn't worry about anybody else noticing the difference. I knew it didn't really matter that I had begun going through her belongings, but a part of me liked having a secret. Mine and hers, something I could have without anyone interfering or looking over my shoulder. I looked forward to snooping on what the laptop beheld, so plugged in the charger and locked it away in the office behind me while I went to say my goodbyes to Dad and Tobin.

I grabbed the keys and made for the door, locking it closed behind me before making my way back into the busy bar area. There, I caught Tobin's pale blue eyes on me the second I entered, but we were both too busy to make our way over towards one another. He was getting one of the younger mums sorted with her request for a downstairs room or at the least, a baby-gate for her toddler, and I could hear him asking one of the prospects to run down to the local shop to try and grab a gate before it closed. I quickly sped through the crowd and intercepted the young guy, Paddy, and eyed Tobin.

"There are actually a few things we'll need, like groceries, and we could do with a new toaster. Why don't we go down ourselves for a quick run and at least then we won't have to do a food shop for a few days?" I asked him, keeping my face straight and my smile small so that the others hopefully wouldn't realise that I was trying to get Tobin alone for as long as I could before he had to go.

"Good plan, Dahl," he replied, using that nickname that made me swoon. "Keys," he ordered to Paddy, holding out his palm and the prospect immediately dropped the ones he was holding into his boss's hand. My dad caught us on our way out the door and clapped a hand on Tobin's shoulder.

"One hour," was all he said, and we both nodded. We didn't care that we were going shopping, something I now knew Tobin loathed. That one hour alone was a welcome treat.

He drove us and we then zoomed up and down the aisles of the nearest supermarket, grabbing tins of easy cupboard essentials and fresh meats, veg, and fruit. It felt so easy with Tobin. Natural. I loved having him close while we did normal things like food shopping. It felt right debating with him over which type of pasta to buy. I was smitten, and I knew it, but wasn't prepared to put on the brakes or back away. Not after everything he'd taught me and shown me. Everything we had, and I believed we could be.

A full to the brim trolley and a few stairgates later, we were heading home. The pair of us walked in the door less than an hour after we'd left, and I saw my father check his watch with a grin.

"Well, on time," I whispered into Tobin's ear, and then gave him a cheeky wink. "Looks like I'm having a good effect on you," I added as we headed to the kitchen to unload the bags of shopping.

"Damn, woman. You're right. I've never been on time my entire life, but a couple of weeks of getting you under my skin has already changed me for the better," he replied, watching me with intrigue. I decided not to shy away from his intense stare or the comments he'd made about me getting under his skin. I liked it I was getting to him because he'd gotten to me too.

When it came to saying goodbye a few short hours later, I held back my tears and remained calm and strong in front of the other women. Tobin seemed to need it too and instead of getting all emotional, we simply kissed each other, and I waved him goodbye as he and my father led the rest of the guys away.

I wasn't going to wilt under the pressure. I was going to be strong. A leader. I called upon that strength both Tobin and my dad had told me was inside of me and used it to keep my emotions in check. I reverted to my introvert ways and forced my anxiety aside, resisting the urge to head inside and hide in my room. I would do that later, when I could recharge my batteries the only way I knew how—in peaceful, quiet solitude.

Chapter Eight

Late that night, after almost everybody had gone to their rooms, I finally had the chance to sneak off back to the office. I'd said goodnight to the other women already and didn't want anyone encroaching on my blissfully quiet evening, so locked the door and took a good look around. I found I liked the small room, feeling as though it was some kind of inner sanctum. Depositing the cans of fizzy drink I'd grabbed on my way, I adjusted the seat to my preference and took a calming breath, going through my mental to-do list. First, I would check the main computer and perhaps do some work while I was at it. I'd recently enrolled in a web design course at the local university to keep me occupied during the quieter days and was glad I had. It gave me a solid reason to sneak away with my laptop or log into whatever computer was close by whenever things were quiet. It'd no doubt provide the perfect distraction from my loneliness while Tobin was away, too.

I then fired up the relatively new PC under the desk and watched as the monitor flickered to life. While it was loading up, I did the same with Dita's now fully charged laptop. It felt odd going into her personal world, as though I was intruding, but I had to see what she'd been working on in those final days, or which emails she had been sending and to whom. I wanted to check her browsing history, read through her favourites, and then snoop at her photos. As if I might finally get to know her by immersing myself in her online world. Sitting there staring at her welcome screen, I realised I didn't really know my sister. I couldn't have told you her favourite colour or go-to band. I couldn't be sure of her reading preferences or if she had even been a reader at all, and as that dawned on me, I felt wretched.

I tried in vain with a couple of password attempts, going with the obvious names or dates of birth, and pushed the laptop aside in a huff after a few minutes. It was going to be harder than I'd thought, so I focused on the main computer that was booted up and ready in front of me instead. It had been restored to its original factory settings and was like new with just the basic software, but there was one added program on the desktop that caught my attention, one that captured camera footage. I opened it and found the widescreen flooded with different views of the large house, both upstairs and down. There were no cameras in the bedrooms but the hallways, outside, and bar area were all covered, and I shook my head even though I wasn't surprised.

"Cheeky bastard," I mumbled, popping open my can of cola as I clicked through the backlog of files. As it turned out, the cameras were motion-activated, only recording when necessary. You could also log into the software from another computer and the cameras could be triggered to watch live whenever needed. I soon found exactly what I was looking for in the backlog, tracking down the files of Tobin and me together and very much alone in the vast house. We were hot. Our homemade porn didn't faze me in the slightest, and I was surprised by my lack of distaste. If anything, I enjoyed watching our shenanigans and was soon feeling a little flushed as I browsed through them.

I moved the files into a password-protected folder and used the same code I had decided on for the safe, figuring that only Tobin and I should be privy to this footage. Without knowing they were safely locked away, I would have to end up deleting them to save myself the infinite shame if my dad ever saw them.

I then spent a little while setting up the PC to connect with my emails and favourite websites, figuring it was easier to use this than always booting up my laptop, and soon I was done and ready to give Dita's computer another try.

It took me ages, finally wracking my brains and going with one of her favourite songs she used to constantly blare from one of the pop bands Dad hated, and the screen suddenly came to life. A sob rose in my throat when I first saw Dita's screensaver. It was her with some of her friends, smiling so brightly that she was utterly beautiful. Tobin was beside her, grinning widely, and his hand was around her waist in the exact same way he had been doing with me the last few days. The protective grip that told others she was his. It had to have been taken during their earlier days, surely?

Forcing myself to ignore the desktop, I connected the Wi-Fi and waited for Dita's emails to load. Nothing of interest, really. I then checked her social media sites but ignored the random messages on her timeline without answering. I couldn't be bothered with explaining how it was I had come on her profile and so instead I snooped into her message inbox. Her friend Sonia had been complaining about her bitchy cousin, while another girl named Karen had been begging Dita to come and visit her in Venice, and her friend Terri had been having an argument with her over whether there was any place for onions in a salad. All normal, day-to-day stuff that randomly made me smile, and for a while I flicked through her photos and read back through her updates. There wasn't a single status or photograph of me. No mention of her family or the club. On the surface, Dita was like any other woman, clinging to her youth and moaning about the weather. I didn't feel remotely closer to her.

After over an hour of general snooping, I headed for my second can of fizzy pop and began checking out her documents, finding copies of many of the photos from her social pages. I almost shut down when I noticed a folder marked 'X'.

Inside were folders marked by the year, going back over the past two, which then expanded into the months. There were documents inside that were labelled simply by dates, and there wasn't one every day, but a fair few. When I clicked on the oldest one from the first folder, the word processor sprang to life in the taskbar. I lifted my head and looked around, checking for what, I wasn't sure. It felt strange snooping further into Dita's personal space, but I couldn't stop myself. If this was what I thought it was, I knew I might finally find the closeness I was hoping for.

A quick skim over the text showed me right away that I was spot-on. The documents I was looking at were Dita's diary. Starting with simple, brief entries, she slowly began to get used to keeping a journal and was soon opening up properly, trusting herself to reveal her true feelings and offload into the pages of her imaginary diary.

She wrote about the guy she was seeing, only ever calling him L, and how it was a big secret that she needed to hide from the club. Reading the events in her own words and scattered thoughts was mesmerising though, and I carried on and on, reading about this man who meant everything to her. The man I'd had no idea even existed. I continued, seeing for myself as over the weeks and months that followed, they had truly fallen in love without her wanting or needing anyone's approval or backing. Unbeknownst to any of us at the club, she'd become her own woman with L to guide her, and I liked the Dita she portrayed on the page. I wish I'd known her…

***

Tuesday 15th July 2014,

Today, Dad came and gave me the sad news that Chuck had died. That man had been more of a father to me than my own dad, and I literally crumbled under the weight of the terrible news. There was no warning and just like that, his life was over. Dad tried to comfort me, but I couldn't believe it. Well, if you'd call a pat on the back as I sobbed my heart out, comfort! I've seen him do it countless times with Dahlia. He wraps her in his arms and holds her so close that I am jealous of her every time he does it. I wish I had been born closer to her, or that I shared the same look that she has. She looks so much like mum did and having been their youngest baby, I'm sure that must be why he wraps her up in cotton wool the way he does. The reason why he dotes on her more than any of us.

Who cares though? I've got L now and we've decided to run away together. I'm going to disappear in the middle of the night and leave no trace and take nothing with me. Simply vanish and leave them no trail to follow. No crumbs to spot. We are just gonna split and never look back. God, I hope we do it. We've talked about it so much, but it always felt like a fantasy. However, L is finally sure he can make it happen. He wants to go for it and I'm with him all the way.

***

I thought back to the July two years earlier, remembering how Dita was hardly ever around, but I had been so wrapped up in finishing my degree that I hadn't bothered to care for her reasons why. But now I thought about it. She hadn't been as wild during that summer. She would be gone for hours but come back clean and sober, when earlier that year she was always falling in high or drunk—or both. It had to have been L. She was going to him and spending her days happy, fulfilled, and full of hope. Readying herself for a better future in which they could be together.

What had changed that? It had to be her relationship with Tobin because, by my reckoning, it was about to begin, but I couldn't understand why she would walk away from L so easily. Not after what she'd said about them planning a life together. I knew I was about to find out, so I opened the next diary entry, readying myself to read her version of the events that followed. I found myself wondering if Tobin had pursued her with the same words he'd wooed me with, jealousy spearing in my gut at the sheer thought of it.

***

Wednesday 23rd July 2014,

Dad came to my room this morning and informed me I must be with Tobin. Don't get me wrong, the guy is seriously hot, but I can't do it. My father will not dictate who I marry or hand me over like something he owns. This is not how life works these days, no matter what he thinks. Garret Proctor does not run the world, nor does he run my life. Not now, not ever!

I can't marry someone else and forget about L, either. We're going to be together, no matter what I must sacrifice to be with him. I screamed and shouted at my father until my lungs hurt. I told him I hated him and would never let Tobin touch me. He revealed the truth about how Tobin was Chuck's son, and it was his wish for him to take his place in the club and be with me. I don't care if Chuck wrote in his will that I'd get a million pounds if I married his bastard son. Life just doesn't work that way. I am not some prize to sweeten Dad's deal with Tobin to entice him into taking the VP position. I'm sure he'll take his father's seat with or without me as part of the deal and I will never let Dad bully me into going there. Since L, I've been with no one else and neither has he. We are so incredibly in love, albeit star-crossed, and yet still so ready to leave everything behind and go follow our dreams. I want to leave sooner than later. I won't let anything come between us this time.

***

There was the fiery woman I'd been expecting. So, she'd told him, setting our father straight, but then how could she have caved in the end? I had to know.

***

Saturday 26th July 2014,

I called things off with L; I had to. I don't think I can ever face him again. After another row with Dad last night, I was so enraged that I let slip about a boyfriend outside the club. He demanded to know who he was, but I'm no fool. I know I'd never see him again. I knew Dad would send his guys to hurt him, or worse, kill him. I cannot have L's death on my conscience. My heart is broken, but I'll do what's right by him now, even if it kills me. Even Nico tried to reason with me, and I know Tobin is his best friend, but fuck, it seemed like he had another agenda for wanting him in the VP's chair.

I stood my ground regardless, which was when Dad showed me just what a monster he could really be. What puppetry he was capable of. He taught me a terrible lesson after our row last night, one I will never forget as long as I live, and I'll hate him forever for it.

I was fast asleep in bed when I heard my bedroom door open, but it was so dark that I couldn't see a thing. I called out, asking who was there, but all I could hear was someone undressing slowly. He took his time, carefully folding each piece of clothing before setting down his belt and leathers in some strange and OCD neat pile I could see by the window. My guest then said nothing as he climbed onto the bed and began pawing at me. He had to have been told to do it. Why else would someone think of sneaking into my room in the dead of night? I'd always been safe here before, but not anymore. Not after last night.

I tried to run away, but he pinned me down. I tried to fight, but it was no use. He beat me so badly I was barely lucid and then raped me. God, I can't believe I'm admitting it, but I know that's what it was. I'm just calling him X in my mind, unable to put any face to him yet because it was pitch black when he did it and not once did he utter so much as one word. He simply took what he'd come for and then left. Punishment in its most primal, brutish form.

I want to curl up in a ball and fade away. I've cried all day, showered God knows how many times, and stayed locked in my room this entire time. I can't bear to see anyone. I know it must be one of the club members, but I don't know which one. Maybe it was even Tobin. I just don't know.

***

I burst into tears. I couldn't believe what I was reading and felt as though I wanted to be sick. Could it have been Tobin? He had done a similar thing in coming to my room that first night, but he'd backed off and waited for me to come around rather than ever force me. He had downright promised never to push me, and I trusted him. Surely, he wasn't the person who had raped Dita in her own bed? No way. Please God, I thought, make it not have been him.

And then there was my father. Had he really instigated the entire thing to teach her a lesson? I couldn't bring myself to believe it. No way would he allow that. No chance in hell could he have let that happen to her. I had to believe he knew nothing about it. For my own sanity, I had to trust in him, even if I was on the fence after Dita's awful testimony.

Although I hated it, I opened the next entry and read on. I had to know for sure just what happened to my poor sister while I stayed oblivious to all of it in my little bubble.

***

Monday 28th July 2014,

X came to my room again last night. It was the same routine of darkness and silence before him, forcing me into submission while he had his way. I begged and cried for him to stop, but he wouldn't. He took me so roughly I started to bleed, but that still didn't stop him. I can't understand what satisfaction he can be getting from this, or his reasons for coming back. I've been hiding away all weekend, so don't understand why I'm still being punished.

I don't feel safe in my own home anymore, but Dad won't let me leave and I can't trust anyone in here. All I can do is hide away and grieve for L. For what we had and could have gone on to have together. It's gone now. All my hopes and dreams have been shattered. I feel so broken, and maybe that's the point?

***

There weren't any more entries for over a week and I dreaded to think what Dita must have been through at that time, because her entire outlook was different by her next entry. She'd been defeated. If she thought she'd been broken before, she was even worse in the entries that'd followed and my heart ached for her, wishing I'd have known and could've helped her. If only I'd realised. If only I'd cared enough to notice her despair. I hung my head and cried for her, fighting the urge to scream and wail.

***

Wednesday 6th August 2014,

I woke up to find my dad sitting on the bed beside me. I was naked under the sheet, curled into a ball, but my back was showing, and I knew he could see all my bruises. He didn't say a word. He just sat there while I cried, sobbing so hard I couldn't breathe. I begged him to stop punishing me and he agreed on one condition—Tobin. I've known for a few days now that my midnight guest was not Dad's new VP and I was relieved, but at the same time, it sickened me even more to discover who Dad was using to send me my awful message. X is someone I know; someone I've trusted for years. I'm such a fool.

I said yes to being with Tobin. Anything is better than this. So, when he left, I got showered, dressed, and headed down for breakfast with the family at his request. I plastered on the fakest smile I could muster and walked in with my head held high. It was the first time anyone had seen me in days and yet no one even asked where I had been the last week or so, either having been fed lies or they simply didn't care. Nico could barely even look at me.

While sitting there, I had to force myself not to lash out and run for the door, especially while watching X talking, laughing, and having fun with my brothers and baby sister. She was laughing at his jokes and grinning up at him like he was one of the nicest guys she'd ever known, when in reality she was standing with a monster. A sick, evil, and twisted monster that now haunts my thoughts day and night.

I decided to take a leaf out of Dahlia's book and stay quiet, and it seemed to work. Dad said he's gonna give me a few days to get used to the idea and then I need to give myself to Tobin, he's ready for me now but Dad apparently told him I'm on my period so wanted to wait.

When did I become this person? Oh yeah, just a couple of weeks ago, thanks to X. Night number one started it all and then he's chipped away at me every day since. Even the thought of having sex disgusts me. I just hope that Tobin will be patient and gentle with me when the time finally comes.

***

I read the entry with bleary eyes, feeling both relief and horror at the revelations Dita had made. Tobin wasn't the man who'd repeatedly hurt her and forced himself on her, but someone else close to me was.

She said I knew him and trusted him. I realised I probably still did, and yet he was the vilest man I could imagine. The worst type of monster, hiding in plain sight without a care or any guilt for what he'd done.

I couldn't believe our father had gone to her and hadn't denied any of it. How could he have treated Dita like that? Letting her be abused under his roof to send her a message? It was downright criminal, and I found myself hating him. Wishing he was there at the clubhouse with me so I could confront him.

Who was I kidding? I knew I could never stand up to my father like that. I was weak back when Dita was going through all her pain, and I was still weak while reading her accounts of what'd happened. I couldn't take on the club, or my dad. He had me exactly where he wanted me, so at least I knew a little of how Dita felt but wished I might never suffer the wrath she had experienced. The torment she'd had to endure.

I hoped that was the end of X and his cruelty. I hoped the next entries would be happier and full of kind words about Tobin and their romance. There was no jealousy now. I wanted to read how she'd fallen madly in love and lived happily ever after, but I knew how that hadn't happened. I just had to hope X had nothing to do with that either.

***

Sunday 10th August 2014,

X hasn't been to my room since Tuesday like my dad promised and so last night I went to Tobin's room after church and waited for him to come up. He seemed surprised to see me, but glad, and we talked for a while. He wants me. He really seems like he does and is such a gentleman that I had sex with him. I didn't cry or push him away, but I did screw my eyes shut as I moaned like I was having the time of my life—when I was far from it. He didn't hurt me or anything. I just can't seem to associate sex with pleasure right now, but he seemed to buy it and I'm giving acting my best shot.

I've been loud, playful, opinionated, and stubborn, just like the old me, but now it isn't real. It's all a front to hide how broken I am and so far, it's working. We spent all day with the club and were congratulated for getting together. Even X came and hugged me, that bastard, and it was all I could do not to kick him in the balls there and then.

I have decided to give this thing with Tobin everything I've got and hope for the best. There's no going back to L. Not now. Not ever. The club owns me. My dad owns me. I guess it just took me a long time to figure that out.

***

An overwhelming urge to ring my dad and give him a piece of my mind came over me in that moment. God, he truly was a bad man. I clearly had never seen that side of him before. I hadn't needed to until that one night when he sent my brothers to make sure I gave up my virginity to the only man he deemed worthy of his daughter's hand in marriage. I had been traumatised by what had transpired that night, but my start with Tobin was far different to Dita's, and I wished she were with me so that I could hug her and tell her I was sorry.

It didn't matter that I had been younger then. I should've noticed and protected my sister. Our brothers should have done something to stop him and X from breaking her down. They should've taken better care of her, but they hadn't. I hated everyone and everything in that moment and was suddenly even gladder that I was alone. I had to stop my hand from reaching for my phone so many times. Ideas for calls I ought to make and texts I should send to Dad or my brothers were filling my head, my anger driving me to feel confident enough to break my silence, but I knew it would do no good to rile any of them up. My father was clearly more of a force to be reckoned with than I'd realised, and I knew I had to be careful not to end up like Dita if I pushed him too far. Perhaps he didn't know how to handle strong women, so had taken her down the only way he knew how—intimidation and violent manipulation. It made me wonder how my mother had coped by his side all those years. Had he broken her, too? I couldn't even begin to let my mind wander of those awful imaginings.

I had to move away from the vengeful thoughts in my head and decided to focus instead on the diary entries that followed Dita's defeat. A quick skim over some more of her and Tobin's first few days showed she was hiding her pain from everyone, especially herself. She wrote about how happy and in love she was with Tobin and how he made her feel amazing, like no one else had ever done before. There were no mentions of L or X, just loved up ranting's that were hard to read because they sounded very much like my own thoughts I'd been having about the very same man. About how wonderful and attentive he was, and how kind and gentle he could be while still being powerful and protective.

Despite being glad that he was not X, I still wanted to vomit. Could I be following my sister down the same rabbit hole? Was I doomed to match her fate, too?

Chapter Nine

Over the next few days, I forced myself to stay calm and refrain from texting or calling Dad or my brothers. I tried to stay as normal as possible with Tobin when he called, but it was hard to hide the pain I was feeling inside. During the nights when I could be alone in the office, I read the remainder of Dita's journal-type documents. For a while, they were consistently positive and happy and even I began to believe that the days of her being taught a lesson by this X guy were behind her. She found her headstrong way again, and some of that fire within she'd once had in abundance. By her own admittance, she and Tobin were far from perfect, but they were making it work. They bickered constantly, and she always had to have the last word, but never disastrously, and never to the point at which she thought they might split up over it. They were happy together.

Well, that was until around eight-months ago when things between her and Tobin seemed to cool off in a heartbeat.

***

Saturday 27th February 2016,

Tobin came back from a run early this morning. He thought I was asleep, but I can never seem to drift off properly whenever I'm alone, not after the nightly visits that still haunt my dreams. Even a year on, every sound still makes me jump awake unless I know he's asleep beside me and last night was no exception. I heard him come in around two-am, dump his bag, and head into the bathroom.

I decided to surprise him and sprang out of bed to go and give him a kiss, but now I wish I hadn't. Tobin was peeling off his dirty clothes and was standing naked by the shower, waiting for it to heat up, and he jumped and covered himself when he saw me, but it was too late. I saw the lipstick marks, and not on his face. He tried to say that it was nothing, but I freaked out. I had a screaming head-fit and trashed the bathroom. God, I feel so stupid. He got the fuck out of our room and went down the hall to one of the spares with just a towel around his waist, leaving me there alone while I cried all night. I know some guys cheat when they're away, but not him. He's never cheated before and I feel so angry I can't even look at him. I've stayed in my room all day and he hasn't bothered to come and see me either, which just adds insult to injury.

Dad stopped by, much to my delight. Not. He warned me against pushing Tobin away. He said that it was my fault he had strayed, and that it was up to me to make sure he didn't do it again. I screamed at him and told him to get the fuck out of my room. I couldn't help myself, but now I'm sitting here wide-awake and refusing to sleep because I know what happens next, and it's making me feel sick. If X comes in here tonight, I'm gonna do everything in my power to fight back. I'll gouge his bloody eyes out if I must, anything to make sure he doesn't touch me again.

***

I felt sick. Worried for her. Was our father going to send X in again? Would he resume her punishment like before, so she'd be more acquiescent to his orders? I had to know. I had to find out the truth, whether it hurt or not.

***

Sunday 29th February 2016,

I slept through the day today, my whole sleep pattern completely messed up, and when I woke up Tobin was here. He apologised, and we made up, mostly because I felt as though I had to. I knew he wanted us to be together again physically, but I just couldn't let him touch me. He backed off when I asked if we could wait before having sex until I was over it and I appreciated that. He's going out with some of the guys tonight and I'm doing the same. Karen and some of her friends are heading out for drinks and I'm sneaking out to go too, it's been far too long. I need this. Some normality and to find the old me again.

***

Monday 28th February 2016,

Last night was amazing. When we were out, I bumped into L of all people. Although things were weird at first, we ended up talking again and I apologised for pulling away before. He knew about me and Tobin but told me how he'd straight away guessed it was my dad's idea for us to pair up. He just got it without me having to drag myself through the ringer, telling him the truth. Like always, he was there for me and understood me in ways I couldn't even begin to imagine. We slept together in the back of his car. I know I shouldn't have, but it was just so right and I kinda needed the payback to Tobin. God, I hope he never finds out. I slept with him when I got home too and he didn't seem to notice, so I think it's all going to be okay. He thinks I can't get enough of him in the bedroom again, despite his unfaithfulness, and I now find myself playing up to the role, letting him believe whatever he wants. It's easier to just do it than fight it anymore. When I close my eyes, I imagine he's L. That we're together and making love. I'll keep those memories safe in my heart. Forever, if I must.

**

I wished I knew who this L guy was. I wracked my brains trying to figure it out, but I came up empty every time. There were no messages in her emails or chats from a guy with that name, starting with that letter. Nothing remotely flirtatious or obvious in her older ones either, and no photos hidden in secret folders of her laptop. The whole story seemed awful, the kind of thing you heard about in magazine articles, but never from those you knew and loved. I couldn't believe her life had been so awful and how none of us had even noticed. That she'd had to hide so much from us all to survive it.

I vowed to read the rest of her entries before Tobin, Dad, and the others got back from wherever they had gone. I had to know the truth before I saw them again, even if it made me see them all in an incredibly different light.

As I sat and read more about how Dita repeatedly

sneaked away to see L, I began creeping up to the most recent document. I found nothing much more than her account of how she and Tobin were trying to rekindle things between them, for appearance's sake. She knew he was cheating on her repeatedly but had given up caring. Mostly because she was cheating too, with L. She started going out with her friends more and more, needing to be away from the club, my dad, and Tobin because she felt as though she was going mad around them.

Then, an entry from just a month before she died made me cry so hard that I was almost sick.

***

Saturday 10th September 2016,

Tobin was really drunk tonight. He got so wasted that when I called him names and let off some steam; he slapped me across the face. I knew I had pushed him, that neither of us loved each other and maybe never had, but I still couldn't believe he hit me. Is this it now? Will my one split lip be the start of things to come, isn't that what they say? Something about if they get away with it once, they'll always do it again? Well, let me just add beaten wife to my wonderful remit.

To top it all off, I then went outside to get some fresh air and X was standing in the shadows. I didn't even see him at first. I was so angry and hurt; I stomped around and mumbled curses under my breath about my darling fiancé. When he stepped out from behind one of Dad's cars, I froze, and he just gave me that sickening grin. I knew what he was after without him even needing to say a word. When he pulled me over behind the club's trucks I didn't bother to beg or scream. I didn't even try to fight back. I was too broken already, and yet he still insisted on knocking me around a little before having his way with me.

When it was over, I cried so hard I puked up. It took forever for me to get myself together enough to go back inside, and I didn't say a word to anyone as I walked back into the house and up to my room. Everyone saw my reddening face but didn't say a word to comfort me. It was as though I didn't exist thanks to the faces that all turned away so that they didn't have to get involved in mine and Tobin's domestic. Just another old lady who'd needed teaching a lesson.

X watched me from the pool table, grinning when I lifted my eyes to his and he even winked. I want to kill him. One of these days I'm gonna take a knife to bed and shove it in his back while he folds up his clothes in their neat little fucking pile.

***

He'd done it again, the bastard. He'd taken Dita simply because he could, and she was so broken by his previous violations that she couldn't even bring herself to fight back. I wanted to kill him. Whoever he was. I wanted him dead and in pieces. I had to find out who he was, no matter what it took. I would avenge her. I would make him pay for what he'd done.

***

Sunday 11th September 2016,

I went to see L today and told him everything. We're going to run away together, just the two of us, and I'm never going to look back. He's getting some money together and a place for us to stay and then we are going to just disappear one night. I can't wait to be free from all of this and will keep my head down and my mouth shut between now and when L gives me the go-ahead. He's been so understanding and amazing. I'm beyond lucky to have someone in my life that believes me and loves me so much. I'm leaving this house. These awful people and their terrible ways. Or else I'll die trying.

***

That last sentence ran through my head repeatedly. Doubts were aching in my gut about her death, and I simply couldn't force them away. I'd had no reason to doubt the cause of her death before, but now I was consumed by questions regarding the 'hit and run' that'd killed her. That'd torn her body to shreds so badly that she couldn't be identified visually, only by her DNA. Could our dad really have found out about Dita's plans and killed her? Was he capable of having his own daughter murdered and then staged an accident to explain it away? As far as I could tell, she and Tobin were well and truly done, and it scared me to know that he was capable of hitting her like he reportedly had. Would he have been angry enough to kill her if she tried to leave? I had to read on. I had to know for sure.

The next few entries were details of her plans to leave and how she was continuing to play the doting daughter and fiancée while waiting for her saviour to give her the call that indicated he was ready. The final document, written the morning of her death, gave me nothing but more questions. Ones that I knew now would never be truly answered.

***

Friday 14th October 2016,

It's my birthday and I'm leaving today. L has everything ready and I'm going to sneak out while Dad and the guys are in church. I'm leaving my room exactly as it always is. I'm taking nothing with me except the clothes on my back and the contents of my handbag. I can't risk anyone knowing that I'm gone until it's already too late. If someone has found my laptop and is somehow reading this, then you must understand my reasons why. Please keep my secrets, or use the truths you have read here to save yourself from the same fate as me.

Dahlia, if it is you, then I'm truly sorry you had to find out this way. I want you to know that I love you and never wanted you to know these things. But please, run away. Run away as soon as you can and do not let Dad push you around or force you into a relationship with any of the guys. Don't let him manipulate you like he did me. Be the strong and true woman I know you are beneath that quiet exterior.

I'm sorry I couldn't have been a better big sister. Goodbye.

***

I couldn't breathe. Sucking in breaths at a rate that was making my head spin, I read and re-read those last few sentences repeatedly. I didn't know how to feel or how to process her words. Dita had run off to be with the man she loved, and then she had died. It couldn't be a coincidence, surely?

The motion detection cameras then suddenly flickered to life on the PC screen in front of me as I continued to sit and stare at Dita's final words. I was meant to read her diary entries. It was as if she'd wanted me to know the truth about what she'd been through. But how could she have known I would be the one to take her computer? Maybe she hadn't, but perhaps in some way she had always hoped that she could tell me the truth yet didn't know how. I wouldn't have listened back then though, so blinded by my love for our father that I was in too deep to be able to see the facts with a clear head. But now, I saw it plainly. I saw the truth behind the lies I'd been fed my entire life and didn't quite know how to make sense of it all. The million thoughts running through my head made me nauseous for the hundredth time since I started reading her diary.

I had no time to process any more of my emotions because, as my eyes moved up towards the cameras, I saw that my dad and his men had just pulled up outside Dahlia's and were walking inside. I quickly stashed the laptop in my bag and grabbed some paperwork I had set to one side in case anyone had come looking for me when I was hiding out with Dita's diaries. After looking at the clock and realising that it was four-am, I face-planted the desk and pretended to have fallen asleep over them.

"Dahlia. Dahl," Tobin's voice whispered after he had unlocked the door and come inside to track me down. "She's fast asleep at the desk. Must've been up late working on stuff," I heard him say to someone and then I felt him lift me up off the chair and into his arms.

"Tobin?" I groaned, blinking groggily, and staring up at him. I was welcomed by a bright smile that made my heart both sing and break at the same time. Could I trust him? Could I trust any of them? I needed time to figure things out and knew that in the meantime, I would have to act as normal as possible. Just like Dita, I'd play my part while processing my inner turmoil. I would utilize my quiet nature, using it to my advantage so no one would question my motives or reasoning for looking into the club's affairs. For snooping at my father's doings. No one could suspect that anything was awry and so I smiled back up at Tobin and buried my face in his shoulder, taking a deep sigh and enjoying the mixture of leather and petrol fumes coming from him.

Tobin carried me to our room, and I watched him undress before heading into the bathroom. I couldn't help myself from doing the same as Dita had when he'd returned from his run, and followed him in, stretching and yawning loudly for effect. I needed to test him. To re-enact the scene she had described, so I'd know if he'd cheated on me like he had her. He didn't jump or try to hide away from me. In fact, he grabbed me close and kissed me so hard that I could taste the cigarette he must've smoked on his way into the house.

When he pulled off my jeans and bent me over the bath, I went with it, sensing just how much he had missed me, and so I let all my fears and doubts about him melt away. He hadn't ever hurt me and, judging by how rampant he was to both give and take pleasure from my body, he hadn't strayed during his days away. I had to hope that he still was one of the good guys in all of this. I had to believe that I could trust Tobin, and so I gave him everything I had to give. He had me willingly and despite my fears, and it felt good to let go of some of the tightness that'd been churning in my gut over the past few days.

When we were exhausted, we showered together and then climbed into bed. As he held me tight, he kissed me softly, stroking his hands up and down my face, back, and thighs. I fell asleep in his embrace and no matter my doubts about the club lingering over me; I felt good for the first time in days.

***

The next morning, Tobin and I were up and ready early, having decided that it would be a nice surprise to make a big breakfast to welcome back the guys who had come home in the middle of the night alongside him and my dad. He mixed up a huge tub of pancake batter while I chopped fruit, ladled syrup and chocolate sauce into bowls, and started the first of no doubt numerous pots of coffee. We chatted, laughed, and worked together so effortlessly that I smiled genuinely in his company. I adored how good it felt. How natural it was to be happy with him. Part of me wanted to block out every treacherous thought that had consumed me for the better part of that week. To overlook all of it. I tried my best to push aside the thoughts tormenting me. To ignore the memories Dita had shown me via her story.

The world around me had gone on turning while I had shut it all out and had been completely consumed by Dita's awful stories. There was a part of me that wanted to take it all back. To throw away her laptop and dismiss everything she had written as lies. While I knew that eventually I would have to deal with them, the part of me that wilted under pressure kicked in, and I pushed it all aside. I was hoping to crawl back into my happy bubble, and I guess it was working, because I was growing icier by the second. Shutting off and reverting to my selfish ways. I was pulling out of my sadness and losing the desire for the truths I knew would hurt me to find. I was taking the easy route but wasn't strong enough to force myself back from that ledge.

I was weak and knew that if I blew, I would ruin everything. So, I bottled it up and stored it so tightly within me that my chest ached, but I would endure it. I would keep my head held high and I would keep on going. Keep living, for her.

With the pancakes made and stacked high upon the table, Tobin pressed me against the kitchen counter and captured my mouth with his. Hands roamed and groans ensued. And it wasn't long before he had gripped one of my thighs and pulled it upwards, evidently needing to have me wrapped around him. I let myself give in to his desire for me, relishing in his need. Yes, I was weak. I knew that already. I couldn't give up on the idea that he and I were meant to be. I couldn't forget how he had made me feel or the life he had promised me we could have together. There had to be a beacon of hope on the otherwise bleak horizon.

"Ha-hum," came a voice from over Tobin's shoulder, and I knew without even looking that it was my dad. I blushed and retreated into myself even more, while Tobin grinned and turned around to greet him, unashamedly tucking his hard-on into his waistband before he went over to join him at the table.

I, on the other hand, was struggling to maintain my cool. I couldn't look at him, so quickly poured my father a cup of coffee and walked over with my eyes on the floor. I then placed the mug down in front of him without a word.

In all honesty, I didn't know what to think or how to feel. Seeing him again for the first time since reading Dita's diaries made me feel strange. Distant from him in ways I couldn't deny, but that terrified me. My head was swimming with questions I couldn't ask and anger I had to try my hardest to force away. And so, I forced my gaze to meet his. To act like everything was normal.

My father slammed his hand down on the bench next to Tobin, making me jump, but then he laughed it off and nodded to the spot where his hand still laid, indicating for me to sit. Tobin shuffled along, his face sour, and I took a seat, albeit begrudgingly.

"Everything okay, Dad?" I asked, watching as he sipped his coffee and eyeballed Tobin with a thoughtful frown. I immediately panicked. Had he caught on to my uncharacteristically extra distant ways? Could he sense that something was up, but that I wasn't ready to talk about it? If he did, it seemed to me that he thought Tobin was what'd caused my upset and I couldn't have that.

My father had to know things were perfect between us. I still couldn't believe how much I wanted to live up to the role he'd forced me into, but I did. I couldn't fight it and knew then how we wanted the same things—for Tobin and me to become something infallible and real. Something no one else could break apart or come between. A union that would never fall to pieces the way his and Dita's relationship had, but I also wanted him to realise that I wouldn't need punishing like she had should things break apart. I was the timid one, the shy one. I was doing as I was told and would continue doing so for as long as I had to. If I could learn to trust his word again, knowing we had my father's approval meant the world to me, even after everything I'd learned.

"You two are getting along well. I think it's time for you to take the next step," he replied, fiddling with the corner of the table absentmindedly, picking at the uneven shards of wood at the edge of it. I waited for him to explain what he'd meant, hoping that surely, he was not insinuating we get married or anything yet, but he kept me guessing for a few more seconds before finally finishing his train of thought. "I think you should go shopping for engagement rings."

"What!" I cried in surprise.

"You heard me. It's time you two made things more official," my father said, watching me intently this time. I didn't reply. I couldn't. After just a few weeks of being left to do our own thing, it seemed I'd become complacent. I'd forgotten that my father was still calling the shots and wasn't against pushing us both around to get his way. Tobin hadn't popped the question, nor had we felt the need to move things along faster, but it appeared my dad wanted more for us. More from us.

I didn't say another word as Tobin slid closer into the gap beside me, boxing me in. He didn't seem surprised at all by my dad's demand, and I knew then how this intervention had to have been planned by the pair of them.

Tobin then turned to face me on the long bench while my father leaned over and took my hand in his. I thought he was going to hold it, but no. He pressed down on the inside of my wrist, seemingly checking my pulse, and

I watched him with a frown. Before I could ask what he was playing at, Tobin spoke up.

"You're acting strange. What's going on with you?" he asked, taking my chin in his hand and turning me to look at him. Dad dropped his head and focussed on my wrist, and I knew without asking that he was reading me via my unspoken reactions. Garret Proctor was a man who knew many things and had various tricks up his sleeve when it came to reading people. No one had ever lied to him and gotten away with it. I'd grown up knowing that from day one.

I knew from Dita's diaries that she had given too much away by shouting her mouth off and not containing her verbal diarrhoea, but my problem was the exact opposite. I internalised everything, so he was getting a read on me in the only way he could—via my inner voice that was always unheard yet raging within—and I freaked out. I wanted to pull away, or to accuse them both of being unreasonable, but knew that would look worse.

I also had to wonder if perhaps they had been keeping a closer eye on me than I'd realised. Maybe watching me via a camera I hadn't known was there while I sat staring at Dita's laptop for hours on end and hiding it from everyone.

I should've been more careful. They had to have questions about how long I'd spent in the office rather than out in the house with the others. I should have taken my time with it and not bombarded my mind with her stories, but I had never in a million years thought I would find something so awful as those diary entries on there. I tried to stay calm, to regulate my breathing and responses, which was when Tobin noted the change and tried his hardest to rile me.

Even he knew me too well. He could tell I was hiding something, and I guessed he was under orders to make me talk whenever my father gave him the nod. I began to panic, shaking my head profusely.

"I'm not acting strange. You two are, though," I tried, doing my best to sound nonchalant, but he was having none of it.

"You have the far-off look of someone hiding in their own skin, Dahlia. We don't keep secrets in this club, and you know it," my father answered, and I was suddenly terrified.

"Kiss me," Tobin muttered before I could respond, turning my body towards him slightly, and I obliged. I cleared my head and let myself think only of him. Of our prearranged future and plans for the new clubhouse and for ourselves. I didn't let myself believe in Dita's tales of him hitting her and my father, allowing her rape and forced submission to the club's rule. I couldn't let it get to me, otherwise I knew I could potentially find myself exactly where she was. I shut all of it out as I kissed Tobin, trying my best to prove to him how I didn't have any fear or hatred towards him, my father, or the club, figuring if he believed me, so too would my father.

Tobin reached his hand down to my breast, cupping it while he kept my mouth on his and I felt the heat spark within me, along with a speed-up of my heartbeat, but that was surely to be expected? When his hand then trailed down between my legs and he slid it over the apex of my jeans, pressing into my core with his fingertips, I gasped against his mouth in shock.

"Why are you doing this?" I groaned, arching into

his hand uncontrollably, even with my father sat silently beside us. My eyes darted over to him, finding his head still down and his breathing slow and steady. He was completely focussed on my heart rate rather than what was happening in the room, so Tobin took things one step further and began kissing my neck.

"It's okay, Dahl. He doesn't care," he said, unbuttoning my shirt so that he could kiss the flesh overflowing from the top of my bra cups.

He stopped before I could protest further, apparently not needing to take things so far that we'd all be left feeling uncomfortable afterwards. At first, I was confused, but then the realisation dawned on me. He had been providing my dad with my rested heart rate, followed by the worried, and then excited beats per minute. He'd been cunningly providing the baseline of comparison for the human lie detector that was his boss. It didn't matter what he wanted, or that I was Garret's daughter, he'd been given an order and was carrying it out.

"Tobin," I mumbled, feeling utterly helpless. "What's all this about?"

"I've got something to confess," he replied, his face still buried in my neck, and he brought it away so that he could look into my eyes. "I slept with someone else this week while I was on the road."

The world fell away from beneath me. Time stood still and all I could hear was my heart pounding loudly in my ears. I stared back into those pale blue eyes that had until then been so loving and kind, hoping he would tell me he was joking. I found myself suddenly glaring at the man who had been so tender and appreciative of everything I had given him, and I wanted to cry.

At first, I was heartbroken and ashamed of him for having fooled me into believing his lies, but then everything turned in a far darker direction. My mouth was suddenly too dry for me to speak. Fear overwhelmed me as my brain filled with images of Dita being taught a lesson by X for her fiancé's infidelity. She had been punished because Tobin had strayed, and I was instantly filled with an incredible sense of despair, dread, and regret. Was I the next Proctor sister to displease their father and receive a visit from the illustrious X? Would I be taught a lesson, just like Dita had?

I wanted to bolt then and there, and felt myself looking at the door, wondering if I might be able to make it before either of them could catch me. I knew I had no chance. I was being held in place by both my father's strong hand on mine and Tobin's sad gaze, and knew I had to face the music. I suddenly had the sensation that I was no longer in charge of my own body. I couldn't run. I couldn't fight. All I could do was crumble in defeat. I began to cry.

Tobin was still so close I could smell his usual musky scent and could feel his breath tickling my neck as he exhaled. I wanted to enjoy those things, but I felt broken. Betrayed. Like a failure.

"What did I do wrong?" I managed to whisper, holding back my tears as I tried to figure out what else I could have done to keep his affection solely on me. We had been so amazing together so far and I wanted to slap him for betraying me, but kept all my emotions at bay, bottled up, and yet I was boiling beneath the surface. My despair had turned to a sort of violent rage I wasn't used to, but the most overwhelming emotion inside of me wasn't anger, though. I was truly terrified of what might happen next. "Are you going to punish me?" I asked, not looking at

Tobin. I was looking at my dad.

"You did nothing wrong, Dahlia. Why would we punish you? Don't be scared," Tobin replied, stroking my cheek tenderly.

"I'm not afraid. I'm furious," I replied, breathing in shallow pants.

"Liar," came my father's voice and his head shot up so he could look into my eyes. The memory of his hard face came to mind from the night I had bolted from the bedroom after Tobin had first come to have his way with me. That image had haunted me—him so detached and cold. I knew I would be greeted with that same look again if I tried to run from him a second time, so I caved. I knew I had to say something, or at least tell the truth, otherwise he'd figure out I was hiding things from him. I gave him the truths I felt able to reveal in a bid to try and work my way back in to his good graces. To hopefully avoid my punishment.

"Okay, I am scared. I'm scared of losing this amazing thing we've started. I'm scared of letting everybody down. I've been terrified of doing or saying the wrong thing for weeks and you realising I'm not the one you want after all. Even with all that fear in me, you still went and cheated on me, so now I feel like a failure," I replied, telling the truth. The fears inside of me spanned way beyond just those few things, but I knew I had to try and express them enough to mollify Dad's curiosity. I don't know why he was hell-bent on testing me but understood there was no getting out of it until he was satisfied.

Between Dad and Tobin, they then asked me a few more questions. Was I going to call things off with Tobin? Was I going to run away? What was I hiding? Thanks to my forced inner calm, I somehow managed to pass those tests, perhaps because my answers were based on the fundamental truth. I knew that there was no other choice in the matter than to stay and be the dutiful girlfriend, no matter what Tobin did behind my back, but it didn't stop me from dying a little inside.

"Do you love me?" Tobin asked, and I shook my head no.

"Liar," Dad replied for me and the tears I had managed to stop crying fell down my cheeks again, refusing to be kept away any longer.

"So, maybe I do, but I wish I didn't. You've broken my heart," I replied, wiping at my cheeks with my free hand. Tobin grabbed my chin and lifted my gaze to his.

"Then let me un-break it," he said, smiling a little. "I was lying, Dahl. I didn't cheat. I wouldn't so much as look at another woman now that I have you. Please believe me. I was just trying to make you angry."

Dad let go of my wrist and focussed on replenishing his coffee while I sat in shock again. Hope rose inside of me, and I looked back and forth between Tobin's eyes, trying to read him, wanting to believe that what he was saying was genuine.

"It's true," Dad said for him, and I turned to jelly. Tobin caught me and wrapped me in his arms, holding on tightly while I had a few moments of pure freak out. He just shushed and rocked me, smoothing his hand up and down my back affectionately while I cried into his shoulder. How could he have done such a thing? I couldn't bear those men and their strange ways of testing people. If my mum were alive, she surely would've never let them treat her daughters that way? There were ways of asking and uncovering truths that weren't tantamount to torture, and yet my father had still gone for the brutal approach, and he'd roped in Tobin to help him break me down.

"I love you too, Dahl," Tobin whispered once I'd had a few minutes to process it all, but I couldn't enjoy those words. It felt like I'd been the butt of some sick joke my dad and he had randomly decided to play on me. I still wasn't entirely sure why as well and knew neither of them would be in any rush to explain themselves.

Chapter Ten

After a few more minutes of tense quiet, I forced myself to calm down and regain my composure. I knew that in those awful moments I'd almost lost everything I had been working hard to achieve and it hurt to think they could let me believe it. In my head, I'd lost the respect of both my father and the club, as well as the love of the man sitting beside me, and most importantly the sense of security and wellbeing in this wrapped up life of mine. I realised then how terrible things must have truly been for Dita when she too had been left feeling so lost and alone, yet powerless to stop any of it. I'd had just a snippet of that and had nearly crumbled to pieces under the pressure of trying my hardest, whilst evidently failing miserably.

Following that realisation, I knew I would never be as strong as she had been, and that awareness hurt me just as much as Tobin's words had done. I was half the woman my sister had been and now she was gone. Dita was in an early grave, and I was evidently filling her shoes as not only the VP's old lady but also as the plaything of both him and the club President.

I pulled away from Tobin's grasp, wiped my face, and went straight into emotionless robot mode. I pushed my feelings down, forcing them away. He and my father weren't going to break me with their strange games. I would allow them to dominate my life and control every aspect of it, but not me. I loved Tobin. It was true, but he couldn't have all of me, nor could he take everything from me in a bid to create the perfect old lady for himself. They weren't going to stop me from being myself and dealing with my angst the only way I knew how—in complete silence while I internalised my turmoil.

I stood and began pulling off the lids covering the then cool pancakes and gave each of the accompaniment bowls a stir. Tobin hated my silence, I could tell. He grew fidgety watching me, but the more he wanted me to speak, the less I felt inclined to. Dad watched me for a few seconds in utter calm and I knew then exactly where I got my introverted nature from. He was exactly like me, only he'd hidden it better over the years. He didn't mind the silence because he drew strength from it too. I would have to find another way to punish him for hurting me, and against my better nature, I found I wanted to.

In stony silence, Dad then stood and opened the door, ushering for those waiting patiently outside to come on in. The club members all filed inside with hungry smiles, not even one bothering to ask what the holdup was. In my head, they were all laughing at me. In on the secrets kept only from me and they too were pawns waiting to be utilised in whatever game my father seemed to be playing. I couldn't figure out why, though. I'd done no wrong. I hadn't even confronted him over the truths I'd uncovered about Dita.

I served the guys' coffee with a forced smile while they helped themselves to their chosen goodies and I wandered the room in silence, grateful for the loud conversation, but I still noticed Dad's and Tobin's eyes on me many times. I wanted to give them both a slap or to tell them to pack it in, but of course I neither said nor did anything of the sort. I seethed and cursed them in my head, refusing to let them hurt me for all to see and then revel in my pain like a pair of sadists. They would just have to get used to upsetting me and dealing with my silent stewing afterwards. My dad didn't want me throwing hissy fits and making a scene anyway, so would just have to deal with the awkward silence.

When they'd each had their fill, the guys drank the last of their brews and brought their plates over to the sink for me to wash. I received many affectionate kisses to the cheek or pats on the shoulder, as well as whispers of thanks in my ear from my extended family, and their little displays of affection made me feel better. I still couldn't explain it but having fed and watered them after their long ride and just a few hours' sleep made me feel good. I liked caring for them all and being appreciated.

I thought I was alone then, the silence filling the void left behind by the leather-clad bikers, when arms wrapped around me from behind and Tobin's soft voice filled my ear.

"Come and sit down. I'll finish this," he murmured, pulling me away from the counter and turning me around to face him. I followed his lead, feeling tired of fighting. Tired of being angry. Part of me still wanted to shove him away. To say no, but I didn't. I simply couldn't.

Captured in his gaze, I became utterly mesmerised by him. I wanted to stay angry and yet despite his games, I knew deep down that Tobin was the only reason I was able to get through all the fraught emotions that'd had me up and down the last couple of weeks. That solemn look of his told me he'd hated upsetting me. Those gorgeous eyes bore into mine and the powerful blast of heat in my belly that always ensued when he was near had me desperate to forget all about the craziness of the past hour or so and the awful secrets Dita's diary had revealed.

He ushered toward the table to reiterate his command and I looked, spotting how he had saved and piled a plate up with sweet pancakes for me. My stomach rumbled loudly. I was starving, I just hadn't realised it until then, and so I followed his lead and sat in the spot on the bench he had been sitting in not long before. Tobin then served me coffee, being the perfect gentleman, while I made quick work of the pancakes.

I hated to admit it to myself, but I caved. In that moment, I cared about nothing but the two of us. I felt no remorse or pain over what Dita had been through, no hatred towards my family—both blooded and extended. When it was just Tobin and me, I felt whole and happy, albeit blinded by those things, but I didn't care. For the first time in my life, I was more than just Garret's daughter. His precious little lady in her ivory tower. Somebody loved me and wanted to take care of me, and I was going to protect it, no matter the costs.

I stared off into the distance, focussing on nothing while my head swam. How would we move on from this? I couldn't make this work while still doubting Tobin and everyone else around me.

Realisation hit me like a punch in the chest. Perhaps the only way to survive was for me to choose them or Dita. I had to live my life and be happy in it, even if that meant giving up on avenging my sister while the dust settled. I still had to survive and if I let her stories continue to consume me, I knew I'd soon be paying a terrible price for my disassociation with the club.

She hadn't cared enough to confide in me in life when I could've actually helped, so, albeit selfishly, I decided I wasn't going to waste any more time fretting over things I could not control. I was going to make things right in my own way by making sure I didn't end up with the same fate. It might be the coward's way out, but I'd already realised that morning how I was, in fact, a coward, so I took it.

"What can I do to make you happy?" Tobin asked as he came over to me, sliding to his knees as I turned around to face him.

"Nothing," I answered coldly. "Just leave me alone." Despite being a coward, I still wanted to punish him, to make him realise I wouldn't just let him off the hook for hurting me, and it worked. Tobin sank back on his heels and stared up at me, his eyes reddening as he took in my icy expression. I stood and headed over to the doorway, intending to leave, but I just couldn't bring myself to walk out. I didn't want to risk the consequences if I took it too far, so turned, glaring back at him, daring him to say more to make me stay. Hoping he would do it and save me from doing something foolish.

"I didn't want to test you, Dahl. Your dad is just paranoid is all," Tobin said as he stood and walked towards me, where he reached a hand up to my face. I didn't pull away, and he breathed a sigh as he stroked my cheek with delicate sweeps of his fingertips. "He told me what to ask you and how to act if he ever gave me the nod that he doubted your intentions. I hadn't expected him to ever make me do it, but then you were acting odd this morning and the next thing I knew, he was giving me the go-ahead.

Garret told me to break your heart, but please trust me when I say I never wanted to hurt you or play tricks on you like that. You seemed devastated by the lie, and I couldn't believe I'd hurt you so much unnecessarily. I never want to do that to you ever again." He was pleading with me to understand, to see it his way, and I caved. "Your dad is a control freak to the max. I hope you can understand that it wasn't my idea, or my doing? You know he's more one for the tough love."

"Tough love? More like rough love!" I replied, watching as he kissed the still red patch on the inside of my wrist where my father had been pressing down to keep check of my pulse. He was so gentle, kind, and I wanted him so much. I needed to have him, to know that he was still all mine. I fixed him with that commanding Proctor look I also seemed to have inherited and narrowed my eyes. His face snapped up to look at me in shock and his breath hitched. It looked like he was scared I was pulling away. Was he scared of losing me? It sure seemed that way.

God, it gave me a rush. I hadn't felt anything like it before but couldn't deny it felt good to have the upper hand.

"Forgive me, please, Dahl," he said. "Or at least say something. I can't bear waiting for you to put me out of my misery. What can I do?" He was begging me, pleading for forgiveness, and for some reason I couldn't fully understand, I felt as if I had the power to make or break us. It was all down to me.

So, apparently, I decided where we were heading and what the rules were. I was the one who had her say at long last, and I was going to make him listen.

"I need to know that you will never cheat on me, Tobin," I replied, not taking my eyes off his for even a split-second. I had to be sure that I was not going to end up like Dita. Whether he knew it or not, his infidelity had cost her so much more than just her dignity and self-worth. Those visits from X had no doubt resulted in her losing her life and I was not going to follow her down that same path.

"Baby, I'm so sorry. I never have and I never will," he said, his expression sincere and full of raw, uncomplicated promise. I believed him.

"You do not even look at other women. No flirting and no straying when you're away on runs. No secret kids across the country. No surprises just waiting to jump out and fuck with my life. If you do, I'm gone, no second chances. Believe me."

"I do. Even the thought of it terrifies me," he said, and kissed me hard. I could feel the pain he was feeling at just the thought of me leaving. "I promise, you're the only one for me, Dahlia. I'd rather die than lose you."

"Then prove it. Show me every day and neither one of us will ever have to worry about a thing," I replied, taking his hand. Without another word or so much as a glance at the men and women we passed on our way, I then led him up to our room.

Inside, we quickly discarded our clothes, and I pushed Tobin down onto the bed, straddling him as our mouths met and he leaned back, ready to let me take control. I took everything that was offered, and then some. His body belonged to me, and I claimed him with every ounce of strength I had.

Riding him hard, I pressed my hands down onto his chest, having my way with him while Tobin lay beneath me, groaning and arching up into me as I slid up and down on his hard length. He let me be in complete control, and I was glad. I needed it and when that strange spot inside of me bloomed with heat, throbbing and clenching around him in the most wonderful, all-consuming orgasm of my life, all I could do was pant and ride the waves of ecstasy I had built.

His voice then brought me back to reality. Tobin was groaning and bucking beneath me, his own release flowing out of him while my body still clenched around him. It was his turn to scream my name for everyone to hear and didn't that just ignite something far deeper inside of me, something carnal and euphoric. He was mine. There wasn't a person in this huge house who wouldn't have heard him come undone for me and, for the first time, I wasn't the least bit embarrassed about it.

Chapter Eleven

For weeks, Tobin and I lived in blissful ignorance of everything and anyone else around us, including my father. We stayed at the new clubhouse, which still felt strange to call Dahlia's, but I was slowly getting used to it. Apart from the regular parties in which Sunny Skye and her friends kept the guys entertained, we had relative privacy and time for ourselves, which was exactly what I'd needed so that we could fight our demons alongside one another and come back whole. Together every day and night, we fell madly in love, and I persisted in blocking out any and all doubts about us, my father's plans for our future, or the awful past that still haunted my nightmares, but I never let in during my waking moments.

We celebrated Christmas there as a large, extended family, and I enjoyed every moment of it, not letting my fears or doubts about the club creep in even once. Dad seemed convinced of my sincerity and didn't test me again, but I kept my distance. He didn't get to treat me like he had and then for things to go back to normal. Either he let go or not, but either way I had my life to lead and thought I was doing a pretty good job of it with Tobin by my side to help keep me strong.

I also kept myself busy doing my online course and

immersing myself in the world of web design, graphic design, and even a bit of blogging. I wrote reviews for the books I had read or the movies I had seen, all while remaining anonymous and posting my graphic art along with my reviews. The response was phenomenal. The worldwide audience seemed to like my work and before I knew it, I had people asking me to buy the rights to my pictures or for me to build them a website. There was money in this. A career I could develop from the comfort of my own home, and I began to realise how much I wanted a job like that. Something I could take anywhere with me to work on day and night around Tobin and his schedule with the club.

I hadn't so much as looked at Dita's laptop again, choosing instead to leave it hidden away in that desk drawer just like her secrets. Gone for a while, but not forever. After all, even I knew the truth always had a habit of rearing its ugly head when you least expected it.

***

"Happy Birthday dear, Nico. Happy Birthday to you," I sang a few days after the new year had begun, greeting my oldest brother with a wide smile and a tight hug. I then made my way downstairs into the packed and busy clubhouse, greeting the birthday boy with genuine affection and happiness. He was the one person I felt I could count on. The constant source of support in the chaotic world I'd found myself in the past few months.

"Cheers, Dahlia," he replied, kissing my cheek and thanking me for his gift—a designer watch that Tobin and I had picked out together. The place was heaving, full to bursting with our friends and family, and every room in the huge house was taken by those who'd come to celebrate my brother's birthday with us. Like with Tobin, Nico would move up into his given position within the club when Dad died or handed over control and had already been our father's protégé for years. Everyone looked up to and respected him, knowing that one day he would be Tobin's Vice President. In my view, he deserved it. He'd cared for me no end of times and I knew it wasn't simply because he was Dad's clear favourite, or my brother—it was because he was a good man.

We had already been partying for hours, but there was no sign of stopping, so I downed another coffee and launched myself into Tobin's arms. He caressed me with his strong hands, wrapping me up in his tight hold as he showered me with kisses and pressed himself into me.

"Baby, will you go check on Calvin for me?" he then asked, leaning in to whisper quietly in my ear. Calvin was Chuck's nephew, so Tobin's cousin, and was one of the club's more recently promoted members. He had gone up to one of the rooms hours ago and had no-doubt fallen asleep up there, but my father was getting ready to deliver his speech and Tobin seemed eager to have everyone together. He couldn't leave the party himself, but I could tell he wanted Calvin there. After having found one another when Tobin had tracked down his father, the two of them had become fast friends and I was pleased he'd come along for the weekend to celebrate Nico's birthday with us. "Tell him to get his arse down here," he added with a roll of his eyes.

I nodded and slipped away with ease, kissing my man's cheek on the way. I don't think anyone even noticed me make an exit. Despite my stronghold atop the female entities of our group, it seemed I was still the quiet, unassuming woman I had always been. Not that I cared or wanted the increased attention, but it surprised me I still wasn't fitting in properly yet. I had to make sure I changed that as soon as possible.

"Calvin?" I whispered as I ducked inside his room after my quiet knocks went unanswered. His room smelled of smoke and beer, despite the window being open, so I made my way around to his bedside to check that he hadn't drank too much and was perhaps lying in a pile of his own vomit. He was fast asleep, no puke in sight, and while I breathed a small sigh of relief, I stroked my hand over his forehead, brushing back his long hair while whispering his name a few more times in an attempt to rouse him.

In a sudden movement uncharacteristic of him, Calvin jumped awake and grabbed me by the throat. In comparison to his huge body, my tiny frame was like a ragdoll, and he quickly had me on my back on his bed, pinned to the covers with him over me while he shook himself awake.

"What the fuck? Dahlia?" he groaned, immediately letting me go when he realised it was me and I groaned as I rubbed at my sore neck where he had held me down so harshly. "What are you doing in here?"

"You're missing the party, so Tobin sent me to get you," I replied, climbing up and turning on the bedside light to brighten the place up in the hopes of waking him a bit more. "My dad's doing a speech soon. Are you coming down?"

"Yeah, I'll be there in a minute. Get outta here," he said, eyeing me as though he feared me or something and I reached my hand out to try and calm him, but he flinched. I was stunned. Had he just flinched as though I might hurt him? I knew he was naked beneath those sheets and possibly felt uneasy being alone there with me, but I wasn't about to try anything.

  I pulled back and walked around the bed towards the door, and on my way, I caught sight of the clothes he had been wearing earlier that day. They were gathered so incredibly neatly in a pile on his dresser, perfectly folded and stacked in a way that made me take immediate notice. Even his belt and watch were atop the almost pristinely stacked neat pile, and I suddenly turned cold from head to toe.

  Good God. No…

  How I didn't fall in a heap before that horrible mound of clothing was beyond me. In that moment, I knew that pile of clothes. That neat and ever so precise folding method. I didn't know them through my own eyes or memories, but I knew them through Dita's words and the realisation hit me like a punch to the throat. I can't remember if Calvin said anything else, but I know I didn't. My mouth was so damned dry that I could barely even swallow, let alone confront him or say anything else.

  Out in the hall, my breath soon began to feel shallower and harder to catch. No matter how hard I tried to gather it, that precious oxygen just didn't find its way into my lungs and soon I was bent double, hands on my knees and my head down as I tried to suck in as much of the smoky air as I could.

  "What happened, Dahlia?" came a voice from halfway up the stairs and I leapt back at the sound, not having realised that I wasn't alone. Nico stood watching me, a beer in one hand and a cigarette in the other, and his face was like thunder. He was furious, seemingly with me, and I just shook my head. I still couldn't speak, and I tried desperately to regain my composure enough to tell him a lie and sneak away to my own room, where I knew my impending breakdown could happen in private. "Don't you dare lie to me," he added, his voice booming as he stepped closer, and I suddenly had an urge to run.

Nico caught my unease. Without another word, he slid his cigarette down into the neck of his beer bottle and placed it on the floor, climbing higher with his hands up as though he meant me no harm. And yet his scowl was still firmly in place. The last time I had seen that look was the night he'd woken me to say he was there to watch over and keep me safe while his best buddy had his wicked way with me. He had said that night how he was there to protect me, but I could see the rage behind that look even then. It was the same look again, but this time there was no mask of protector and brother, just a powerful adversary who seemed to know exactly what I was freaking out about without me having to utter a word, which clearly meant that he knew the truth about Dita and X, who I was now positive must have been Calvin.

"Nothing, let's go back to the party," I eventually managed to reply, although rather than go towards him, I stepped away and then headed to mine and Tobin's room. Nico was hot on my heels and when I reached my door and flung myself inside, he refused to respect my privacy. In fact, I think he might've kicked the door in if I had managed to get it closed behind me. He burst in straight after me as though he had run or leapt the last couple of steps and length of the hallway right behind me. Before I could even ask him what was going on, my biggest brother pinned me down on the bed and got right in my face.

"Dahlia, tell me what happened," he insisted, almost growling. Although I couldn't see his eyes in the pitch-black darkness, I felt them burning into me from above and cringed. He had to know what Calvin had done to Dita, surely? I couldn't answer. I was terrified of the repercussions I might be forced to face if I spoke the truth now, but Nico didn't stop. "I need you to tell me exactly what Calvin just said to you, or what he did. I need you to tell me right now or so help me God I'm gonna go in there and beat the living shit out of him."

That wasn't what I'd expected to hear.

"What? I don't understand?" I breathed. His response had shocked me, and I couldn't tell whether he was angry with Calvin or me. "He didn't do anything. I just had a moment, that's all." I tried my best to stay calm and try to convince Nico that nothing untoward was going on, but he was having none of it.

"Did he try and touch you? Has he ever touched you? I need you to tell me the truth, Dahlia." He let go of the tight grip on me ever so slightly but didn't move or let me sit up. My brother just kept me at his mercy, waiting for my walls to come crashing down, and a sob finally caught in my throat and gave me away. He knew I was hiding something. There was no going back and so I knew I had to be honest.

"No, he has never touched me. But I know what he did to Dita," I replied, making Nico groan and pull away from me at long last. He then flicked on the light and began pacing the room, running his hands through his dark hair with a pained look on his face. It was as though he felt guilty, and I had to wonder what part he too might've played in our sister's punishment.

"You were never supposed to find out, even Tobin doesn't know," he replied after a few tense minutes, and that one piece of truth from my big brother made me feel so elated I couldn't even begin to describe it. Tobin hadn't known what my sister had been through. He hadn't been in on her abuse, and she had clearly done a good job at hiding it from him. That realisation gave me strength. "I told Calvin he wasn't allowed anywhere near you and I'm glad to hear that he has followed his orders this time."

"This time? So, did Dad tell him to rape her or not?" I blurted out, stopping Nico mid-pace, and he looked at me in horror.

"No, he would never do that!" he cried, his loyalty to our father etched clearly on his face despite his pain having risen. "Calvin was meant to scare her, rough Dita up a bit, but nothing too bad. She was a fucking livewire, Dahlia. She could be a crazy bitch at times, but you never saw her when she went mad like that. The only thing that could calm her down when she was bad was a fucking sedative, and she refused to take them that night. She told Dad she was leaving, and she would take him and the club down when she did."

Nico stepped closer to me, hesitating before resting a hand on my shoulder. "He needed to take things further to scare her into doing as she was told. She was never like you, Dahlia. She revelled in his disapproval. I'm sure of it. Dita enjoyed winding him up, causing trouble for him, and then watching him squirm. But that night, Dad just snapped. Calvin roughed her up and then he lost himself in the moment. He took things way too far and since then I've kept an eye on him to make sure that it didn't happen again.

When he snaps, he doesn't even know who he is, let alone what he's doing."

I wondered how my brother could possibly know all those things. How he could carry on as if nothing had happened when he knew what Calvin had done to Dita. Even one time was too many, and yet I had the sneaking suspicion Nico didn't quite know all the facts.

"Nico," I whispered, shaking my head in shock. "He didn't just do it once. He did it repeatedly. Dita was sure Dad was sending him to her room when she'd been bad or when Tobin started losing interest. He raped her so many times that she stopped fighting him. All the while, she was dying inside because she thought you were all behind it. She begged Dad to stop him, but he said it would only stop when she had learned to behave. He knew all about what Calvin was doing."

Nico fell to the ground, his legs seemingly giving way beneath him, and his eyes went wide with shock. We sat in silence for a few seconds, him taking in what I'd just said, and vice versa.

"How do you know all of this?" he asked, grabbing his stomach as though it was suddenly hurting him and I told a white lie, not wanting to give up the laptop just yet.

"She told me. Dita never said who it was, but near the end she told me about all the times she'd endured him coming into her room, beating, and violating her while I was asleep a few doors away. How could no one know?" I replied and paled at the thought that perhaps none of this had been planned how Dita had thought. Calvin might have been doing all of it alone for his own kicks.

"I'm gonna fuck him over for this. Make no mistake about that. He told me over and over how he never touched her again, lying right to my face, and now I hear this. From you?! I think I'm gonna be sick," Nico said, running into the en-suite while I sat on the bed and rocked back and forth, my pent-up emotion suddenly releasing.

I was in complete and utter turmoil. I didn't know who to believe or what to think. There was always a part of me that knew Dita's diaries would only tell her side of the story, of course, but I had taken her word for it that Dad must have been sending Calvin to her all those times to teach her a lesson.

Thinking about it after Nico's version of events, I came to realise she had to have been wrong. She'd automatically assumed that Dad had instigated those cruel punishments simply because she hated him so very much and would've always thought that of him. Her hatred would have overridden any logical response to those visits, and perhaps Calvin had played on those feelings she'd always had towards our father. It wasn't like she hid them, so maybe he was the one who told her Dad had sent him. I knew I might never know for sure, but I had to trust in Nico's story, too. Part of me desperately wanted to believe that Dad and Tobin were still the innocent parties in Dita's abusive history.

There was something else I needed though, and I hoped that between Nico and me, we could figure out a way to keep our realisations a secret. I needed more time. To do it properly.

"I want to do this carefully," I said as he emerged from the bathroom, swaying until he plonked himself down on the chair beside my dresser. "If what you're saying is true, Calvin is the only one who needs to be punished, and so we need to go about this the right way. I want him to suffer, but I want to shame and humiliate him first. I want to get him kicked out of the club, his family, and maybe even this entire country for what he's done to our sister. We do this right, Nico. We do it the clever way."

"Fuck, where did this girl come from?" Nico replied, seeming surprised at my sly plan in comparison to his violent desire to teach our enemy a lesson, but I could tell he was instantly on board.

"Don't worry, you're not the only one who has underestimated me all these years, Nico. But trust me, we're going to take him down, and when we do, he will wish for death. Are you in?"

"Yeah, I'm in," he replied, leaning forward to offer me his hand, and I shook it with a devious smile. All thoughts of shock and worry were gone. Instead, I felt strong and full of resolve. I would avenge my sister. I would do one thing right by her in my entire life and when it was all done and dusted, I decided I'd simply carry on with my life, because I was also going to make sure that no one knew it was me who had done it, even if it meant blackmailing Nico to ensure his silence in the end.

We had each underestimated Calvin. I'd not gotten to know him all that well over the years, but he'd seemed like such a nice guy. Always the joker of the group. He had come across a gentle soul as well though, calm and quiet natured much like me, but we had always gotten along. I remember how glad I had been when my father had allowed him a proper place in the club after his couple of years being a prospect.

Not anymore. From that moment on, he was my enemy, someone to be defeated and left to rot in the wake of our battle.

God, how naïve I was, thinking I was capable of such things…

Chapter Twelve

Once we'd finally emerged, Nico and I put on the bravest faces we could and went down to re-join the party. I wasn't sure what our next step would be, but I knew we could do this. That we could see it through and come out on top. I also knew that when Calvin was defeated, we would know, even if no one else did, that we were a force to be reckoned with. A Vice President and a President's old lady who could reign over their father's empire with unending strength once he was gone.

Nico stopped halfway down the stairs and turned to face me, our noses the same height thanks to me being a step higher than him. I was about to ask him what was wrong when he wrapped his arms around me and held on tight. So tight the wind rushed from my lungs, but I didn't fight his hold. He clearly needed it. My protective big brother needed a moment to be weak, and I let him.

"You're happy with Tobin, aren't you?" he asked me quietly, resting his chin on my shoulder. "We did the right thing putting the two of you together?"

"That first night was the worst, Nico. Don't ever do that to me, or anyone else, again," I told him honestly, using my newly found strength to spur me on. He didn't answer me back or move away. Nico just took his miniscule telling off with grace, and I was glad he wasn't going to argue with me about the rights and wrongs of that night. "But yes. I'm happy with Tobin. We're right together and he's brought me out of myself in ways I didn't know I'd needed. Shown me a life I hadn't realised I was missing."

Nico breathed a sigh of relief and lowered his arms. He then took me in for a moment, his eyes scanning my face with a wistful, youthful look I hadn't seen on him in years.

"You look so much like mum," he told me before letting out a sigh. "She would've been so proud of you, Dahlia." I wanted to cry. No one ever spoke of her anymore, as if the memory of our fallen matriarch was too much for any of us to handle. Although I knew I resembled her more than any of us, it made my heart ache to think how Nico had watched me grow up, looking more and more like her, but not once feeling able to tell me. Being able to openly mourn her. I wish I could properly remember her. In truth, I had very few memories of our mother, having been three when she'd died, but he must've had so many as he would've been a teenager. While I envied him for having spent longer with her, I also couldn't envy the loss he must've felt at her passing.

Before I could answer, he turned and bounded down the last few steps toward the muffled voices and music in the bar. I hung back a moment, stifling my tears, and then jumped when I heard the stomping of heavy feet from behind me.

Calvin rounded the corner and headed towards me, reaching the bottom right as I did. He was grinning playfully, back to his normal self again, and I forced myself to play along. To hide my hatred and fear from the man who I knew had ruined my sister's life.

"You waiting for me, babe?" he asked me with a wink. Inside, I cringed. How could he ever think I'd be interested in him? Not just because of what I knew about his nights spent forcing himself on Dita either, but also because I was seeing his cousin. I certainly wasn't going to play along with any game he was trying to lure me into.

"Nah, I bumped into Nico. They're all inside," I answered, opening the door for Calvin, and then following him through it. I was glad to be back in the busy bar rather than alone in the hall with him and veered straight towards where Tobin was standing beside my father and brothers, ready to toast Nico's special day.

The guys closest to him had lined up shots and Nico was back to his old self again, like our conversation upstairs or out in the hall hadn't happened, but I knew he wouldn't forget our pact. Like him, I would act the same as always and give nothing away, while plotting secretly to bring down Calvin in whatever way I could, but for now, I would drink and be merry with my family and friends. I would celebrate and smile, because deep down, I was still in a much better place than I had been. I was glad to have discovered the truth about who X was. Watching him fall from the pedestal he'd put himself on was going to be fun, or so I convinced myself.

***

A couple of days after the party, I was lazing with Tobin on the sofa beneath the window, his hands leisurely stroking their way up over my knees to my thighs and then back again. Most of the club members had headed back to the city but Thomas and Brad had stayed, along with a couple of prospects, and they were putting the new guys to good use by having them clean and tidy Dahlia's after the chaos of the weekend. Tobin and I were ignoring everyone, doing our own thing, and I guess perhaps I was being a little too giggly and girlie, but I was happy with him. Safe. Tobin made me feel like a supermodel or a star, or something. I don't know, but I did know I felt more alive than I had my entire life before.

"Fucking hell," I heard Brad mutter under his breath as he walked into the living area. I then watched as he did an about-turn and headed back in the direction of the kitchen. Enough was enough. I'd had it with his apparent distaste of seeing Tobin and me together, so decided to confront him. I didn't make a big deal out of it as I slid from my man's grasp, pretending I needed to pee, but then plodded out and toward the old kitchen, rather than to the bathroom.

"What's wrong, Brad?" I asked, opting for the gentler approach rather than to ask him outright what his problem was with me and Tobin. He rolled his eyes but didn't answer me, so I stepped closer. "Brad. I feel you've barely said a word to me in weeks. And now you can't even look at me?" I demanded, feeling angrier by the second. I was right. He was looking everywhere but at me, so I grabbed his chin and climbed up onto my tiptoes so we were eye to eye.

"I can't, Dahl. I promised Dad," he answered, much to my chagrin.

"Don't do this to me," I begged, shaking my head. "Don't make me lose you when I don't know what I've done to make you hate me." I was sure he had to. What else could it be? Maybe he'd had a harder time letting me become a woman than our father had, and I just hadn't seen it before? I couldn't fathom another reason for me being in his bad books.

I was pleased when my brother softened and leaned into me, crumbling against me. He wrapped his arms around my waist and laid his head on my shoulder, showing me he didn't hate me at all. It was a relief, but I still couldn't understand.

"The first night we came here; do you know why we stood guard?" Brad asked. I groaned, not wanting to relive that strange night, so I simply shook my head against him. "We were there because Dad needed to know you'd gone through with things and been willing, but also for another reason…"

"Tell me," I implored him, desperate to know the truth. It felt like forever before Brad answered me, and what he said made me recoil in disgust. I finally knew how all our lives had been touched by the evil soul within our midst and to what extent his reach had gone.

"I was the first one to notice the bruises," Brad finally answered, his head still buried in my neck. His voice reached my ears and was quiet and muffled, but clear enough. "I saw them on Dita's wrists and neck. He'd been rough with her. I knew it, and it wasn't the last time. She was scared all the time, Dahlia. I think he was hurting her."

I wanted to cry. Bradley had been beating himself up all this time because he too had noticed the changes in Dita, as well as the abuse she had thought she was successfully hiding. But it wasn't Tobin giving her those bruises. It was Calvin. However, I couldn't tell him, so without blowing the secret, Nico and I had already agreed we were going to keep. All I could do was lie through my teeth, but I did what I had to. Tobin deserved to be absolved of the sins he hadn't committed.

"It wasn't Tobin," I whispered back, watching as Brad lifted his head in surprise. The hazel eyes that matched mine fixed me with a scowl, so I continued with my white lie. "The bruises were from someone else, she told me."

"So, it's true? She was seeing someone behind Tobin's back?" he asked, and I decided to go with it.

"Yes, but it was all consensual. She wanted what Tobin couldn't give her, but the other guy could. That's why they were close to breaking up," I told him, which was almost the truth. She'd been madly in love with L after all—ready to run off into the sunset with him.

"Who was he?" Bradley asked, but I shook my head.

"I honestly don't know," I replied, telling at least one whole truth. Brad shrugged it off. I guess figuring it was too late now, anyway. "So, he's never hurt you, not even once?"

"Not even once," I said, hugging him again. "Trust me."

Chapter Thirteen

I laid awake for hours that night, plotting and scheming in my head as Tobin lay beside me, fast asleep. His body was curled against mine, his hands somehow instinctively caressing my naked skin, even in his sleep. I wanted a future for us. A safe future. I didn't want to have secrets to hide, so decided I was going to get straight to work on bringing Calvin down. But how? I wracked my brains, following trains of thought I figured could work, but all of them either incriminated myself, my family, or Tobin in the end. He would figure me out if I wasn't cunning about it and if Calvin really did have a violent side, he wasn't afraid to unleash. The last thing I wanted was to put anyone I loved in danger. He'd already taken Dita from us.

As I began to drift off to sleep, a dark shadow swept across the room, either a figment of my imagination or the passing of a car outside, but either way, it scared the shit out of me. I jumped, making Tobin do the same, but he settled back to sleep as soon as I shushed him.

"It's okay, just a nightmare," I whispered, curling my body against his. Yes, just a nightmare. An illusion manifested by the paranoia haunting me in the dark hours of the night. Right then, I realised I had it. I knew exactly what I was going to do, albeit with a rather childish approach at taking my vengeance. I was going to haunt Calvin, or should I say, Dita was. I was going to make him think she was coming through from the other side to complete her unfinished business and torment him in ways he could not control. Yes, I was going to let the monster ruin himself just as much as I intended to rip him to shreds from the shadows of his torment. It was going to be fun. Almost easy...

The next morning, I woke early thanks to Tobin's alarm. He needed to get up and head out with my father for a few hours, so I stirred long enough to enjoy a morning quickie with him before dozing and listening to the sound of him taking a shower in our en-suite. After he blew me a kiss goodbye, I watched him leave with a sour expression and buried my head in the pillow but perked up right away when I heard him chatting to someone out in the hall. Clambering to my feet, I pressed my ear against the door. Being nosy, but not caring. I was glad I did.

"Hey, what you up to?" Calvin was asking him, and I heard Tobin answer with his plans. "Don't envy you mate, I'm heading to the shitter then I'll be back to sleep for at least another couple of hours," I heard Calvin add and Tobin laughed before leaving his cousin to it.

An idea hit me. It was perfect. My first chance to do something to mess with Calvin while he was in the bathroom, so I scanned my room, desperate to think of something I could do as my first attempt at riling Dita's abuser up. I spied my backpack and ran to it, quickly finding the item I had hoped was still wedged in the bottom of it—a small vial of Dita's perfume. No one else wore the same scent, and I hadn't been able to use it either as it reminded me too much of her, so had left it there.

Slipping on my robe, I ran across the hall directly into Calvin's empty room and sprayed just a couple of times in there before turning to leave again. In my fear at being caught in the act, the blood was whooshing through my ears, my head pounding. I wanted out of there right away, but that was until I saw his perfectly neat pile of things again and saw red. I shoved them, tipping the stack over so his clothes and accessories fell across the unit. There, now, it was perfect. The room smelled of Dita and while his things had been moved, nothing had been taken. Calvin couldn't go around asking who'd been in his room going by just those two things without sounding like a madman, could he?

I was across the hall, back in my room, and snuggled in bed just a few seconds later, but I needn't have worried. It was another five minutes before I heard the communal bathroom toilet flush and him pad back down to his room. I held my breath and waited. It seemed like forever, but then suddenly there was a slam from one of the rooms and I heard as footsteps thundered downstairs. It had to be Calvin, surely? I cracked my door open an inch and peered out to where his room was, and lo-and-behold, the door was wide open and natural sunlight was streaming in through what had to be its open curtains. Had he flung open the window to clear the smell? I imagined him coming in and freaking out before throwing on his clothes and making a run for it. When I then heard a bike start and speed away, I was sure I was right, and a huge smile spread across my face at the sheer thought of him panicking and feeling like he had to take off.

It's far from over yet, X, I thought. He was going to pay his debts, and when he was finally broken, I'd find a way to make him confess his sins. He'd never know what hit him.

***

That evening, we all got ready to head back to the city and Dad insisted Tobin and I went too. I'd kinda hoped for some time alone, but couldn't deny my father's wishes, just like Tobin couldn't refuse his President's command. I was horny. Like crazy horny. I wanted my gorgeous man to take me every which way he knew how, and knew I was still riding the high after my successful first attempt to rile Calvin. He'd left ahead of the others and gone back to the old house without a word to anyone, however Tobin told me he'd seemed off when he'd called but wouldn't explain his sudden disappearing act.

"I'm sure he's fine, babe," I said, sliding in behind him on the bike after everything had been locked up and we were ready to go. The cars and other bikes were already on their way back, so it was just me, Tobin, and Nico left. I could tell my brother wanted to ask me how I was doing after our crazily intense talk at his party, but he also seemed to like seeing me happy so decided against sneaking a minute with me to try and discuss any suspicions he might have as to Calvin's sudden disappearance.

Nico gave us a nod and then sped away, while Tobin took his time getting himself ready to leave. "What's the matter?" I finally asked, and he answered by twisting me around over his hip, so I was suddenly straddling him instead of the bike. The front of the chassis dug into my back like it had before, so I arched my body against his, giggling when I heard him groan from beneath his visor. I pulled mine off and he did the same, revealing those immense blue eyes that had me flushed red hot in a second.

"I don't want to share you anymore, Dahl. I want to stay here and fuck your brains out..." he groaned. I wanted the exact same thing, and he knew it. Tobin then lifted me off his bike and carried me around the back of the house. I was surprised he hadn't taken us back in the main entrance to sneak some time alone, but then realised we weren't heading back inside, only out of the view of the main road.

Tobin eventually set me down next to one of the back walls not lit by the security light. There, he pressed himself against me and began kissing me with such ferocity I was soon gasping for breath, coming undone at his command. He was rough, as if he could barely control himself. I'd never seen him that way, but I didn't mind one little bit. In fact, he was seducing the dark side of me, luring her out. I gave in and ground my hips against his, telling him I needed him inside of me, which was when he began ripping at my clothes in a bid to gain access to my flesh.

The cold air of the late winter made me hiss, my nipples going rock hard the second he had my shirt open and my bra cups yanked down. He sucked on them in turn, the wetness only making them colder, and I grabbed his hand, pulling his finger to my neglected nipple so he could warm it with his touch. As he went to town, sucking and tweaking them roughly, I moaned loudly. The sound seemed to spark something inside of him and Tobin suddenly lifted the hand, caressing my right breast. Up it went, over my collar to my neck, where he wrapped it around me in a gentle yet firm hold. His other hand was unbuttoning my jeans, which he then slid down my thighs to my knees. He then yanked my knickers aside and slipped two fingers inside me, caressing me with harsh plunges that only served to make me hotter and wetter for him.

I stood there, pinned to the wall by Tobin's hands, one holding me down and the other driving pleasure through my core at an alarming rate. I was utterly at his command, but I wasn't afraid, and he knew it. When I came, I screamed his name for all to hear, and for the first time since we'd started being together, he didn't want to hear it. Tobin put his hand over my mouth, lifting his head up to meet mine while he unbuttoned his jeans and released his erection. "I love you, Dahlia, but so help me, God. All I want to hear right now is the sound of your body taking me inside of it." His voice was a deep, rumbling growl that sent me over the edge. He'd never been rough before, but I liked the game we were somehow both playing and I decided to make him wait to fuck me, only in the best way possible.

I shoved my jeans back up to my hips and slid to the floor, landing face-to-face with his cock, so I did the only thing I could, given the circumstances—I slid my mouth over the head and sucked on it. With his palms against the wall behind me, I was trapped as he began to move, and before I knew it, he was hitting the back of my throat and I was fighting my gag reflex in a desperate attempt to accommodate him. I'd sucked him off before, but never like that. Not all the way back. It was the hottest blowjob I'd ever given him.

When he reached one hand down and cupped the back of my head, I instinctively knew what was about to happen and tried to ready myself as best I could. Hot cum spurted down my throat, filling me with his release, and I gagged as he withdrew, still not used to the taste of it. I thought I might be sick, but luckily managed to subdue my nausea. I'd wanted to please Tobin and was glad he'd let himself go with me. I didn't want him to feel bad or as if I hadn't liked what he'd done, even if it'd been rougher than I was used to.

"Tobin," I whispered, climbing to my feet with his help. I wasn't sure what to say next, so peered up into his face, hoping to find answers there. His heated stare told me he'd enjoyed himself, and I grinned.

"That wasn't what I'd had in mind when I said I wanted to be inside you," he told me, mirroring my smile. I shrugged and turned to walk back to the bike, figuring our stolen moment was over now that we'd both reached our climaxes. I was blissfully wrong. Tobin grabbed me and pulled me over to where a lonely picnic bench sat in the shadows. "Bend over," he commanded, and I immediately obliged. I gripped the edge of the wood and said nothing as he pushed my jeans and knickers over my hips and down below my knees, but I was sure to arch my back seductively so he knew he was welcome to dive right in. The cool night air was nothing. I didn't feel it. I only felt him. Tobin was inside of me in a second, pummelling me so hard I had to brace myself against the table or else I knew I'd fall over.

The wood was coarse against my palms, sharp splinters digging into my skin, however I refused to stop his deliciously rough lovemaking session. I came so hard my knees buckled, but Tobin held me up and continued, eliciting one more orgasm from me before he too reached his high.

By the time he pulled away, I was jelly. My legs were

shaking and my hands were tingling with fresh sores. I was panting so hard my throat hurt and when I'd pulled my jeans and underwear back up, I had to sit down and take a moment to regain my composure. I closed my eyes and leaned back into the table I'd just been fucked over, sucking in deep breaths. "You're amazing, Dahl," Tobin's haughty voice pierced the silence, and I opened my eyes, watching as he lit a cigarette and then took a deep drag.

"You're pretty damn amazing yourself, you know?" I replied, grinning up at him. I swear he actually blushed. It was dark, so I couldn't tell for sure, but he definitely offered me a coy smile in return before taking another drag. I watched his hand fiddle with the smoke and wondered what it was like. I'd never tried them. It was always something the guys in my family did, so I had followed Dita's lead and not smoked, but it wasn't because I hadn't felt tempted. I'd often felt like asking for a try but knew my dad would kill me if I did.

I didn't mind the strong scent of it on Tobin, though. It was downright sexy as hell now that I got to smell it on my official boyfriend after he'd just fucked me raw.

Tobin flicked the butt to the ground and put out his hand to me, pulling me into his embrace the moment I took it. He held me for a moment, kissing me tenderly, before leading me back toward where his bike sat waiting for us.

"Back to reality, babe," he muttered as we both mounted it, sounding a little disheartened at the thought of us heading back to the city. I wrapped my arms around his waist, holding him tight.

"As long as we're together, reality is fine with me," I answered, and meant it. I didn't care where we were or what was going on. If we had each other, that was all that mattered.

Chapter Fourteen

We arrived back at my dad's house just over half an hour later and I winced as I climbed off the bike, reminding myself not to ride right after a session like that again. I was sore as hell but hid it as I straightened myself up and followed Tobin inside. Calvin was at the door, evidently waiting for us, and he immediately pulled Tobin to one side. I overheard Tobin asking his cousin what'd happened and wanted to hear more but figured it wouldn't look right if I were openly eavesdropping, so I eventually walked away, heading towards where Bradley was chatting with one of the prospects.

"Hey, sis," he said, greeting me with a kiss to the cheek. I was so glad he'd sorted out his attitude towards Tobin and me at last, and loved having my kind and gentle brother back, rather than the grumpy git he'd turned into back in those earlier days of our relationship. "Where's Nico?" he then asked, looking behind me towards the door. My heart sunk.

"He left ages before us," I replied, looking around the room. "We had… stuff to sort out, so he went on ahead. Hasn't he come back yet?" Brad shook his head no, and I immediately reached into my pocket for my phone. I pulled up Nico's number and hit the call button, my hand shaking as I lifted it to my ear. The call wasn't answered, so I tried again and again. When someone finally answered, I began to tremble the moment I realised it wasn't my brother. "Hello? Who is this?"

"Hello, my name's Sarah and I'm a nurse at the Royal Hospital. Who's calling please?" a woman's voice chimed through the speaker.

This couldn't be happening. My throat was dry, and I had to swallow a huge lump that'd formed in my throat as I tried to answer her. Brad was staring at me, clearly having realised the situation wasn't what he might've initially thought. Nico hadn't stopped for a drink or to grab a bite to eat. He was somehow in hospital.

"I'm Dahlia, Nico's sister. Is he hurt?" I eventually managed to ask the nurse.

"I'm afraid I can't give you any details over the phone, but if you could come here with some identification, we can give you an update."

"Is my brother alive, surely you can at least tell me that?" I bellowed, making every head in the room turn towards us.

"He is alive, Miss Procter, but he's in a bad way. Please come to the hospital and we can give you a proper update here," she answered before dropping the call. I then stood there staring at my phone for a second or two as the information sunk in.

"Where's Dad?" I eventually asked, turning towards Brad. I was suddenly in robot mode. Nothing was more important than getting the news to our father and going to see what'd happened to Nico. No one was moving nearly fast enough, and I was growing impatient. We should be out the door already. "Get Thomas," I commanded.

Brad nodded in the direction of the club's meeting room, which doubled as Dad's office. Of course, he was in there, and for the first time in years, and I headed straight over and walked in without knocking or being escorted. I wasn't a club member, so had been told I wasn't allowed in there from a young age, but it didn't matter now. All that mattered was our family, and one of them was in a bad way. Inside, Hadley was on her knees in front of my dad, sucking his cock like her life depended on it. She was the same tramp who had tried to get away with giving me a mouthful that night and Dad had told me to beat the shit out of her the next time, so I was surprised to find him indulging in some of the few skills she had to offer. He was a red-blooded man after all though, so I couldn't be angry. In fact, I didn't feel anything. I wasn't disgusted or shocked. I just wanted Hadley out of there so I could talk with my father and brothers alone.

"Get outta here," Dad told her, zipping up. She grumbled and groaned but did as she was told, and I waited until the room was clear before I finally crumbled. I slumped into Nico's chair to the left of my father and held my head in my hands. "What is it, Dahlia?" he asked me sincerely, reminding me of the man I'd grown up with and had been so close with before he'd passed that torch to Tobin.

"Nico. He... he didn't come back. He's been in an accident."

"What?" Dad cried, standing so fast his chair scatted away behind him. The door then opened and my brothers joined us, but not for long. "Get Tobin in here now!" they were ordered before they could get comfortable.

When the three of them were inside, I relayed the

message the nurse had given me about Nico having been in an accident. It didn't feel real. Surely it was an elaborate hoax or some sick joke? Nico had to be fine. There wasn't a world I could live in without him there with me. Not after Dita.

Tobin came over and grabbed me, pulling me to him in a bid to calm and soothe me. I appreciated the gesture, but still felt numb. I couldn't cry or scream or wail. I had to be strong for Nico. I had to get us on our way to him, so he'd know he was loved and that we'd be by his side when he woke up.

"I'll go get Jodie and meet you at the hospital," Thomas informed us, climbing to his feet, car keys at the ready. Dad jumped to attention at my brother's words and started directing the rest of us to one of the larger cars we owned, insisting we travel there together. Tobin was the most with it of us all, and he took the wheel while I climbed into the passenger seat beside him.

I felt awful. There we were, fucking and enjoying ourselves while my brother had evidently been in an accident and then hauled off to the hospital without anyone having realised. Why hadn't we seen it on the journey home? Had Nico taken another route? Questions were whizzing around in my head, and I barely registered the drive there. It was only when we arrived and Tobin took my hand in his that I finally started to crumble. The walls of my icy resolve were melting, and he could see it, but he held me close and let me do things in my own way and, most importantly, my own time. I'd barely said a word to him, but he seemed to know what I needed, and I loved that about him.

"We're here because my son was brought in after an accident. Nico Procter," Dad informed the Accident and

Emergency receptionist, who looked him up on her system.

"Yes, he's in surgery right now, but if you'd like to take a seat, I'll let the doctors know you've arrived," was all she replied, giving nothing away. Part of me wanted to scream and beg her for more information, but I didn't. I remained my usual calm self and followed my dad into the waiting area with Tobin and Bradley, where we all took a seat and stared off into the relatively empty room in silence.

It felt like forever until someone came over, clipboard in hand. The doctor seemed uneasy approaching us, eyeing my father's cut warily. He then looked at the rest of us and I saw him do a double take as he realised the other guys were wearing club leathers as well.

"Mr Proctor?" he asked timidly and then seemed surprised when my father stood and shook his hand courteously in introduction. Even in times of chaos, my father never forgot his sense of decorum, and I softened the part of my heart that'd hardened towards him. He had his ways, but overall, he was a good man. He simply had to be. "We tried the emergency contact on your son's phone, but there was no answer. I apologise for the way you all found out, but one of the trauma nurses heard the phone ringing in your son's jacket pocket so decided to answer it, hoping to find a relative on the other end." He then fiddled with the clipboard, taking a quick look at the notes either he or someone else had made on it before staring back up in my father's dark brown eyes. "We believe your son came off his bike at seventy miles an hour on a dual carriageway, before sliding into the centre and narrowly missing the traffic on the other side."

"You believe so? What does that mean?" Dad asked him and I watched as the man squirmed.

"There were no witnesses, and your son is yet to regain consciousness. Dispatch thinks the call to the emergency services was placed by a passer-by as no one but your son was on the scene when we arrived. He's lucky it was so late and that he was on a quiet stretch of the road."

None of it felt right. I had one hundred questions I couldn't bring myself to ask and could feel myself shaking, rocking back and forth slightly as the doctor's words washed over me. Nico had been all alone there, lying in the street and almost dead, when Tobin and I should've been with him. The guilt made me want to vomit.

"What now?" Dad was being super calm, urging the doctor to carry on, while the rest of us sat in silence, letting him take the lead as always.

"He's had surgery to repair internal bleeding in his abdomen caused by a blow to the gut we think was caused by him flying over the handlebars. His organs on the right side took the brunt of the damage but have stabilised and there are some extensive injuries to his right arm and leg where he skidded across the cement. His leathers saved him from anything too awful, but he's still required stitches in places where they tore." I gagged and Tobin rubbed my back gently, shushing me.

"He'll be okay, Dahl," he told me, but I wasn't convinced. I peered up at the doctor, silently pleading with him to tell me some good news. He noticed and turned to me, his soft gaze making me want to cry.

"Are you Dahlia?" he asked, surprising us all. I nodded. "He was calling your name as they brought him in, pleading with the paramedic for you to find someone called Elle?" Everyone looked at me, hoping I would tell them who Elle was, but I couldn't. I knew it was L. Not some fictitious woman. He wanted me to find Dita's lover, and it seemed it'd been the one wish on his lips as he lay potentially dying in the back of an ambulance. Evidently, L had more to tell me about my sister's traumatic last few months of life. Whether Nico pulled through or not, I knew I had to honour his request. It was time I stopped being selfish and went in search of him.

I shook my head, feigning confusion, but couldn't listen to anymore. I stood and ran for the bathroom, where I threw up in such a violent way all I could do was cry into the toilet bowl.

"Baby, are you okay?" Tobin asked me when I finally emerged, his face bleak as he took me in. I shook my head no.

"I don't know if it's the shock or what, but I feel awful," I replied, following him back to the chairs where I curled up and somehow managed to get comfortable lying in his lap.

I must've dozed off because the next thing I knew, Jodie was there with Thomas, and she was sitting beside me. I sat up and gave her hand a squeeze, which then turned into a full-blown hug when she turned towards me and threw herself into my arms. We cried together, our worry for Nico pouring out of us, and none of the men accompanying us brought attention to our typical feminine reaction to such times.

"I can't believe it," Jodie groaned in my hold.

"He'll be okay," I replied, trying to give her strength even though I had no certainties as to my brother's wellbeing.

"He has to be," she answered, pulling back from my embrace, and I watched as her hand reached down to her stomach and then rested there. I nodded, silently telling her I understood. They were expecting a child together. The first in the next generation of Proctor children, and even I was damned certain Nico sure as hell had better pull through and be there to raise his kid.

We all breathed a collective sigh when the doctor returned and told us he had come through his surgery and was going into recovery, where they were hopeful he'd be waking up not too long after. Jodie and my dad went with the doctor to wait by Nico's side while he came around, the rest of us being forced to sit and wait for more news again. It was torture, but at least I had Tobin with me, which I knew was more than Jodie had. She was facing a future without the love of her life in it, and I didn't envy her. Nico was going to make it. The doctor had said so himself. We were going to be back to normal in no time.

In the early hours of the next morning, Dad and Jodie returned, telling the small group how Nico was awake and wanted to see all of us. At the doctor's insistence, only two at a time went in so after Thomas and Bradley had taken a few minutes to check in with him, it was mine and Tobin's turn.

Nico looked like shit. The colour had drained from him and he was clearly in pain, but tried his best to talk normally, while we all knew he was in bad shape. He might as well have been bandaged from the neck down thanks to his various injuries, but I just kept thanking God for bringing him through it. I hadn't put much stock in prayers before, especially since Dita had died, but couldn't deny my prayers had been answered the night before.

"What's this cryptic message you told the paramedic to give Dahlia?" Tobin asked once we'd gone over the details of how things had happened. All Nico could remember was that his bike had choked, and he'd been thrown. The rest was apparently a blur. "Something about someone called Elle?"

Nico looked horrified. It seemed clear to me he hadn't remembered saying those things to the medics seeing to him on the road, and he frowned as if it hurt his head trying to come up with a lie to tell his best friend.

"I dunno, mate," he eventually said, and even I knew that wouldn't be enough. If anything, his dismissive answer made him look even more suspicious. Nico gathered some strength and, in a sudden burst, grabbed Tobin by his shirt and pulled him to him so they were nose-to-nose. "You keep her safe, Tobin. You keep Dahlia protected and safe from harm. Do you hear me?"

"I hear you, Nico," Tobin replied, and I watched as he stared back into my brother's dark gaze in surprise. "What the fuck is going on, man?"

"You swear. Swear it to me here and now that you'll protect her with your life. That no one will harm her under your care." Nico wasn't backing down, regardless of his waning strength, so Tobin nodded. He pressed his head to Nico's and put his hand around the back of his neck, holding him there.

"I promise, Nico. I'll protect her until my dying breath." I guessed Tobin must've been thinking about how Dita's life had ended. It seemed like he was promising not to let me down like he had her, while I was thinking of the days, weeks, and months before. The times when a monster had visited her room repeatedly without anyone noticing or caring. The days she'd spent lying to everyone around her and hiding her pain. He hadn't been able to protect her, but would he if he had known? I liked to think he would.

Tobin left the two of us alone then, and it was my turn to make a promise to my big brother. We didn't need the swearing or the theatrics. We each knew how the other felt.

"I don't know how long I'll be here, Dahl. I don't want you doing anything about the things we discussed the other night, do you hear me?" Nico said, and I nodded, fiddling with the white, starchy hospital duvet he was laying under. "No messing with him and no digging into Dita's past."

"So, I'm not to go and find L?" I demanded in a hushed tone. "Because it seemed as though that was your dying wish, Nico. Why?"

"I guess I thought it would bring you peace to find the man she loved. The man who you said would have made her blissfully happy. I thought if you found him, you wouldn't go off on a mission for revenge all alone."

"I already messed with him a little," I told him, deciding on honesty. Nico groaned and shifted his weight on the bed, reaching towards me so he could take my hand in his. I explained my little game and Nico laughed but told me in no uncertain terms not to do anything like it again, and I agreed. Not having my brother there as backup was a scary thought, and I realised I wasn't as brave as I might've once thought.

We left things there. I would stop messing with Calvin, for the time being at least, but I was going to dig just a little. I needed to know who L was. It was an itch within me that simply wouldn't go away. A thirst I couldn't quench no matter how much I had tried to force it aside.

Chapter Fifteen

The next afternoon, I locked myself away in my old bedroom with Dita's laptop and trawled through every folder I could find looking for a secret file with photos in, or better yet, some saved emails or messages from the illustrious L. None of the club members I knew of who had with names starting in L matched the profile she had described in her diary entries, and I began to wonder if his name even began with that letter at all. Calvin had become X in her eyes, so in a way, almost anyone could be her secret lover.

I exhausted myself with the search and eventually fell asleep on my bed, cradling her laptop to my chest. Later, I woke to find Tobin standing over me, gently pulling the computer out of my grasp. I knew he didn't realise it was Dita's and not mine, but wasn't about to reveal the truth to him, even in my sleepy haze.

Tobin had spent the day going back and forth between the hospital and Jodie's house, taking care of my brother and his fiancée without complaint. Doing his part for both the club and for Nico as his best friend. He was a good man. I could see it in every moment he spent being selfless or kind. I admired his strength and ability to be able to care so strongly for those he held dear. I also felt privileged to know I counted among those he would always put above others—including himself. There was no backing out from what we had together. I knew without a doubt that we would be married and live happily ever after. That was the only future I saw for us and refused to believe in anything else.

"I was going to climb into bed with you and snuggle, but I've accidentally woken you up," Tobin said with a sly smile. I had the distinct impression he'd purposely been noisy and disruptive, hoping I'd wake up and pay him some attention. And do you know what? I was more than happy to.

"Get in, baby," I whispered as I kicked off my clothes and climbed under the sheets, turning onto my side before lifting the duvet invitingly. Tobin undressed in a heartbeat and was in with me a second later, spooning me from behind. He was cold, like he'd been outside, and I guessed he'd not long got back. I was glad he'd come straight to see me rather than head to the bar, and although being against him gave me a chill, it also warmed me from within. I arched my back against him, pushing my bum against his swelling cock. "You're cold. Let me warm you up," I groaned, pushing my entire body up against his.

Tobin pushed his arm under my top one and reached back, placing the flat of his palm against the centre of my chest. His mouth was on my neck as his knee pushed mine up at a right angle and then opened them slightly. The head of his cock was stroking at my core, demanding entry, but he held back. He waited, and while it was torture, I couldn't deny I loved simply having his body against mine. We'd had our share of nights together, but he still drove me wild and while sometimes I wanted him hard and rough, it wasn't that time. "Make love to me, baby."

Tobin thrust, entering me with one deep, fluid stab. My body welcomed him without complaint, the inner muscles already having been willing before he'd taken the plunge. Rather than the usual in and out routine, he then did something new to me. He stayed inside, rocking back and forth while keeping me full to bursting. My body clenched and released him over and over, desperate for the usual stroking, but still Tobin didn't withdraw. He seemed insistent on going slow and sensual, making love to me like I'd asked him to.

It took longer than usual to reach my orgasm, I guess because the stimulation was different that time, but when I did, it took my breath away. I cried out, curling my knees up higher on the bed, while Tobin continued to press himself into me, riding the waves of my release along with me. When I was finished, he wasn't, so began rubbing my clit from behind in relentless circular motions while he continued to move slowly inside me. I came again and this time he was right there with me, emptying with a deep, rumbling groan.

"Fuuuuck," he breathed, falling over me as he withdrew and then pulled me into his embrace. I turned and wrapped myself in him, each of us well and truly warmed up. "That was amazing," he then told me with a contented smile.

I had to agree, but words evaded me. All I could do was press my lips against his chest, taking his nipples into my mouth before laying soft kisses against his tattooed chest and neck. I eventually reached his mouth, showing rather than telling Tobin how I felt, and he responded by sticking two fingers in my pussy. I yelped, not having expected it, but then found myself riding them with reckless abandon. I didn't care that I was already spent, and Tobin didn't seem to mind that I was soaked in a combination of our releases. He buried them deep inside of me, stroking his way over my g-spot and then back down until I began bucking with yet another climax. "I want to photograph you, Dahlia. Like this." He yanked off the covers and splayed my legs open, showing off my body with such admiration I couldn't deny him.

"Why?" I managed to ask, still floating on my cloud.

"Why?" Tobin replied with a gruff laugh, snapping me back to reality. "Because of this body that has me so fucking ruined, Dahl. I always want you with me, even if all I have are the pictures. I want to see those flushed cheeks and sweet smile. I need to have this." He reached down and strummed my clit, eliciting a moan from me. I giggled, feeling shy at the thought of him grabbing a camera and shooting, but couldn't resist those puppy-dog eyes of his he then fixed on me. I nodded, and Tobin wasted no time in diving off the bed to grab his phone from his jacket pocket. He loaded the camera and held it steady in one hand while he got back to work with the other. I was shy at first, hiding my face, but eventually got into it, especially when I came for him and he captured it on the small screen in his hand.

Tobin was then back inside me, holding the phone directly over where he was impaling me, filming as he fucked me with a relentless rhythm. When we were both finally spent, he didn't stop photographing me. Tobin took stills of my flushed, naked body and then close ups of my face and breasts. He then laid down with me and showed me his handiwork.

They were amazing, and while I shied away from the truly graphic shots, I couldn't deny he had taken some wonderful pictures of me. He had a good eye and had captured my natural shyness without making me look foolish. My favourite shot was a picture of his tattooed hand over my breast, the nipple just poking out between his deft fingers.

"You have a talent behind the camera, Tobin," I told him, flicking through them again. I kept going through his camera roll, not sure what I was expecting to find there, but gasped at what his phone was filled with. "Me. They're all of me?" I asked, looking over at him incredulously.

"Of course, they are," he answered, looking a little shy. "I told you how obsessed I am with you. Did you think I was joking?" Tobin added with a laugh. He was messing around to hide his true feelings, but I didn't mind. We both had our secrets, and that was fine, so if he felt the need to shy away because I'd uncovered one of his, I didn't care. I continued scrolling. Spying various nights we'd spent together in both the company of others and just the two of us. Tobin had caught me sitting alone beneath the huge bay window at the clubhouse, working at my laptop. There were more than a few like that one when I'd been alone and he had sneaked a photo, and they were lovely. Me in natural poses and genuine smiles.

"They're beautiful," I answered, and I was sure he sighed in relief. "I just wish we had some of the both of us—outside the bedroom!"

Tobin took the phone from me and looked back through the feed.

"Here," he handed it back to me, and I could see numerous shots of us sitting together at Nico's birthday party. And then again a week later when we were surrounded by just the club members and their old ladies. "Brad took some for me. He came to me and apologised for being rude, offering to take some when he caught me shooting you." I smiled. Tobin must've known I'd had a talk with my brother, but he didn't ask me about it, and I appreciated that. He didn't seem one to pry, and I liked my privacy, which was just another of the ways we seemed so perfect together.

I flicked through them with a smile, but then frowned when I noticed a trend there. In a few of them, Calvin was watching Tobin and me intently, like he was interested in us or was listening in on a conversation. His girlfriend Shannon was hanging off him, not seeming to notice that his attention was elsewhere, but he wasn't bothered. I thought he had to have been interested in Tobin and me, but then I flicked to the next picture and saw a shot of me on my own, with Calvin still hovering close by, watching me with a dark, emotionless expression. My blood ran cold. Did he know? Could he have been onto me the whole time and simply played nice like I had been? All I'd done was mess with him the one time. Surely, he couldn't have known it was me? Paranoia was a bitch who came crashing down on me like a ton of bricks, suddenly feeling too heavy to bear.

A hundred and one questions filled my mind, and I was aware that Tobin was still lying next to me, watching me flick through the photos on his phone. If he knew a thing about Calvin's dark side, he hadn't seemed to react to the photo, so I chose not to bring it up. I didn't even know how to broach the subject with him about Calvin and his violently sadistic ways. Instead, I resorted to my old tricks of forcing the thoughts away and retreating into myself.

"I can't wait to make more memories with you, Tobin," was all I told him, handing back the phone before snuggling into his hold and we both fell into an exhausted sleep.

***

The next day, I was helping clean and tidy up at my dad's while he, Tobin, and my brothers were at the hospital seeing Nico when I came across a set of car keys I didn't recognize. I popped them in my pocket, thinking I'd figure out their owner later, and carried on straightening the place up. Dad was gathering the club members that evening, so I wanted it nice for when my extended family came round. I guessed it was that need to care for them kicking in again, but I found myself putting a lot of effort into the task, going as far as lighting candles and spraying some fabric freshener on the sofas.

My family arrived in perfect time to dive right into the evening meal the housekeeper had made for everyone—a huge bowl of chili over tortilla chips and rice—and I joined them, listening to the light conversation going back and forth around the table.

"Nico's going stir crazy in that place," Tobin told me, grabbing another handful of nachos so he could scoop at his dinner. "He was ready to come home days ago, but they won't let him. He's still at risk of infection," he told me, but then quickly shook his head when a fearful look swept over my face. "He's fine, trust me. The doctors are just being extra careful is all."

"Good," I replied, tucking into my small mound of

food. A few of the others then began arriving for church and they hovered on the periphery, waiting for their leader to invite them to enjoy the meal. Calvin was there, and this time I felt him watching me. I looked up and caught his eye, smiling in greeting like I always did, and he shot me back his trademark grin. It was as if nothing was wrong between us, and of course I couldn't be sure if he was onto me or not, but doubt was forcing me to tread carefully, just in case.

After dinner, they disappeared for just over an hour while I curled up on the sofa and read a book. I planned to wait for Tobin, but he and my father stayed behind, talking in private after their club meeting was over. It was late, and I was tired, but I forced myself to stay and wait for my man.

While sitting there engrossed in my novel, I could hear some of the guys teasing and joking around and looked up to find that Calvin was the butt of their jibes.

"Who loses the keys to the President's new truck the day after it's delivered?" Ethan, one of the junior members, asked another, nudging him with his elbow. "Oh yeah, this guy!" He pointed to Calvin, who laughed it off, but I could see he hated it. The conversation went on and on, mostly banter, but I learned enough. Dad had had a new truck delivered the evening before, ready for Nico to drive when he came home, and Calvin had been asked to give it a tune up but had then apparently lost the keys.

I felt like I might burst out laughing at any moment, feeling the heaviness in my pocket of the set of keys I had found while cleaning up. They had to be the ones, and I couldn't resist keeping that nugget of truth to myself. Dad would undoubtedly be furious with Calvin for having misplaced them and I relished in the idea that he'd been given a grilling and was now in my father's bad books. He deserved it, the bastard. And then some.

I bided my time, waiting for the opportune moment to sneak away unnoticed, and then made for the kitchen, where I ducked out the back into the huge garden. The bikes and cars were all lined up in neat rows alongside one another and I reached into my pocket for the keys, pressing down on the fob. I was right. The gleaming new truck halfway down the line beeped to respond to the unlock button having been pressed, and I saw the lights turn on inside. I slunk over to it, checking my periphery. I wasn't entirely sure what I wanted to do with the keys. Maybe I should've just tossed them into the bushes, but I felt brave. I wanted them to be discovered and get Calvin in more trouble, so I opened the door and threw them into the footwell of the passenger seat before closing it silently behind me.

As I then headed back to the house, I heard clapping hands coming from the shadows over by the back door. My heart sunk. Dread halted me in my tracks. I knew who was there before he'd even emerged from the darkness of the back porch and readied myself, unsure how he might be going to react to my trickery.

"And there was me thinking the devious, rotten sister had gone and only the meek, gentle, and naïve sister remained. How wrong I was about you, Dahlia," Calvin said as he stepped closer. "How wrong we all were." He laughed, eyeing me curiously. "But not Tobin. He sees you, doesn't he? Brings out the free spirit in you, I bet?"

"I know what you did to her. I know how you beat and raped her time and again, fooling her into thinking you'd been sent to teach her a lesson, when all the while you were just having your deviant way without a care for her wellbeing." I couldn't hold my tongue or my anger. I shoved his shoulders hard, catching him off guard, but not for long. Calvin lunged for me, grabbing me by the neck and heaving me into one of the trucks. My head span with the rush of it, but I still squirmed, intent on fighting him back. Not letting him win.

"You think you know me, or the things I've done? You have no idea, sweetheart, but you will. You'll know soon enough," he growled before letting me go. "I suggest you quit messing with me, or mark my words, something terrible will happen. Something even the sweet and innocent Dahlia can't come back from…"

Calvin then sauntered away as if he didn't have a care in the world, while I crumpled in a heap on the floor.

I wrapped my arms around myself and curled my knees up to my chest. My breathing was ragged, my head spinning, and all I wanted to do was get away. I wanted to go home, not my dad's house, but my home. Dahlia's. Just me and Tobin.

Gathering myself together, I forced my fears away, stood tall, and took a deep breath. I then headed straight back inside, being careful to sneak up to my room unnoticed before I then flung myself onto the bed and screamed into the pillow with all my might.

Chapter Sixteen

Tobin didn't come up to bed until late and he was drunk, so rather than try and talk or gain any closeness, I just pretended to be asleep. He undressed noisily, but then fell into bed beside me. He was snoring in a second and I just lay there, contemplating my life, my family, and my future. But most of all, the predicament I had found myself in with Calvin. He knew I was onto him, that I had uncovered some of his misgivings, and yet he didn't care. Calvin knew I wasn't going to tell anyone, otherwise I would've done it already. He thought he had won and yes, he'd bested me for the time being, but not forever. I decided then and there that I would find out everything I could while staying as far away from Calvin as possible. I wouldn't give him the opportunity to corner me again. As the saying went, he might've won the battle, but he wasn't going to win the war.

The next day, I heightened my efforts to find L. I read back through Dita's messages with her friends, hoping to find something helpful, but still I came up empty. She hadn't confided in anyone. Why? L had to have been someone she had to see under the radar. Someone completely out from the club and our father's gaze. There must've been a good reason for that. I browsed through her contacts list again, looking for any clue, which was when I found a profile locked down and containing nothing more than a red flower as the cover photo. The name wasn't anything distinguishable either, being simply called Jane Doe, so I opened the message box and wracked my brains, thinking of a suitable way to introduce myself. Being brave, I typed in the small window, writing Jane Doe a message from Dita's posthumous profile.

I know you loved her…

I hit send.

Nothing. I waited ages, and the message wasn't even opened by whoever Jane Doe was. I figured perhaps I was wrong after all, so closed the laptop and stowed it away, figuring I'd come back and look later. It turned out it was a good call because just as I stood to head downstairs, a sharp knock came at the door and my father walked straight inside.

"Hey Dad, everything okay?" I asked him, feeling on edge. He didn't answer me right away. He just closed the door behind him and stepped closer, eyeing me with that hardened stare.

"No," he answered, coming closer. "You're not yourself. You haven't been since Nico's accident. All you do is hide yourself away and everyone is noticing. What's wrong?"

"Nothing," I answered a little too quickly and saw the disappointment on my father's face.

"I thought you knew better than to try and lie to me, Dahlia?" he said, reaching out and taking my hand in his. He then pressed his forefinger into the same spot on my wrist where he'd held me before. The place he could use to determine my innermost reactions via his craftily honed skills at reading people. I wasn't about to let him repeat the exercise though, so yanked it back without a care for my usual calm nature.

"Enough with the weird lie-detector thing! I'm sad and angry and I'm allowed to be, okay?" He was understandably shocked and stood there, his dark brown eyes boring into mine.

"Why?" he eventually breathed, and I had to look away. There was no lie I could tell him. No truth I could exploit. I had to do it. To tell him at least part of what I'd learned about Dita's torment. He had to know, for my safety as well as my need for the truth.

"Because under your roof, Dita was raped and beaten repeatedly without you or anyone else putting a stop to it. Without you helping her. You sat back and did nothing while she was hurting. While she was in pain day after day." I felt a sob rattle my chest and let it out as I rubbed my stinging eyes. "Not even when she begged you to…"

"What?" he asked me, and his deep voice more like a whisper. "How do you know all this?" I couldn't answer without giving up the precious laptop I was still hoping Jane Doe might message me on, but I also didn't want to give up Dita's diaries. They were private. Something only she and I had read, and I wanted it to stay that way.

Sensing my refusal, Dad took a deep breath and sat down on my bed, his body sagging as though he were exhausted. "I knew she was seeing someone behind Tobin's back and yes, I saw the bruises. I figured she liked it rough with the guy she was cheating with, but thought it was consensual. She and I weren't close like we are, Dahlia. I couldn't just come right out and ask her, so I left it for a while, but decided to take Tobin away on a run with me so they could have some space. I got him laid and made it clear I was behind him if he wanted to break things off with Dita and he was glad. He knew they were over but hadn't known how to tell me."

"So, you just left them to continue the façade of their relationship while suffering at the hands of her abuser? She was riddled with guilt because of it and that burden drove her crazy."

"I didn't know!" Dad bellowed, raising his voice to me for the first time in years. I crumbled. Taking a seat next to him atop my thick duvet, I took his hand in mine and leaned my head down onto his shoulder, curling my body against his. It wasn't the sort of hugs we used to always have, but it was the closest to it I felt comfortable doing. "I didn't know," he repeated.

"None of it adds up, Dad. She told me she begged you to stop him and you agreed to it. That she had completed her punishment, so you stepped in?"

"You're believing a one-sided version of events, Dahlia. She asked me to stop punishing her. I remember that night, but I thought she meant something else. I figured I'd been being too hard on her, so lessened my hold a little. I decided to let her make her own decisions and was surprised when she then strengthened her relationship with Tobin rather than walk away."

"She did it out of fear," I murmured, feeling sadder than ever.

"I didn't know. Please believe me," Dad said again, and his words had been so heartfelt I had to. I realised then that perhaps things really weren't as they'd seemed. No matter how much I wanted to believe every word of Dita's account, I knew I was seeing the world through her eyes. Through the eyes of a woman who had lost the love of her life and had been abused.

Of course, things would be skewed.

I also realised in that moment how much older my father had become. As if overnight, he'd aged a decade and the all-knowing man atop our empire seemed lost. The mighty strongman was suddenly weak. The all-powerful patriarch had been defeated. Trodden on by life itself and with no one to turn to because he was a lone wolf—the alpha at the head of his pack.

"I do believe you," I told him, and meant it.

Chapter Seventeen

Nico came out of hospital the following afternoon and I went with Dad to collect him. Jodie was by his side as he walked slowly towards us, and they snuggled against one another so lovingly that I knew my brother's near death experience had brought them even closer. They'd been together for years and even though I had been told their exciting news, they hadn't told anyone outside the family yet, so I hadn't been able to celebrate the impending arrival of my first niece or nephew. Nico still had some healing to do and so they'd focused on his care first and foremost, which was understandable given how his insides were still mending after being given a battering in the crash.

I turned my head back and watched the pair of them as they left the revolving door of the hospital and approached the truck. They took the back seat, our father evidently having checked in with Nico and told him the plan beforehand, and then we got ready to set off.

Nico folded his still huge body into the seat, moving slowly and carefully, and I realised then just why Dad had made the purchase. It wasn't just for Nico to drive while he was recuperating, but also something strong and big. A vehicle sturdy, like the son Garret Proctor, had almost lost. It was beyond important that Nico stay safe, but now that he was heading home, I foolishly thought the danger had passed. So, when the conversation turned dark on the drive back, I was understandably shocked.

"The police haven't found any clues, but they've confirmed how the engine failure was initially caused by a fault in the cooling system," Nico said, updating us, and I bit my tongue. I'd had no idea they were even treating the crash as suspicious, let alone having had it investigated. As far as I'd known, Nico had lost control. End of story. "I cleaned that bike and gave it a tune up every other week. There's no way I would've missed a fault. It was tampered with, Dad. I know it."

Jodie gave a little yelp and Nico tucked her under his arm, sheltering her from the truth it seemed he needed to get off his chest while we had some quiet time to talk.

"Who?" I asked, turning in my seat to glare at Nico. He and I both knew Calvin was a threat to our safety and his words came back to me from that night by the trucks. He said I didn't know the things he had done. Could he have been the one to tamper with Nico's bike? Perhaps he'd thought Nico was the one who had sprayed Dita's perfume in his room and tossed his pile of clothes? If so, it stood to reason that he would've been out for revenge. Had he then retaliated by messing with his bike? It could easily have been the case, but Dad trusted Calvin, as did Nico. Even having known the truth about his treatment of our sister, Nico had still favoured him, but surely he was suspect number one?

Nico shrugged, narrowing his eyes at me. I knew he was telling me to leave it, that he was on my train of thought, so I turned back and stared out the front windscreen. We'd talk about my suspicions eventually, I knew, but not there in the car with the others.

"It can't have happened the day of the accident as I was parked at Dahlia's all along, but the evening before, I'd been running errands for Jodie in town. Maybe one of the Red's spotted me and took a shot at messing with my bike? They've been getting cocky lately?"

Dad hummed, and it came out like a growl. There had been more and more trouble with the rival gang and regardless of my surety that it had to have been Calvin, I began to wonder if I was being a little blind sighted. I was so convinced we had the monster I needed to watch out for in our midst but considered how I was missing all of those who still lurked on the periphery. Those who my father had sent us to the new clubhouse to hide from a couple of times already.

He himself had told me to steer clear of the Red's. But then again, he'd also told me time and again that he and the President, Alexander, were on good terms. Their club was younger but also family run just like ours and it seemed to me like they felt they had something to prove, when surely it wasn't necessary. I couldn't understand why the shows of force or the fighting between their guys and ours even happened. I guess my gentler nature was testament to that naïveté, but I still couldn't see why we didn't just get along. It had to be more about business than bikes and turf. I still wasn't one hundred per-cent sure what my family did for a living but remembered back to my conversations with Dita such a long time before. Was my brother still a dealer? If so, did that make my father a drug lord? Were the Red Reapers creating competition for the drug money in our city? They had to be, otherwise I couldn't fathom what else might be causing their rifts.

We reached Dad's house, and I was still none the

wiser, but decided against grilling Nico about the answer he'd offered up in the car. He had enough on his plate, and I was feeling tired. We'd been so busy I was exhausted, especially with all the back and forth to the new clubhouse, so I gave Tobin a kiss and headed for my room, deciding to take a nap before dinner.

I awoke to the sound of my mobile phone ringing, which was unusual given only a dozen or so people knew the number and they were all downstairs.

"Hello?" I asked as I answered the call from a withheld number, feeling groggy but alert.

"I got your message," said a voice from the other end. It certainly wasn't anyone genuinely called Jane Doe, so I knew right away I had to have been right. It was L. It had to be. He was rough sounding, deep and raw. There was also an edge to his voice that I didn't recognise. Something not from our area of the UK, that much I was sure of. I wondered if he might be foreign, maybe Eastern European.

"I need to talk with you. I have to know if she truly suffered, or whether you made her happy towards the end." Words were tumbling from my mouth at an alarming rate, and I forced myself to slow down. To calm my anxious unease. "I... I read her diaries." L sucked in a hiss.

"You shouldn't have done that," he told me, and my blood ran cold. "You should have left it. Burned that laptop so no one could ever know what she went through. How she suffered."

"Why? Don't you want me to avenge her?" I demanded, growing annoyed at how he could possibly have wanted me to forget all about my sister and the truths she had told me via her diary entries.

"There is no such thing as vengeance, Dahlia. Only

pain and torment. We can love one another and hope for more, but it does nothing other than tear us all apart in the end. The monsters always win. The only way to put an end to your useless suffering is to let them." L sounded so defeated. As broken as Dita had seemed in the end and my heart broke for him.

"I can't. Don't you understand? I'm lost and afraid, but I need to know the truth. I need to do right by her."

"There is no truth. No right. Only wrong," he answered, before hanging up the call.

***

I was out of sorts for days after that phone call. Who the hell was he and why hadn't he at least put my mind at ease? If all he was calling for was to tell me to drop it, what was the point? He had to have loved her, otherwise there was no way he would've spoken about his broken hopes and dreams so dejectedly. Not that I would've believed him if he'd told me he hadn't cared for her. That Dita was nothing more than a diva with a crazy crush on her forbidden fuckbuddy. If anything, L had only succeeded in making me worse. My need for the truth only more powerful.

I went through the motions while I replayed our conversation in my head repeatedly, running on autopilot with everything and everyone around me. Tobin could tell I was off but didn't pressure me to talk. For a fiery guy with an open and honest way about him, he didn't seem to want to lash out with me or force me to be someone I wasn't. He made me believe he respected the woman I was on the inside, and I loved him more for it.

"I have to go to college for an exam tomorrow," I informed him as we climbed into bed and snuggled against each other's naked bodies. It was for an end of term assessment to see how both myself and the other people on the course were doing, which wasn't anything new to me, given my numerous A-levels and the couple of degrees already under my belt. God, I'd been bored all those years. There had been nothing better to do, so I'd studied hard, passing the time with my head in books and on my laptop working towards the next goal and the next.

None of those successes had meant a thing. I wasn't going to jet off to other countries where I could put my learned languages to good use. There would be no chance of me ever writing my first novel or ever putting my hand to poetry utilising the philosophy I'd learned. I came to realise it was all something I'd used to pass the time, but not anymore. Not after my life had changed dramatically following Dita's death and my time with Tobin. The new course was something entirely different to my others. It was something I could see myself pursuing. A job I wanted to do when I was 'grown up.'

"I'll drop you off, okay?" Tobin answered, and I nodded.

"That'd be great, thanks. We'll have to drive though, because I need to take some coursework with me," I replied.

"What is it?"

"Nothing much, just some mock-ups for graphic design and stuff," I said, remaining blasé. I'd still not told him or any of the others about my website and blog, or my plans business I wanted to create utilising them. For some reason, I wanted to keep it all to myself. I guess a lot like

Dita had kept her diaries to herself. Maybe one day I'd come clean, but only when it felt safe. Only when I felt safe.

"Sure thing, Dahl," he said, running his rough hands over my body. I knew what he wanted and curled into him, pressing my back against his stomach. He was rock hard and ready for me, but held back, his pale blue eyes piercing me with a serious stare. "I'll stay until you're done, though. The others will be fine without me."

"No, baby," I replied, and shook my head. "I'll be there all day 'cos I have to have a tutor appraisal as well. I'll just call you when I'm done."

The matter agreed, Tobin took me in his embrace and buried himself inside of me. He had me moaning his name in moments and delivered my pleasure readily. There was no holding back or hesitating. Not anymore, and it was perfect.

Tobin dropped me off, and I carried my printouts and laptop with presentation at the ready into the busy college foyer. There, I knew exactly where I was going and found the IT suite with ease, having been to it numerous times before.

After settling in behind one of the school PCs, I looked around, spying some faces I recognised from induction day. One was a girl a couple of years younger than me, and she grinned over before heading in my direction, her own laptop pressed to her chest like I often carried mine. She had kind eyes and her hair was that type of blonde that had been shaded with a dull grey, but I liked it. She suited the look.

"Hey, are you here for the exam too?" she asked, and I nodded, offering her the seat next to me. "I'm

Gemma," she added, offering me her hand.

"Dahlia," I replied, taking her in. She had to only just be eighteen, and while she was dressed in a way that showed off her slim body in skinny jeans and a tight shirt, she seemed shy. I wondered if perhaps she too had chosen a distance learning based course like me because she couldn't bear to be around people too much. Either that, or she was just another geek like me and most of the other guys in our group. Many of the others seemed so socially inept it was cringe worthy, but I didn't think we were the same, or at least I hoped not.

As the morning went on, I barely stressed over the examination or my usually introvert ways. I breezed through it and during the quiet times, Gemma and I chatted a little, both of us stopping here and there when the conversation reached a natural pause, but I found I liked talking with her. We didn't make small talk. We talked about HTML and the coding we'd tried out so far. We debated the best platforms for social media reach and compared notes on our tried and tested methods in graphic design. Gemma was the first person I'd ever spoken to that way, and it was refreshing.

"I'm working on a fully illustrated graphic novel for my coursework assignment," she told me, showing off her impressive work after she'd completed her appraisal with our tutor. "How about you?"

I showed her my portfolio of various website designs and the graphic work I had done so far.

"I want to branch out more, but I just haven't had the time," I answered honestly, which felt good. I genuinely hadn't been able to throw myself into the studying and was glad the reason for that had been a more than worthy one. Tobin had kept me nice and busy the past few months, which was fine by me.

We ended up staying in the IT suite so long we missed lunch, so when we were knocked off mid-afternoon, I offered to take Gemma over the road to a pub I had visited with Bradley the last time I'd been at the college. "They do amazing all-day breakfasts," I said, and had to contain my happiness when she nodded her head.

"Don't take this the wrong way, but I'm so pleased I came over," she said as we walked across the courtyard and out of the college grounds. I frowned, thinking how I could've taken it the wrong way, when Gemma elaborated. "I mean; I wasn't sure 'cos you looked kinda mean. Like you didn't want to be approached, but when you smiled back at me, I thought I'd take the plunge and I'm glad I did." She giggled and I couldn't help but join in.

"Me, mean? I wouldn't know how to be!" I cried, still laughing. "Maybe I have that bitchy resting face thing?"

"Yep, that'll be it," Gemma answered, still grinning. I nudged her with my shoulder as we walked off campus and crossed the road, both of us laughing and joking like old friends.

As we reached the Prince of Wales pub, I grabbed us a couple of drinks and thought nothing of ordering us a bottle of wine to share. I realised how times had changed, but it was just nice to sit with a new friend and have a laugh. Even Gemma seemed pleasantly surprised by our sudden friendship, and I hoped it could continue.

Two huge plates of sausage, egg, bacon, beans, toast, and tomatoes later, we finished our wine, and I checked my phone. It was getting late, so I figured I'd best not push my luck.

"I'll just text my boyfriend and let him know where

I am in case he starts to worry. I hadn't told him a time to come and collect me, but he's working anyway, so there's no rush," I explained, typing a quick message to Tobin. Gemma nodded, watching my hands as I hit send and then stashed my phone back in my pocket.

"What's he like?" she asked, her eyes turning wistful. I wanted to play it cool and act like it was no big deal, but I couldn't. I went all gooey inside and felt my cheeks burn just thinking about him.

"He's so amazing it hurts," I replied with a smile and a dreamy sigh. It was nice being able to talk boys with someone. Especially someone who wasn't my big brother or one of their girlfriends. "He's eight years older than me, but it doesn't seem like it when we're together. We started seeing each other a few months ago, but I've known him for years because he works for my dad," I explained, adding a little detail to my story.

"I've never had a boyfriend," Gemma said, blushing.

"How old are you?"

"Eighteen."

"Well then, you've got nothing to worry about. Tobin's my first boyfriend and I'm twenty," I replied, making her smile again. "Books before boys, that was my motto!" Gemma nodded in agreement and then climbed up out of her seat, heading to the bar to grab us one last drink before we called it a night.

When she came back, she stopped in her tracks, staring at the doorway. I swear if her chin could've dropped any more, it would have, and I turned to follow her gaze. I had to see what had her gawping like she'd just spotted her favourite celebrity and laughed when I saw Tobin standing in the doorway of the pub, shaking the rain out of his dirty blond hair. He looked like a god with that skin somehow still dark regardless of the cooler weather and his detailed ink peeking up over the collar of his cut. How I hadn't noticed it all those years baffled me, but he was seriously hot. "Shit, Gemma. Don't make me fall out with you for staring at my man," I told her, watching as she flushed bright red and took her seat.

I was only half kidding, but had to admit, Tobin sure was a sight to behold. Every woman in the place had noticed him, not just my new friend, and I couldn't help the smile that spread over my face as I watched him scan the crowd. Tobin wasn't looking at any of the men or women openly staring at him. He was looking for someone. Me. God, it felt amazing to know he was mine, and I was his. I knew I was about to become the envy of every woman in the place, but at the same time, I no longer cared about them. My Tobin-tunnel-vision had kicked in and I raised my hand to signal where I was.

"Hey, babe," he said as he reached me, delivering a kiss to my still smiling lips. "Who's your friend?"

"This is Gemma," I answered, indicating to my suddenly mute companion with my hand. Tobin seemed to decide on a half wave rather than try to get her to say something or shake his hand. He clearly knew the affect he was having on her and I was pleased he'd decided against embarrassing her because of it.

"I'm gonna grab a beer. You two want another?" I shook my head, thinking we'd had a few glasses of wine already and I didn't much fancy going home swaying. I watched him leave and turned to Gemma with a grin.

"Is that really your boyfriend?" she hissed, reaching

her hand across the table to high-five me. "Where can I get one of those?" she added, giggling and fanning herself with her hand.

I watched Tobin as he chatted to the barman, using his natural charm to ensure we didn't have any trouble, just like he had in the town around Dahlia's. I'd noticed his methods for some time now, and not only since I'd started seeing Tobin. My brothers and father always played nice too, and it occurred to me how even in our hometown, there was still a bad reputation with bikers. I'd seen the news reports about shootings and rival gangs laying waste to one another's family and friends, not just the club members themselves. My dad didn't seem to want the Black Knights to be like those clubs, so it appeared he demanded a certain amount of etiquette as well as their loyalty from a prospect and adherence to the rules and regulations of the club itself.

As VP, Tobin was the epitome of that persona. The young face of the brand my father had created. He had the barman laughing and joking with him in an instant, and for the first time, I could imagine him as a soldier. He had a way about him that told you he was strong, and you could bet your life on him. That he had your back in a fight, but also that he would keep you laughing through the bad times. He was a quick wit and had super-sharp bantering skills, even with relative strangers, like the man serving him a beer as I watched.

"He's one of a kind, Gemma," I eventually answered, snapping out of my reverie. "So, now you know a little more about me, I've something to ask you. Do you recognise his jacket?" I had to ask, having wondered when a good time might be to bring up my place within the club. Gemma nodded.

"I've seen guys on bikes wearing them and around town. Is he in some kind of motorbike club?"

"Yes, and he's the second in command of it," I told her, watching as Gemma's eyes widened a little. I figured, in for a penny, in for a pound, so told her the rest. "And my dad is the leader. The club President. You remember when I said I'd been kept away from outsiders my entire life? Wrapped in cotton wool?" Gemma nodded, and I figured she was thinking back to our earlier chat about why I'd done so many online courses and yet still hadn't had a job.

"They protect you, don't they, the club members that is?" she asked incredulously, and sighed when I nodded. "I wish someone protected me the way they do you. That someone cared as much about my wellbeing..."

I saw red. It didn't matter I'd only just met her, Gemma was the closest thing I had to a friend and the thought of her not being taken proper care of made my blood boil.

"You're welcome at my place any time, Gemma. You can come and work from there and kick my arse when I need it," I told her in all seriousness, but lightened the tone a little as well. "Where are your family?"

"My parents each work forty hours a week and haven't cared what I do with my days for years. Not since they didn't have to worry about getting me a childminder. It's like I'm their afterthought, not the centre of their world. I envy you," Gemma replied, looking down at her hands.

"My life is far from perfect, trust me," I said, bringing her gaze back up. Gemma smiled across at me and shrugged.

"Wow, we get deep and meaningful after a few drinks, don't we?" she said, lightening the mood in an instant.

"Yeah, you can tell we're both recluses who have finally found a friend. We don't quite know what to do with ourselves!" I was glad we were back to joking around, and by the time Tobin came back over, we'd finished our drinks and were ready to go.

Gemma barely said a word to him, her lack of experience with the opposite sex showing, but she managed the odd word before saying goodbye.

We'd agreed to meet back at the same pub a few days later for a study session and another couple of drinks, and I was looking forward to seeing her again. It was nice to finally have a friend.

"Now then, if you'd have told me you'd made a new geek friend, I would've flipped my shit imagining some nerdy guy with glasses and a bow-tie. It's a good thing I met her for myself, hey?" Tobin joked with me as we headed out into the cool evening air, and he directed me towards where he'd parked the car.

"Careful, or I might think you're jealous," I teased, settling into the passenger seat with my laptop and bag on my lap.

"Always, babe. I told you, when it comes to you, I'm downright crazy. A man fucking obsessed and only falling deeper and deeper down that rabbit hole."

Chapter Eighteen

Over the next couple of weeks, Gemma swiftly became my best friend. We just clicked and things felt natural between us, so much so that we regularly met up at the college for study sessions, which invariably ended up with a trip to our new favourite pub afterwards. The time flew by, and we kept each other dedicated to our work, inspiring one another and being that go-to we each needed. She and I talked every day via text or online, and thankfully Tobin seemed to understand my need for a true friend outside the club, so encouraged me to keep it up. I think he liked me being suitably distracted as it meant he could go about his club business guilt-free, but he hadn't said so, and I chose to simply leave things that way. We were solid, that much I did know, so didn't feel the need to sit him down and go over the deep and meaningful.

My work was getting better and better. My inspiration and passion for it increasing with each day. There were even times when I let myself forget about Dita and L. I was too busy to fret over a past I couldn't change, so I didn't. I simply focused on my family and friends, letting only the good vibes in.

Gemma was talented, but lonely, I could tell. I think she would've spent every day with me if I let her, but she settled for what I could give her and seemed to understand how it would have to be enough, at least for now. Despite my initial promise, she was welcome at Dad's house any time, I actually held off with inviting her over. I wanted to keep her separate from the club. Someone of my own.

I was impressed Dad hadn't asked me to bring her round so he could question and vet her. Him having done so in the past so I wouldn't have put it past him. I figured Tobin had already vouched for my new friend and as my new protector, maybe his word was enough to appease my father's need to control every aspect of my life.

One Friday afternoon, a couple of weeks later, we headed straight for the Prince of Wales and ordered a bottle of wine. Gemma was stressing over something, so we decided to forgo the pretence of an extra study session and go straight to the drinking.

"My dad says he wants us to move to London!" she exclaimed as we took our seats and waited for John, the barman, to bring us over some food we'd ordered. We were fast becoming regulars there, and I loved how they knew us by name and treated us like old friends whenever Gemma and I came in. Even the not so regular members of staff were getting to know us, which I decided to take as a compliment rather than a testament to whatever drinking problem I feared I might be developing.

"Calm down," I replied, putting my hands on hers across the table. "Why does he want to move? What does your mum say? And surely you don't have to go with them if you don't want to?" I began firing questions at her, needing the rest of the information before I could offer any advice.

"He's got a new job, and she said she can put in for

a transfer. I don't want to go, though. But you're right. I'm an adult now and could stay here if I wanted to. Maybe rent a flat or something?"

"See, there's the logic." I knew Gemma had her own income from a part-time job she did in IT, plus there was the potential for her design work to take off and then she'd be set. "Do what you feel is right, honey. The possibilities are endless," I added brightly, but then told myself to calm the hell down. Who was I to talk? I was still coddled and hadn't worked a day in my life, much less fully considered branching out on my own and taking responsibility for myself. I didn't know how to pay bills or budget a monthly wage. I still used the same bank account I'd had since I was twelve years old and didn't ever need to wonder how much I had in there. Dad or Nico had always kept it topped up for me, having called the fund my pocket money even though we all knew I did no chores or work to warrant it.

The food arrived, and we then chatted some more, and Gemma thankfully calmed down a little, opting for the good old 'wait and see what happens' approach. I considered offering her a place to stay, but didn't want to make another empty promise, so decided against it. She didn't need to get her hopes up, and I certainly didn't want to have to follow through on something I hadn't been authorised to offer, or worse, must tell her no and undoubtedly ruin our friendship because of it.

"Hey ladies," John said, coming over with two glasses of wine for us. We hadn't ordered them, so I was immediately on alert. I wasn't about to accept a drink from a stranger because I knew if I did, I was expected to tell them thank you or worse, must fend off their advances.

John spotted my puzzled frown and grinned. "Relax, it's just a freebie for my favourite customers." Feeling assured, I accepted the drink and thanked him, and was surprised when he then took a seat at our table. "I'm taking five minutes to have a fag and then we're setting up for a gig in here tonight. You're more than welcome to stay, but ought to be warned, they're a heavy rock tribute band."

"I grew up listening to rock music, Johnny Boy. Don't worry about hurting my delicate ears," I teased in reply, but was still glad he'd given us a heads up.

After polishing off our burgers and chips, Gemma and I decided to go and sit outside while the bar staff and the band did their thing, settling in under one of the patio heaters they'd thankfully turned on for those wanting to sit in the beer garden. Despite spring having sprung, there was still a chill in the air, so I had my thick wool jumper on and my leather jacket, and beneath the heater I was perfectly toasty. Gemma, on the other hand, hadn't come prepared for the cooler weather. She was still shivering in her thin jacket, and I was about to suggest we head home when John came over and offered her his coat.

She thanked him profusely, and I caught the glint in her eye that told me Gemma enjoyed our regular trips to the pub for more than just my company and the cheap booze. "Do you like him?" I asked when he'd gone, watching as she flushed red and shrugged.

"Yeah, I guess," was her answer, so I shot her a stern look, one eyebrow raised. I figured it was the infamous Proctor stare because she immediately caved. "We always chat when I'm at the bar, but I always thought he's just being friendly. Not flirting."

"He's not like that with the other girls who come in

here, nor have I ever seen him buy anyone a drink before," I replied, leaving that point hanging. "And then there's the jacket…"

Gemma giggled and pulled his large, padded coat around her tighter, enveloping herself in it.

"We'll see," was all she said, and I dropped the subject. If she didn't know what to say or do next, I wasn't about to push her. I was no matchmaker and knew I lacked any knowledge in the romance department. Tobin had done all the chasing, my dad's help notwithstanding, so I had no clue how to flirt or to make a move on a guy.

With him on my mind, I pinged him a quick text to say we were staying to watch a band play and that he should join us if he could make it. I hoped he could. It'd be nice to have somewhat of a date after us having only spent time with my family the past few weeks. He and Dad had been so busy I doubted either of them minded me having been distracted by my new friend's company, but I missed them—both. But Tobin more so.

By the time the band started playing, the pub was packed. They evidently had a following and I couldn't deny they were good. Only young, the four guys were playing all sorts, from the classic rock to modern hits, and I enjoyed singing along to the tracks I knew while me and Gemma danced on the outskirts of the crowded dancefloor. She seemed to know a few of them too, despite her being more into pop music, and it was fun letting loose. A few guys tried dancing with us but soon got the hint when we moved away from them and remained focused on just one another.

When the set was over, I followed Gemma to one side, where she gave John a wide smile and accepted a bottle of water from him. I took one too and downed it as we propped ourselves against the wooden bar. Gemma was up close and personal with our barman, and I couldn't hear them over the din, but saw them talking quietly, leaning closer to each other, and hoped he was making his move.

The bar was rammed, and it had grown stuffy, so I decided to get some air. I also figured I should check in with Tobin, so headed out the back door to where Gemma and I had been sat together earlier, catching the strong smell of cigarette smoke as I ducked out into the dark garden.

A group of men were sat in a circle there, each of them chatting loudly and laughing with one another, but they weren't sat under the security light, so it was hard to make out how many were there. I paid them no attention and took a seat on the bench right beneath the security light, focusing on the phone in my hands, but soon noticed when everything suddenly went quiet.

"Look at this bit of skirt, sitting there all alone. I think someone should keep her company…" one of the men barked, clearly directing his voice towards me, and I cringed. I should've realised not to go out there alone, but I guess I'd gotten complacent and had taken my regularity at the pub for granted. There was no one inside who would hear me shout for help and certainly no one out in the garden who would step in if the guys got rough with me, and so I hit the call button, ringing Tobin. There was no answer, and I inwardly cursed him.

"She thinks we don't know who she is," another added, which got my attention. I turned and looked at them, spying just another group of guys like any other. That was when one of them stood up and walked towards me, his leather cut coming into view. I spotted the patch with a red

ROUGH LOVE

ghoul emblazoned on it first and didn't need to read what was written above to know which club the man, and undoubtedly his friends, belonged to. "Did Daddy let you out for once, sweetheart? Let you be a big girl and finally come out into the wide world to play with the rest of us?"

I didn't answer. For one, I wasn't sure how best to respond. Should I bite and tell them to go fuck themselves? Or should I smile sweetly and play dumb? I was clueless. "She's not playing," the same man said, still standing just a couple of feet away, staring at me with a pout.

No. He was right, I wasn't playing. I'd had enough and decided to just leave before things got out of hand. The last thing I needed was to cause more of a fight between my club and the Red Reapers. I stood and tried to walk to the door that led back inside, but the man blocked me. He was tall, much taller than me, and when I peered up into his eyes, I could see nothing but darkness in them.

"Bring her here. I'll make her talk," one of the other men taunted in a thickly accented voice. The others sniggered, clearly enjoying their little game of cat and mouse.

"She doesn't need to talk. I could enjoy just making her scream," the man blocking me answered his friend, leaning down so our faces were just inches apart. Fear gripped my gut. What was he planning to do to me? I wanted to ask him. To demand he release me, but my mouth ran dry. I still hadn't uttered a word, and no longer thought I even could. I'd never been in a situation like this before and didn't know how to act or how to stick up for myself. I was the perfect prey and wanted to kick myself for being so weak.

"Leave her," a deep, rumbling voice then boomed

from within the group, and unlike when the others had spoken, this voice was more authoritative than conversational. The man holding me couldn't seem to refuse the order.

"Your sister was much more fun," he said, before turning and walking away, playing the big I am as if he hadn't been told to do it by who I assumed had to be one of the higher up members of their club. I wanted to ask him what he'd meant by it, or how he could've possibly known Dita, but I was still mute. Scared stiff and frozen in place, I then yelped when a man in the centre of the group stood and let out a loud whistle.

"We're leaving," he told the rest of them, and I realised it was the same man who had told his comrade to leave me alone. The Reds all sauntered away, sidling around the back of the building to a side exit I hadn't known was there, but the man remained. He was watching me intently, and all I could do was stare back at him, shaken and confused. "You shouldn't have done that, Dahlia," he then said, stepping closer to me. I recognised that voice. That deep, accented sound. Where did I know it from? Where had I heard it before?

"Done what?" I asked, finally gathering the strength to speak now that he and I were alone. For some reason, I wasn't scared of him like I had been the others. I was glad he had protected me from his friends' advances but didn't understand why.

"Let the monsters get to you," he answered, and my knees suddenly turned to jelly. The man then took in a deep breath and stepped into the light so I could see him. His bald head caught the glow of the lamp, and I was surprised by the contrasting thick beard that covered his jaw and neck. He was handsome, probably in his early thirties, but had a rough look of someone weary beyond his years. He had seen a lot in his time, perhaps too much.

"What's your name?" I asked, needing to know if he was who I thought he might be.

"Liev," he answered, putting out his hand. I extended a shaking palm and shook his, watching him intently. His name was Liev. L. I knew that voice because he was the one who had called me a few weeks before. He was the man Dita had loved and wanted to run away with, I was sure of it. "Yes," he said, as though having read my mind.

"Is that all you're going to say to me?" I demanded, finding strength from somewhere deep inside.

"There's nothing else to say, Dahlia. What's done is done. She's gone…" I slapped him across the face in rage, but Liev didn't reply, nor did he let it anger him. He simply walked away while I had to steady myself against the wall, sucking in breaths at a rate of knots.

I'd found him. Liev was the last man I would've thought Dita would fall for, but at the same time, he was the perfect opposite of the men she knew and distrusted from our club. The way she'd spoken of him had made me care for him too, and I knew he couldn't have meant it. That he couldn't have forgotten her so easily. I ran to where I'd watched him walk, hoping to find him there and none of his friends.

Liev was leaning against the wall, his head turned up to the heavens as though saying a prayer. He'd needed a moment to steady himself too, and I knew I'd been right not to believe his front. I hugged him, throwing my arms around a man I didn't know, but felt connected to. Kindred grieving souls finding one another in the darkness.

"I'm sorry, Liev. You should've had your life together. You deserved to be happy," I whispered, but knew he'd heard me.

"It's your future you need to take care of now, Dahlia," he replied, letting me go and heading over to a gate that led out onto the main road beside the pub. "Stay safe and be happy. Do it for her, okay?"

"Okay," I replied, before turning and going back inside the then half empty pub to track down Gemma and call my brother for a pickup.

Chapter Nineteen

Thomas came to collect me, looking rather sour at how drunk he proclaimed I was. I didn't feel drunk in the slightest but let him believe what he wanted to. I wasn't in the mood for a fight.

"Where's Tobin?" I asked, slumping in the front while Gemma climbed in the back. I'd had to pry her away from John and their new budding relationship but was still pleased he'd made the move on her at last. They had been kissing when I'd come back from the garden. Completely oblivious to how long I had been gone, or the frozen, sorry state I was in. I'd chosen not to enlighten them on the subject.

"Brad got into some trouble down south, so Dad and Tobin had to head down there to bail him out," he answered, not giving anything away about the kind of trouble our brother was in, and I didn't question him further. Thomas was a lot like Dad and me in the quiet department, only giving away what he'd felt necessary, so I knew the conversation on the subject was over as far as he was concerned. "Where does your friend need dropping off?" he then added, and I gave him Gemma's address. We sped away, the car remaining silent as we drove the short distance to her house. When we got there, I climbed out of the car and gave her a hug.

"So?" I asked, bouncing on the balls of my feet excitedly. Gemma knew exactly what I was getting at and beamed.

"He's taking me out tomorrow. Dinner and a few drinks in town," she replied, blushing. "I really like him and said we need to go slow, like you said. He seemed to understand." I was glad. John had seemed a good egg right from that first time we'd met him and I trusted in him to keep things that way.

"Good," I replied, hugging her. "Well, have fun, and make sure you tell me all about it afterwards," I added with a smirk, before jumping back in Thomas's car and heading home.

It seemed almost too quiet at Dad's house, especially without him or Tobin there. I wasn't sure what to do with myself, but it was late enough for me to get away with heading to bed, so I climbed up in a daze, the wine finally affecting my sluggish body. When I reached the top step, for some bizarre reason, I didn't go into my room. I went into Dita's.

Still kept otherwise untouched, it was strangely reassuring to be amongst her things, and I sat on the bed, staring at the wall where her photos had been taped up in a collage. I'd found him. Liev—the man Dita had truly loved and wanted to spend her life with. He was mourning her. Hurting, just like me. But even more so. Liev had seemed lost, broken, and beaten down by life.

Tears suddenly began falling from my eyes. God, I wished things had been different between us. Why hadn't we been close in real life? Why had it taken for Dita to die before I could finally feel a connection with her?

I had my hands over my face, rocking back and forth while sobbing uncontrollably, and the sleeves of my jumper soaked in a matter of seconds. I turned to look for a tissue box or something, which was when I realised, I'd left the door wide open.

A couple of the guys were stood there watching me in shock, clearly not knowing how to act or what to say to me. They were the younger ones, and certainly none I wanted to confide in, so I simply stood and shut the door in their faces, which was when I saw who was at the back of the group. Calvin. The dark look on his face gave me the creeps, and I glowered right back at him, but he made no attempt to hide his disdain, while the others showed me nothing but concern. Slamming the door, I flung myself down on Dita's bed, burying my face in her pillow.

That evil bastard is going to get what's coming to him one of these days, I thought, making her a silent promise. He was going to pay. It didn't matter that I was still scared of him or what he might be capable of. He simply couldn't win, and that was that.

***

After going back to my room and managing a fretful couple of hours' sleep, I heard the door to my bedroom open and close almost silently and jumped awake. I thought it had to be Tobin coming back, and opened my eyes, trying my best to adjust to the complete and utter darkness.

"Tobin?" I whispered hoarsely and turned to flick the switch on my bedside lamp but was stopped in my tracks. Strong hands caught mine before I could reach the light, and I knew right away who was with me in my room. X had come to teach me a lesson. "Please, no," I groaned, whimpering in fear. His face then came into view as he pushed my arms above my head and held them in place, climbing over me on the bed. I felt beyond vulnerable, given the fact that I was naked, but I didn't let that stop me from fighting against his hold. He wasn't going to have me that easily, but I also noticed he'd kept his clothes on. They weren't stacked up neatly in wait for him to have his way with me and I hoped he was only there to scare me off, rather than show me by force how he'd meant what he'd threatened before.

Calvin's knees pinned me at either side of my hips, pressing into me, and his face was just inches away from mine. The look in his eye was wild, full of rage, and pure evil. He said nothing. Instead, he just watched me, drinking in the sight of his captive. Calvin then reached his free hand down and placed it around my throat, causing me to go straight into fight-or-flight mode. I kicked and bucked against him, but he wouldn't bloody move. He was like a rock, and I was nothing in comparison to him. There was no way I could escape him, and we both knew it.

"I'm watching you, Dahlia," he whispered, and I could smell the beer on his breath. "Don't tell anyone our secret, otherwise next time I'm taking my frustration out on your body in ways Tobin's never even dreamed of. You'll learn to let me, just like she did, but for now I'm giving you one last chance to be a good girl…"

Quick as a flash, Calvin was off me again and out the door, and I dived out of bed into the en-suite, where I puked my guts up and cried my heart out.

How did I get here? When had the situation become so completely out of my control? I didn't know, but I knew I had to get that control back again. I had to be the one to come out on top, because even in my sorry state, there was one thing I was certain of. Calvin wasn't going to leave me alone, no matter what I did. He was going to keep pushing me and keep threatening until the day he decided he'd had enough of the games and was going to take me how he'd promised—whether I was willing or not. He wasn't going to stop; I could see that.

I needed help and knew exactly who I had to turn to if I wanted to get it.

The same person my sister had gone to. L.

Chapter Twenty

The first thing I did when I woke the next morning was open Dita's laptop and I loaded up the message screen, ignoring the notifications from the people who still insisted on tagging her in remembrance posts. I loaded up the message to Jane Doe, staring at the blinking curser for a few seconds before eventually writing my message.

I need your help. Please.

No reply came, not that I was expecting one, so I closed it and headed off to my en-suite to take a hot shower. I stayed in there ages, attempting to cleanse away the memories of the night before, but nothing could stop the images of Calvin leaning over me, holding me down via my wrists and neck, from coming back over and over again. He was truly a monster, and one who needed to be taken care of. Tobin would be heartbroken when the truth about his cousin was revealed, but I had to do it. For my own safety as well as the safety of numerous other women, he might've also hurt. There had to have been others.

I suddenly thought about his girlfriend, Shannon. Was he abusing her, too? He couldn't be, otherwise his dark side would be common knowledge to the club and surely she wouldn't stay with him? But then again, I guessed women did stay with their abusers and had read the stories and seen the news. I knew how, once manipulated and sucked into an abusive relationship, the abuser could often take all the power, regardless of how strong the victim tries to remain. Perhaps Shannon was the same. Maybe Calvin had beaten it into her to do as she was told and smile falsely while in our company. I decided I would have to try speaking to her on the sly. Figure out what was going on behind closed doors and no matter his warnings, I decided I would help Shannon leave him if she asked me to.

Tobin returned around lunchtime, looking and smelling like he'd been up all night. Dad and Bradley followed behind, Tobin having been faster as usual, and they too looked shattered. I helped our housekeeper feed and water them, listening to Bradley tell the story of how he had been dragged into a police station during his visit to one of our affiliated clubs.

"They were trying to get me done for speeding and tried to tag on reckless driving, but after hours of waiting, they couldn't charge me because of some technicality, so here I am!" he said, looking pleased with himself, and I turned to check out Dad and Tobin's faces. They weren't happy.

"That's no accomplishment, son," Dad groaned, finishing his coffee before throwing the mug across the room, where it smashed against the wall. "I sent you on a simple run and you get yourself locked up? It looks bad on you, on me, and on the club!" He stood and stormed out, all of us staring after him in shock. I'd heard him shout and tell the guys off before, but this was different. Dad seemed even more highly strung than usual, and just like I used to, I stood and followed him into his office.

"Dad? Are you ok?" I asked, rounding the door quietly. He was slumped in his armchair, nursing a glass of whiskey I guessed he'd just poured. He shook his head, grabbing a handful of ice cubes and dropping them into a second glass, along with a splash of the amber liquid.

"Here," he handed me the tumbler, and I accepted, staring down into it as I swirled the ice over the whiskey. I took a sip, strangely enjoying the burn it gave my throat, and then peered up at him. Dad had been watching me intently the entire time, but he wasn't smiling or considering me with his usual warmth. In fact, he seemed cold and distant. "You're not a little girl anymore, are you?" his voice was just a croak, but I understood what he was getting at.

"No. I'm not," I replied, and took another swig. "I drink and I swear. I have a steady boyfriend, a career I'm building and a life I intend to live outside of these walls you've protected me within for the past twenty years." I finished my glass and set it down on the side-table. "But, despite all that, I still need you to care for me. To honour the promises you made me by remembering that I'll always be your little girl, Dad. The only way you'll lose me is if you push me away."

"Like I did with Dita?" His sad reply caught me off guard and I wasn't sure how to respond, so I simply stared at him, taking in the sudden oldness to his face and posture.

"I didn't say that," I eventually replied, breaking the tense silence.

"You didn't need to. I know she and I went from bad to worse over the last few years, and I couldn't bear it if things went that way with you as well," he said, and beckoned me over to him. I didn't climb into his lap, but instead I perched on the arm of his huge leather chair and refilled both our glasses.

I considered him for a moment and had to wonder what had kept him going outside the family and the club all these years. There seemed to be nothing, and I began to think perhaps I had him a little more figured out. He'd been so worried about Nico that he'd made a mistake by letting Bradley go on a run alone, which had ended up with him effectively needing rescuing. He was angry with us for making him worry, but there wasn't anything me or the boys could do to stop him from having that concern for us. He was our sole surviving parent and had just lost his eldest daughter, so I guessed the thought of him losing any more of us had overwhelmed him.

"I know you've had a lot on your plate, Dad, but please don't let it get to you. Nico is getting better each day and Brad made it home safe after all," I said, hoping I was on the right track. Dad lifted his eyes to mine, his eyebrows drawn.

"So intuitive, aren't you?" he told me, smiling at last. "But there's more than that to my sorrow, Dahl. One of the lads told me they caught you in Dita's room last night, crying your heart out…"

My stomach dropped, but I refused to deny a thing. I was allowed to grieve for her, even if it was a surprise to the others as to how I did it.

"I've been thinking about her a lot. Wishing things had been different between us. I'd had a fair bit to drink last night and ended up in her room, hating how she'd been a stranger to me," I told him honestly.

"She was a stranger to me too," Dad replied, taking my hand in his. "To all of us. I just want to make sure you don't go the same way."

"I'd never," I replied in surprise. "I plan on setting up my web design business to work from home so I can stay with Tobin at Dahlia's and bring my work here. I'm not going anywhere." Dad's face immediately brightened, and he kissed the back of my hand before dropping it.

"I hadn't realised you were serious about the graphic design stuff," he told me, and I appreciated the honesty. We then chatted a little bit about my plans and the ideas Gemma and I had started putting together for our business. He didn't understand it all, but got the general concept, and I was overjoyed when he offered to install whatever extra monitors and equipment I might need in my office at the new clubhouse. "I also want to meet this Gemma," he told me with a knowing stare. "No use keeping her away if you're going to go into business with her. I get it, you want a friend away from the club, but that won't work if she's gonna be your partner."

Dad always knew. He'd probably known since I'd first met her and hadn't brought Gemma back to his that I wanted to keep her separate from the club. That I didn't want to taint her by letting her in, or potentially scare her away by introducing her to my extended family. I conceded, letting Dad know I'd invite Gemma over soon, before climbing up and leaving him alone. He needed his peace and quiet just like I often did, but I hoped I'd helped at least a little bit.

Tobin wasn't at the table when I returned, and Thomas informed me he'd gone upstairs to take a shower. I followed, heading into my room where I found him stripping off and muttering under his breath.

"Oh, so now I'm worth your time?" he growled when he spotted me. "Daddy always comes first though, eh?" Tobin flung his dirty clothes in the wash basket and stalked into the en-suite, not even bothering to listen to any response I might have to his harsh words.

I followed him but wasn't at all sure how to deal with his anger. Tobin washed up, ignoring me as he rubbed the soapsuds over his entire body and then washed it clean. When his eyes were closed, the shampoo rinsing out of his hair; I stripped off and climbed in with him and pressed my body against his. His cock was suddenly rock hard in response to my presence, his breathing quickening, but he continued to ignore me. Tobin kept his face turned up towards the jet of water, rinsing his hair and face regardless of them already being clean. I figured I had some making up to do. There was no way I'd put my dad before Tobin, but I could understand how he might be upset by me going chasing after him like that. We were still figuring out our relationship, and he needed to know I would be always by his side, not disappearing off after my father whenever he threw a paddy.

I leaned forward and started kissing Tobin's chest, letting my tongue stroke at his deliciously clean and wet skin. Moving to his right nipple, he hissed when I bit down, even though I'd only done it gently, and I figured he was feeling sensitive in both mind and body. I continued nibbling and kissing him as I reached my hands down and gripped his cock, wrapping both palms around his long erection. I then moved up and down, opting for a hard, rough rhythm, and he didn't stop me. Like when Tobin had taken me outside the club, I knew how he liked it this way sometimes, and was willing to get a little bit more adventurous when it came to our exploits, if that was what he needed from me.

I then fell to my knees and sucked his cock, driving it into the back of my throat while forcing my body to accept the intrusion. Tobin didn't stop me. If anything, he pushed it deeper to punish me somehow, fisting his hands in my wet hair and driving himself into me over and over until he came down my throat.

When he was finished, I kneeled back and stared up into the cascading water at him, suddenly feeling desperate for him to look at me or to say something kind. I had no idea what make up sex was, or whether that's what we were doing, but I knew I simply couldn't bear him being mad at me any longer, and that I would gladly do whatever he wanted of me if it would make things better.

"Always you, Tobin. Before anyone else," I told him, wrapping my arms around myself against the cool of the shower floor.

Quick as a flash, he reached down for me, yanking me up into his arms and turning, so I ended up directly beneath the hot water, my trembling immediately ceasing. Tobin's hands roved over my body, warming me with his touch while he took a moment to gather his thoughts before finally saying something.

"I know, Dahl," he whispered against me, holding me closer. "I just hate having to share you with your dad and brothers. I want to take you far away from all of them. To keep you all for myself, but I know I can't."

I didn't understand it. Why couldn't he see that what we had was incredibly different to the relationships I had with my family? I panicked, wondering if I'd somehow neglected Tobin without realising it, but I also knew he'd had my utmost attention every day that we'd been together. I'd put him first right from the start, so no, he hadn't been neglected. He was being selfish.

"You're just gonna have to get used to it, baby," I replied, and he pulled back, staring down at me in surprise. "You can't date your boss's daughter and think you get to keep her all to yourself. You have to share, just like I have to share you with them."

I then opened the shower door and walked out, leaving him behind to mull over my words. I was his, just as he was mine, but there had to be some kind of middleground. Tobin had to know he couldn't control every aspect of my life. Wrapping a towel around my body, I headed straight out into the bedroom where I dried off and climbed under the sheets, not bothering to dry my hair.

Tobin followed me a few minutes later and climbed into bed, and I half expected him to turn away from me, stewing on my reluctance at letting him win our first fight, but he didn't. He flipped me onto my back and climbed over me, kissing me roughly while his hands trailed up and down my body. I let him, feeling hot and ready for him as always, and before I could so much as ask him how he felt about things, he disappeared beneath the duvet. Tobin lifted my hips with his hands, his mouth finding my clit while his fingers delved inside of me, and I cried out, writhing and bucking against him as he pleasured me relentlessly.

When I came down from the orgasm he'd delivered, Tobin reappeared, and I was pleased to see him smiling at long last.

"As long as I get this, Dahl. Me and you, just us…"

"You have it, Tobin. I'm all yours," I told him, kissing his wet lips. He was ready for me, and I didn't hold back. I guided his hard-on straight inside of me and my body clenched at the intrusion but didn't refuse him. I wanted him there, nestled inside my body and making love to me. I could do it ten times a day and it would never be enough. It was then I realised what'd happened to me without me noticing. "I'm obsessed with you too, Tobin. I love you," I groaned, coming undone one more time.

"I love you, too. And I always will."

I hoped he meant it, especially given the favour I was about to ask of Liev.

Chapter Twenty-One

The next morning, I awoke to the feeling of Tobin grinding against me from behind. It didn't seem to matter that we'd had plenty of sex the evening before. He evidently wanted me again and took me the moment he knew I was awake and was up for some more. Since we'd been together that first time, I'd never denied him, and couldn't see that I ever would, but I was also no fool. There would come a day when we'd argue, or I wasn't feeling up for it, so I was keen not to leave him feeling like I was always a sure thing in the sack. Tobin's horniness couldn't be the deciding factor in whether we did anything or not, and I told myself again never to lie back and take it. If I had done so that first night, our relationship would be different by a mile, and I knew I'd never let myself forget to be strong and decisive when it came to my future. Tobin had always said he respected and valued my opinion, so I hoped he would live up to those promises whenever the time came for us to disagree on anything.

"Yes, yes..." I breathed, climaxing uncontrollably while Tobin continued thrusting back and into me repeatedly. When he stilled and I could feel his release throbbing into me, he bit down on my shoulder gently and pulled me against him, showing me he was still a little raw from the previous night. I took the hint. I needed to show him he was first on my list of priorities, but especially how he was above my brothers and father.

I decided to take some time away from my pursuit of an answer from Liev and my course to spend the day with him, and we took a ride out to Dahlia's together. It was his idea, but I agreed immediately and was looking forward to getting away and clearing my head, so gladly went along.

When we arrived, it was late afternoon, so Tobin called the Indian restaurant he'd taken me to on our first official date and ordered us a takeaway.

"I'll be back in fifteen minutes," he promised as he left, being sure to lock the door behind him so I felt safe. I decided to check on the cameras while he was gone so unlocked the office and booted up the PC, loading up the camera software while fiddling with my phone, pinging Gemma a quick text to let her know I was otherwise indisposed. She replied with nothing but a winking face, making me giggle. That girl already knew me so damn well.

After skimming over the various recordings from the time we'd last spent at the new clubhouse, I then loaded up the footage from the back garden and found a suitably graphic recording of Tobin and I enjoying our last bit of freedom before heading back to the city. Damn we were hot, and I didn't shy away from the images of us in various erotic displays. Saving that file in my password protected folder along with our others, I then decided to have a quick look back through the rest of the recordings and hit rewind on the keyboard.

No one had been out the back all day leading up to me and Tobin being there, and I almost gave up bothering. I jumped back in hour-long segments, when footage of two people I was shocked to find together filled the screen. Nico and Calvin were stood having a cigarette the night before I'd gone into Calvin's room with Dita's perfume in a bid to fuck with his head. They were talking, laughing, and joking like old pals. As if nothing had happened to drive any kind of a wedge between the pair of them. While I knew Nico had chosen to protect Calvin and not reveal his indiscretions to the club, I still couldn't understand it. And I certainly couldn't understand how they could still be such good friends after I'd revealed the truth about how many times Calvin had raped Dita just months before the footage I was watching had been filmed.

There was no audio, but I could see them grinning, sharing some kind of joke, and I almost turned it off. I didn't want to see my brother associating with his sisters' tormentor. Calvin had also threatened me and violated my privacy. He was a monster, not some buddy to joke around with.

Suddenly, the on-screen mood changed between them. They stopped chatting and glared at each other, the mood tense. Before I could even begin to fathom what was going on, they were kissing. Like lovers who couldn't get enough of one another, they were passionate and intense, and certainly not new to having their tongues down one another's throats. Calvin was then bent over the same table I had been the following night while Nico was fucking him from behind. I could see him driving his cock into him repeatedly. His face screwed up like he was in pain, but I could tell he wasn't. Nico was enjoying having his way with Calvin.

In fact, they both loved it. I was shocked to watch as Calvin came onto the wooden table after nothing but their fucking. Nico hadn't so much as given him a reach around, nor had Calvin touched himself. His pleasure had been driven purely by Nico driving in and out of his arsehole and I couldn't take my eyes off it as he stilled, coming inside of him. It was just a moment before they were tucking their cocks back in their jeans and rearranging themselves like nothing had even happened.

Well, except for more kissing. On the screen, Calvin was peering up at Nico, his hands on his face while he caressed him tenderly, and Nico kissed him back for a few seconds before shoving him away. Their moment was over as far as my brother was concerned, and I could tell from their body language that Calvin wanted more from Nico. Perhaps he even loved him, but it wasn't reciprocated. My brother seemed confused by his feelings towards another man, and it looked like he was willing to keep fighting them in spite of the physical act that'd just happened between the pair of them.

I was in utter shock. Watching with a hand over my open mouth as Nico stormed away and Calvin stared after him, his face like thunder. He certainly was an unstable and violent man. I could see it in his eyes and knew for sure that he had to be stopped.

So that was the reason Nico had continually protected Calvin, even from our father. Dad had no idea about Dita and her violent oppressor because Nico had covered for him. I could imagine him whispering in my father's ear about how she liked it rough and had gone elsewhere to get it because she and Tobin weren't compatible in the sack. I wanted to scream!

Yes, I might've been overreacting, but it still didn't change the fact that Nico had protected Calvin purely to save his own skin. He'd done it for himself and no one else. The fucking bastard.

My phone chimed in my pocket, making me jump out of my skin, and I looked down to find a text from Tobin telling me he was on his way back. I didn't answer. I was still glued to the image on the screen of Calvin's hatred and envy etched clearly on his face. He'd wanted Nico, and I wondered just how desperate he might've been to prove it. Desperate enough to mess with his bike's cooling system? Desperate enough to punish me to get Nico's attention? Yes. Both were entirely likely, and I knew it.

I saved the video to another password protected folder and shut down the PC before shaking off my shock and plastering a smile on my face.

By the time Tobin returned with our food, I was in the kitchen pouring him a beer and warming our plates. I wasn't going to let my revelation ruin our time together. If anything, I realised it'd given me more leverage, and it felt good to finally be uncovering some of the truths my family couldn't deny.

***

Tobin and I stayed alone at the new clubhouse for two blissful days before the other club members joined us. It felt strange being in a house full of men, especially given my recent unease with a certain member, but I didn't let it bother me. I just stayed close to Tobin while maintaining my usual quiet and watching everyone around us, suddenly more interested in reading everyone's body language than ever. As far as I recalled, none of their friends had ever made jokes about Calvin's preference for the far-less-fairer sex, or

Nico's evident bisexuality, and this time was no different.

I watched as Nico went about the place like usual and everyone respected him, listening to his guidance wherever he offered it. He loved Jodie, I knew that, but he also had needs it seemed he indulged every now and again. Urges he hadn't confided in any other member of their club than his secret boy-toy.

Nico was finally feeling better, and he truly seemed himself again, though. I was glad to see it, and still found myself enjoying his company and watching intently as he, Thomas, and Brad resumed their usual banter. It was good to see them laughing and joking around like old times. Never having let the dark days get to them, I followed suit and pushed myself to do the same.

I didn't get a moment alone with Nico that night but wasn't really sure how I wanted to go about revealing what I knew to him, anyway. Should I just come out and say it, or should I bide my time and use it as leverage at a convenient moment? I wasn't sure, so sat on the knowledge, pushing my feelings aside.

"Baby, I'm gonna go up to bed," I told Tobin when I'd had enough and was ready to leave the guys to it. He eyed me, as though checking I was okay, but conceded, and wrapped his arms around me and kissed me deeply, regardless of our audience.

He then escorted me up, giving me one last kiss before disappearing back downstairs, and I couldn't help but smile to myself as I climbed into bed and grabbed the laptop I'd brought with us to the new clubhouse. It was Dita's, of course. I hadn't been able to bring myself to leave it behind, so loaded up the messenger service and checked for a reply from Jane Doe. There was nothing, not that I expected one.

You're a fucking coward.

I hoped that'd get Liev's attention. Perhaps get him angry enough to respond at least. I then closed the laptop and lay down, snuggling into the familiar sheets that felt like home. Like they were mine. Ours.

I fell asleep listening to the sounds of chatter beneath me, the din loud enough to reach me yet indistinct enough for me not to listen to it. The white noise washed over me and brought with it a haze of tiredness, and I gave in.

That was the first night I dreamed of Dita. In my dream, she was happy, smiling, and free. Nothing like she had been in life. It was wonderful, and when I woke a few hours later thanks to Tobin crashing around the room in his drunken attempt to undress, I knew I was smiling too. I hoped wherever she was, she looked like I'd imagined her. That she was truly free at last, and that she was happy.

Chapter Twenty-Two

The next two days passed by in a blur. I messaged Liev two more times, each one more daring than the last, but still, I got no response. He'd left me behind. I was sure of it, so instead of wallowing in self-pity, I threw myself into overcoming the hurdles life had thrown in my path over the last few months. I put Tobin first and really made the effort to make sure he knew he was on top of my 'most important people' list.

Nico had left for a night but turned up with Jodie the following day, and I watched him fawn over her with interest. No matter what I'd seen on that camera footage, my brother really seemed to love her, and I figured he was like most men—he slipped every now and again. But rather than cheat with other girls, it seemed Nico had a thirst another woman couldn't quench. Something he'd decided Calvin was the man to help him with. However, for the time being, it seemed my brother had put Jodie to the top of his list too and he'd finally proposed.

She showed off her impressive engagement ring while beaming and glowing with the pregnancy, and I couldn't be happier for them. I could also tell they were back to being a sexually active couple again because I heard them going at it in the bedroom when I then went up to take a bath in the main restroom that was next to their room. I was pleased to know he was back to normal following his crash though, so popped my music on and ignored the noises coming through the wall.

Tobin then joined me, climbing in at the opposite end of the full and flowery scented water. I'd used a bath bomb, and the water wasn't only heavily fragrant, but also a deep shade of sparkly purple he seemed surprised by. I just laughed, figuring he hadn't been one for taking long and aromatic baths in the past. We simply stared at one another, me tracing the lines of his ink while he had his eyes on my breasts as I breathed, dipping them in and out of the dark water with each inhale and exhale.

"When did you have those done?" I eventually asked, and Tobin looked down at his chest, following my line of sight. He lifted one hand and pointed to the tattoos on his body and the tops of his arms.

"These were started years ago while I was still in the army. I had some done while based in Germany and others once I came back to the UK," he told me, and I grinned. "The rest I added over the past few years since getting out."

"I can't imagine you in a uniform," I replied, leaning forward so I could take his hand in mine, tracing the lines of the roses on the back of his left one. I'd seen the soldiers in their kit and, like most women, couldn't deny a man in uniform was a sexy sight, but he wasn't a soldier in my eyes. He was a biker, through and through. Chuck's prodigal son, who had returned in time to spend his final years together. "I think I'd like to see you in your kit though."

"I'll show you some of my old photos if you like?" Tobin offered, and I nodded profusely. I wanted to know the man he'd once been. I wanted to see his friend who had died and learn about how Tobin had coped with the loss. He didn't seem to have PTSD anymore, but I knew it was common in soldiers who'd returned from war, having seen and experienced things I couldn't even begin to comprehend.

"I want to know everything about you, baby. I want to see your life, both the good and bad," I replied honestly, and Tobin seemed glad. As if he too had secrets he hadn't felt able to tell me, and I just wished that one day I might finally be able to open up to him and reveal the things I had learned about my sister and his abusive cousin.

The next morning, Tobin took Dad out to meet with a few local mechanics. I could tell it was a business meeting, probably to discuss the club's needs for local contacts for their bike repairs. That side of the club business bored me, so I said goodbye and headed to the kitchen in search of some breakfast. My brothers then came downstairs and joined me and were soon chatting loudly while I made them coffee and bacon sandwiches. When Thomas and Brad were done, they thanked me and disappeared back into the bar, while Nico stayed behind, watching me intently from the large table as he finished his brew. As I was taking a large bite of brown sauce covered bacon, he stood and refilled our mugs, both of us enjoying the comfortable quiet.

"Are you okay, Dahlia?" he then asked, taking his seat opposite me again.

"I'm fine," I answered, but I could tell he wasn't convinced. Nico seemed to have the same insight as our father and could tell something was up with me, even though I'd done my best to hide it. "Just been doing a lot of soul-searching lately. A lot of thinking."

"About what?"

"Dita…"

"Still?" he seemed uneasy by my answer, and now I knew why.

"Yeah," I answered. I tried to think how best to come out and say what was on my mind, so I started slow, trying to gather the courage to finally tell him the things that were haunting me. "Calvin hurt her over and over. I can't help but wonder why. It doesn't make sense that it'd be just about the sex or the power he wanted over her. I think he wanted to have power over someone else as well, to punish them."

"Like Tobin? Maybe he was pissed off with him and thought that by hurting Dita he could hurt him too?" I shook my head. "Then who?" Nico was playing the game, but we both knew who Calvin had been trying to punish, and I was looking right at him.

"You," I answered coldly. I'd had to detach myself from the idea to cope with it, but there was also a huge part of me that needed to know if my hunch was true. If Nico was the reason behind Calvin's torturous ways. "I know about the two of you, and I know that's why you protected him rather than tell everyone what he'd done to Dita."

Nico went white. He let his mug clatter onto the wooden tabletop and stared at me incredulously. I didn't move a muscle as he shook his head, and when I didn't back down, he lowered it and began rocking back and forth. "How long have you been fucking him, Nico?" I demanded quietly, trying my hardest to keep from screaming it at him.

He didn't answer me right away. Nico simply

continued to stare at the table, his head in his hands. But I didn't let him off the hook. I stared him down, waiting for what felt like forever for my answer.

"About two years," he finally responded in a strangled tone, as though the tense silence was killing him, and he'd had to say something.

"Do you love him," I needed to ask.

"No, but for some reason, I keep going back. It's like I can't help myself, even though I know what he did to Dita."

"Did he do it to punish you?"

"Yes, the first time, at least. I told him we were over, and he flipped his shit. All I know is that he was in the right place at the wrong time and Dad ended up confiding in him about how off the rails Dita was getting. Calvin talked him into letting him rough her up in a bid to scare her, which was when he… you know," I certainly did. I clutched my chest over where my heart was beating ten to the dozen.

"How did you find out?"

"He told me the next day. Said he had to punish me every time I hurt his feelings because he loved me so much, and I caved. I let him dictate when and where we met up, knowing he was unstable. Knowing I should've called it off and sent him away, but he hid the truth from me after that first time. He was punishing me in secret by ruining her, and I had no idea until you told me the night of Thomas's party." Nico finally looked at me, his brown eyes bloodshot and suddenly weary. It'd been weighing on him, I could tell, and so I reached across the table and took his hand in mine. It couldn't be easy on him, so I remained supportive rather than letting myself be angry with him for having kept his secret. Didn't we all hide the truths to save ourselves the shame of coming clean? I knew I too had told white lies to suit my own agenda, so couldn't begrudge him. "I stayed quiet and protected our secret rather than say a word to anyone about what you told me that night. I should've told Dad or gone to Tobin, or at least told Jodie the truth, but I couldn't. I even told you to wait. To bide your time, because I knew he might punish you too, and I couldn't bear it if he treated you the same as he had Dita."

"Do you think he messed with your bike?" I replied, and Nico looked surprised at my question, his brows furrowing. "I fucked with him that same morning. Maybe he thought it was you? Maybe he took it as you trying to freak him out, so he decided to fuck you right back?"

Nico jumped up from the table and began to pace, his hands on his head as he thought about my question. I don't think he'd even considered it before I'd said, and I watched as something snapped within him. Something primal and dominative.

"Stay here, Dahlia. Do not come outside, got it?" I nodded but wasn't sure what he was getting at and wasn't given an explanation either. Nico stormed out of the kitchen without another word, and he stalked over to where Calvin was playing pool with some of the guys. He barely said a word to him, but I saw Nico indicate for him to meet him outside, and I had to force myself to keep my promise. Instead, I charged into the office and loaded up the security software, watching my brother as he continued his pacing outside on the gravelled parking lot.

Calvin appeared, and I watched them talking for a few moments before things quickly became heated. They were soon arguing and while I couldn't hear what was being said, I could tell via a spot of simple lip-reading that Nico was furious and Calvin was pleading with him for forgiveness.

I'm sorry, please! I could see him mouthing, but Nico was having none of it. Clearly, I'd been right. Calvin had been the one responsible for his crash, and Nico now knew it. I then watched, open-mouthed, as he lunged for Calvin and punched him repeatedly while tackling him to the ground. Calvin took it at first, but then his rage seemed to take over and he retaliated, fighting back with strength and skill I was shocked to see. He sure knew how to fight, and before I knew it, they were both black, blue, and bloody.

Each lying on their backs, staring up at the sky, I then watched them talking quietly, the row evidently over with, and was surprised to see Calvin's hand reach for Nico's. I was even more stunned when my brother took it, caressing his fingers with his for just a moment before jumping up and storming back inside without another word or a backwards glance.

I didn't see Nico again that day. He took Jodie and went home, the official story having been that he and Calvin had been talking and had a disagreement, which was dealt with the only way the men in my life apparently knew how—by having a good old-fashioned fight.

"Sometimes we have to clear the air and so long as neither of you are hurt permanently, a few punches can be quite cathartic," Brad told me over lunch when I couldn't help but snoop.

"What was it about?" I asked him, and he shrugged.

"Could be any number of things. Nico's been stressed lately, so maybe something small set him off and it just happened to be Calvin who got it." I knew then how Brad had no idea what had been going on between Nico and Calvin, and I wondered if anyone knew. Could they really have done such a good job of hiding their gay affair from everyone? Surely someone had to have noticed.

After I'd finished eating, I made my excuses and then disappeared off to the office so I could do some more investigating. There, I trawled through some more of the recordings but found nothing. I knew there were no cameras at Dad's house, so guessed they hadn't counted on being caught before, but now they would know. Nico had to have realised how I had found him out, or at least he soon would, so I decided to lie to him. I'd say I'd delete the files, when I would secretively keep them in case I ever needed them for leverage against Calvin. I even made backups on my work hard drive in case Nico decided to make sure by wiping the computer's memory.

I then booted up Dita's laptop and read through some of her diaries again. She really had hidden the details of her relationship with Liev as best she could, and I finally understood why. They would never have been accepted. Not only for her having defied our father's wishes by not seeing things through with Tobin, but also for her having fallen for the enemy.

The Red Reapers were Dad's rivals for not only turf and business but also for his daughter's loyalty, or so it seemed. There hadn't been much information come my way about them over the years, but I'd heard rumours of them having been responsible for the death of one of our prospects a few years back. I'd also been warned never to put any information regarding my whereabouts online, especially after one of the girls who frequented our club had been beaten and raped by a member of the Reds who had stalked her on social media and then attacked her after finding out she was shagging a member of our club. They were monsters capable of anything, or so I'd always believed, and yet Dita had loved one of them. She'd repeatedly met up with him and they had tried to run away into the sunset together. She had trusted him, so I had to as well.

Making my mind up, I did a search for their clubhouse and made a note of the address. Liev wasn't answering my messages, so I would simply have to go straight there. I wasn't going to make it easy for him to ignore me. But first, I sent one last message.

I'm scared. I think I might be next...

Chapter Twenty-Three

A week later, I found myself in a cab on the way to the address I'd found for the Red Reaper's clubhouse. Gemma had been busy with her official boyfriend John while I'd been at the new clubhouse, and even now that we'd all come back and were staying at Dad's, I'd hardly seen her. I didn't mind though. There was a lot on my plate that I was still determined not to drag her into, so we just caught up via text and she kept me updated on the budding romance she was now having with our friendly barman, while I made sure to sound interested and not get distracted by my own woes. But, as I seemed to do, I couldn't switch off from the matter at hand. I couldn't forget what Calvin had done or what Nico was doing with him behind Jodie's back. Their fight had been and gone without mention or consequence. The guys all treated it as if the air had been cleared and that was that. No one even pried as to what it was all about, so I couldn't get away with keeping on pressing the club members as to their assumptions behind the fight.

I'd come back to the city and decided to go it alone again, so had sneakily asked for a lift from Bradley once Tobin and Dad had gone out for the day. I obviously couldn't tell him where I planned to go, so had gotten him to drop me off at the college and told him I'd be there for the day. After waiting fifteen minutes to be sure he'd gone again, I'd then jumped in a taxi and given the driver the chosen address, but I wasn't going in blind, and I certainly wasn't going to take any chances.

"Will you wait for me?" I asked the cabbie, offering him a handful of cash when we arrived. He looked out at the windscreen at the clubhouse and then back at me in surprise but accepted the payment.

"You sure you want to go in there alone, duck?" he asked, eyeing the bikes all lined up outside. Grinning at his use of local pet name, I nodded and opened the door, stopping only to take a deep, steadying breath. "No matter how long, I'll wait for you," the driver then called after me, restoring my faith in humanity a little. I thanked him and then crossed the road, heading inside before I could lose my nerve.

"You must be in the wrong place," a voice called to me as I stepped into the lion's den. I had a good look around, taking it all in. Their clubhouse was much like ours. They had a large communal bar area with staircases leading up into what I knew had to be their meeting room and offices. I took in the red and black décor, along with a mural dedicated to their club. Someone had taken the time to recreate their emblem in fine detail in the centre, along with drawings of bikes I knew the makes and models of, having been around them my entire life.

"Get lost, little girl," said another of the members, but I refused. Peering around at the dozen or so men stood staring at me in surprise, I searched for Liev's face, but he wasn't there. I looked again, hoping and praying to find him. No such luck. My heart sunk.

"She's not lost, are you?" another man asked, and when the crowd parted, my earlier tenacity wilted even more. The same man who had trapped me in his grasp at the pub was walking towards me with a satisfied smile on his lips. He seemed to think I might be there for him, like I might've actually enjoyed our interaction the last time. As if. "I think she liked what she saw the other night so came looking for more. Is that right, lisichka?" he added as he reached me, his hand going up to my hair where he twirled one of my auburn locks around his fingers.

"You wish," I replied as I stepped away from him, opting to go deeper into the still surprised gathering of club members rather than let him corner me again. "I'm here to see Liev. Where is he please?" I asked the others, but they all remained quiet.

"When your sister came here, she always let us have some fun with her. She often danced for us," my admirer told me as he followed me into the group. He then stopped right behind me and pressed his chest against my shoulder blades. "She would get high and take off her clothes. And then she'd wear Liev's cut to tell your father to go fuck himself. She showed us we could trust her not to go running home and tell him our secrets. Are you going to do the same? I don't think so…"

"I don't need to do the same. Liev already knows he can trust me." I looked around the room, looking for a more friendly face, but couldn't be sure about any of them, and began to panic. "Tell your boss I came by and ask him to call me. It's important." Turning on my heel, I headed for the door, when my new friend grabbed the top of my arm, turned me to face him, and then yanked me into his hold. The others sniggered as I yelped and tried in vain to pry myself free. None of them would help me, and I began to panic. I should've known better than to go I there alone and unprepared. Liev wasn't even there, so I'd wasted the opportunity, anyway.

"One—you don't tell me or any other member of this club to do anything," the man growled, walking forward with me in his hold, so I had no choice other than to step back along with him. When my back hit the wall, he finally released his grip on my arms and glowered at me. "Two—Liev isn't my boss, or at least he won't be for much longer." I frowned, staring up into his face, and he seemed to enjoy my confusion. He'd liked delivering the news to me, but I couldn't fathom why.

"Is he moving to another chapter?" I asked timidly, trying to ignore the sensation of the strange and scary man as he pressed himself harder against me. He wanted me, that much I couldn't ignore, and yet I refused to let it shake me. He wasn't going to win. Not this time.

"No," he eventually answered, stroking his hand through my hair again. Despite his malicious taunts, I got the feeling he was quite taken with me, but he lacked anything I would've been attracted to in a lover, not to mention I wasn't looking for anyone new anyway.

"What's your name?" I mumbled, feeling lightheaded thanks to his firm hold over me.

"Oscar," he replied, finally turning slightly gentler. His dark brown eyes roved my body, and I knew he wasn't being nicer for the hell of it. He was doing it because he thought he might be about to get lucky with me. Not a chance.

"Well, Oscar. Care to tell me what's going on with Liev?" He let out a small groan, evidently realising that he wasn't going to get anywhere with me, but I was glad when he didn't resort back to his cruel ways.

"He's leaving the club for good. Moving away to live on a farm or some shit like that. Had enough, or so he says. Ever since your sister died, he hasn't been the same…"

"None of us have," I replied, putting my hands on his chest to silently ask him to back off, and I was surprised when he did. Oscar then actually walked me out. No messing and no more taunts. He did, however, take one last opportunity to rile me before letting me walk back across the street to my thankfully sincere cabbie.

"Don't ever come back here, Dahlia. You're not safe at the clubhouse, no matter what you think Liev will do to protect you. He couldn't save her, and he won't save you," he said, making me wonder again if perhaps Dita's death wasn't quite the accident I'd been led to believe.

***

When I got home, Tobin was back, and he immediately ushered me to one side, his brows pulled tight.

"Where have you been?" he demanded, and while I hated lying to him, I knew I had to.

"I went to college for a while. What's the matter?"

"You hadn't told me you were going out today, Dahl. I at least thought you might send me a message to let me know you wouldn't be here when I got back. Even Gemma didn't know where you were when usually she'd be there with you…"

"Oh, so you felt the need to get my friend involved rather than trust me?" I replied angrily, my guilt making me come across madder than I'd intended. I didn't want Tobin snooping on me but hated that he actually had a good reason to. I'd disappeared for the day and hadn't answered my calls or texts until I was long gone from the Red Reaper's clubhouse, when usually I was reliably contactable.

Tobin was understandably shocked by my outburst, and I saw unmistakable rage flash across his face. He then stormed away, swearing loudly to himself before disappearing out one of the back doors.

I went to follow but was intercepted by my brother Bradley. I made to step round him, but he continued to block me.

"No matter what you promised me about him not having hurt you, Dahlia, you're not going out there. I've seen him rage and do not want you anywhere near him if he's kicking off," he instructed. It reminded me of the conversation we'd had months before when I'd had to reassure him that Tobin hadn't been physical with me. He, too, had seen things that hadn't made sense about Tobin and Dita's relationship, but his assumptions had been wrong. Well, mostly wrong, if Dita's diary was to be believed regarding the night when Tobin had slapped her across the face.

Nodding in understanding, I turned and wandered off in the opposite direction, where I was given two options on where to go—upstairs, or into the busy living area with the others. Not feeling much like company, I went up to my room, where I laid on the bed and stared up at the ceiling while a million thoughts buzzed through my head. I didn't want to add another worry to my already full plate, so decided to make things right with Tobin. He didn't deserve to be on the receiving end of my stress when it wasn't him causing it. I grabbed my mobile phone and sent him a quick text, figuring he could reply or ignore it as he saw fit.

I'm sorry I flew off the handle. I'm upstairs whenever you want to talk.

I then sat back again and resumed my overthinking.

At some point over the few minutes that'd followed, I fell asleep. When I woke up, it was an hour later and roasting hot in my bedroom, so I pulled off my cardigan and padded into the en-suite to brush my teeth. They felt rough and dry, like I'd been asleep for longer, so I ducked my head and brushed away, not paying attention to my reflection in the mirror until I'd cleaned up and thought I'd best check my makeup hadn't smudged. That was when I noticed the bruises on the tops of my arms. They were exactly where Oscar had held me tightly at his clubhouse and were clearly in the shape of handprints.

I cursed him and stormed back into the bedroom so I could cover back up, which was when I came face-to-face with Tobin. He was clearly drunk and was swaying slightly, watching me with a blank expression. His eyes were red with the drink, and I didn't like the air he'd carried in with him. He seemed indifferent to me, rather than madly in love like we'd been thus far. I couldn't tell if he was about to forgive me or shout at me and realised when he saw the bruises that I might never find out his initial reasons for having come to me.

"We're over, Dahlia," he groaned, shaking his head wildly as though trying to force some awful thought away. "I'm not doing this again."

"Doing what?" I exclaimed as I reached up and tried to touch his face. Tobin pulled away from me, storming over to the chest of drawers, where he began throwing his things out onto the floor. "What have I done wrong, Tobin?" I shrieked and hated how desperate my voice sounded.

"I should've known you'd be the same. I opened my heart to you and now all you do is keep secrets, just like Dita did. You disappear on me and turn up with bruises all over you, and ones I know I didn't put there. Who's had their hands on you, Dahlia? Who've you been fucking behind my back, like she did?" Still swaying, Tobin watched me with a sad look before he crumpled in a heap on the bed.

"I'm not fucking anyone, I promise," I tried to tell him, but Tobin refused to listen. He shook his head, staring at the floor. He needed more truth from me, not more lies, so I decided to reveal at least a little bit of what I'd been hiding. For the sake of our relationship and his trust in me, I had to come clean. "I went looking for someone I thought might give me some answers, but all I found were dead ends. That's where I was today, and where someone grabbed me by the arm." I showed him the bruise and put my hand over the mark to show where Oscar had gripped me a little too tightly. "I hadn't realised it'd bruised until just now, but that's the only one, I promise. No others and certainly nothing I'd want to hide from you."

I sank to my knees before him and was glad when Tobin didn't pull away from my touch this time. "There are things I'm not ready to share with you yet, but I will when the time is right. You can either give me the benefit of the doubt, or you can walk away, but please trust me when I say I'm not cheating on you. I never have and never will."

"Then show me," he answered, making me think he meant by making love there and then, but it appeared Tobin had other ideas. "I want to see your phone and laptop. I wanna read your messages."

No matter his suffering, I wasn't going to allow Tobin to invade my privacy, not that he'd really find anything as the evidence was all on Dita's laptop, but for the sake of my self-respect, I still shook my head no.

"That's not how this works," I replied as I pulled away and climbed to my feet. With a heavy heart, I then packed a bag and grabbed my phone and its charger from the nightstand. After yanking on my cardigan, I then left without another word to Tobin, who was still sat on the bed, staring at the floor in a daze.

Downstairs, I tried to be invisible as I crept over to where Nico was chatting with our father. I needed some space from Tobin but knew that both he and my dad wouldn't let me go just anywhere. "Do you have a minute?" I asked Nico once the conversation reached a lull, and my big brother turned to me, as though shocked to find me there. I guessed I'd blended in a little too well.

"What's up?" he asked, his eyes roving my face, taking me in. Nico could tell something was going on with me, and I was glad when he took my hand and led me from the room without making a fuss or letting on to any of the others.

Out in the garden, he sat me down on one of the benches and put an arm across my shoulders. "What happened?"

"Tobin and I had a fight," I answered with a shaky voice. I'd been bottling it all up but was feeling kinda heartbroken. I was sad that we'd fought, but also terrified of him forcing me to reveal all or else lose him forever. I wanted things to go back to how they'd been before, when we were freshly in love, and nothing could touch us.

Yes, Dita had cheated on him, but Tobin had been

unfaithful as well. He wasn't innocent in their breakdown, so couldn't take it out on me a year down the line. "Can I come and stay at yours?" I then asked him.

Nico nodded and pulled his mobile phone from his jacket pocket. I then watched as he dialled his fiancée and gave her the lowdown. I could hear her response from where I was sitting, that of course I was welcome, and I smiled. I always knew I could count on Jodie. She would help get me through our argument with a clear head. Mine and Tobin's first, and hopefully not last, fight.

Jodie came to collect me, and I left with her straight away, no fussing or making a scene about it. At Nico's request, we didn't say a word to any of the others inside, not even our father. We both knew he would demand to know everything and then probably still wouldn't let me walk away, not even if I begged. No matter me knowing he hadn't sent Calvin after Dita with the awful punishment in mind, I knew he might still go as far as punishing me for potentially ruining things between us. He had this fixation that his VP had to be with one of his daughters, hence his weird and old-fashioned actions the first night we'd been at the new clubhouse, and I wouldn't put it past him to do the same as he'd done the last time. If Dad took Tobin off to get him laid elsewhere, I knew I'd never forgive him. This wasn't like with Dita. I hadn't done anything behind Tobin's back and would stand my ground, even if it meant we were over.

Chapter Twenty-Four

I explained as much as I could to Jodie, leaving out the parts about Liev, Calvin and, of course, Nico's part in all the chaos. All I told her was how I'd been digging into Dita's past and had uncovered some awful truths about her final days. Jodie seemed to know more than she said too, protecting Dita's memory, or perhaps herself. I couldn't be sure. Either way, we each said only what we felt we could, and then I explained the horrible conversation Tobin and I had had in the bedroom.

"I couldn't believe it when he just said we were over without any explanation why. Who does that? One wrong move and then you're done?"

"Oh, believe me, it'll happen time and again, Dahlia," Jodie replied with a kind smile. "This is your first fight, and it's going to feel like the end of the world. Like you'll never come back from it, but you will. We all have these moments where you think you've passed the point of no return. When you're so angry with them, you can't fathom everything being back to how it was before. But then, suddenly, your anger fades, as will his. The pair of you just need to let the dust settle and then talk. You'll see."

I couldn't imagine either of us simply backing off and things going back to how they were. With the threat of leaving me, Tobin had also delivered a chilling reminder: I was disposable. Temporary. Not a member of the club or an official old lady. Just another girl clinging onto the Black Knights Motorbike Club because she loved one of the members and was related to a handful of the others.

"Do you think Dad would let me move out on my own, like Nico did?" I then asked, and I indicated to their shared flat. It hadn't always been Jodie's too. Nico had bought it and had lived there for almost two years before inviting her to move in with him, and part of me wondered if I might be able to do the same. Even if I had to go into the same block of upmarket apartments, I would. At least then I'd be away from the club and out from under my dad's nose. I could run my design business and make a life for myself without him controlling me.

The sheer idea made me smile again, thinking that even if Tobin and I were done, there were still other passions in my life, and it brought me comfort to know I was more than just another old lady in the making. I had aspirations and dreams. I was ambitious and ready to fight for the life I wanted for myself, with or without Tobin by my side.

"Dahlia." Jodie's soft voice broke my reverie, and I turned to peer into her soft blue eyes. "He won't ever let you go. You see that, don't you? Please tell me you're aware just how much your father dictates your life?"

"Don't say that," I retorted, feeling a flush of anger hit me in the gut. "He's already backed off and agreed to let me live with Tobin. He's seen for himself how well I can cope and that I'm a woman now, not a child anymore."

"I hope you're right," she replied dejectedly. Jodie ran her hand down my hair and across my shoulder, and I could tell she was trying to bite her tongue. To not say the things she truly wanted to.

"What is it?" I had to know.

"I just hope this strong and determined woman doesn't get locked away again, that's all," she told me, and I knew it was a lie. There had been more she'd wanted to say, but evidently felt she couldn't. Jodie seemed timid at that moment, as though scared. Of Nico or of our father, I couldn't be sure, but I didn't want to put her under any more stress given her condition, so didn't pry. We simply sat in silence for a little while before I made my excuses and went to bed in their spare room.

At four in the morning, I awoke to hear voices coming from across the other side of the flat. Opening the door, I peered down the hall and listened hard, hoping to figure out what was happening without having to head towards the living room to find out.

There was the sound of glass breaking and at first, I feared for Jodie's safety, wondering if perhaps Nico had come back and was acting out for some reason.

"Fuck, man," I then heard my brother say relatively calmly. "What happened?"

"Your bloody table is wonky," I heard Tobin's slurred reply. I froze. Nico had to have told him I was hiding out at his place and invited him back, but why? I thought we'd have a little bit more time to let the dust settle after our fight and then talk again the following day. Not that Tobin would follow me to the place I'd run to so I could get away from him.

"What the fuck is he doing here?" I demanded as I stalked into the living room, pointing at Tobin. Both men froze in shock, their eyes boring into me. "Did you tell him what you said to me?" I then asked Tobin.

"Yeah, he did," my brother replied for him. "And he told me how stupid he was for demanding shit from you. How he was sorry that he treated you so badly and how he wished he hadn't let you walk away."

I glowered at Tobin, tears pricking at my eyes.

"Is that true?" I mumbled, wrapping my arms around myself protectively.

"Yeah, Dahl. Of course it's true." He then downed one of the shots lined up before him on Nico's coffee table. "I'm not here to fight or to drag you back to your dad's. I'm here to tell you I'm sorry for not trusting you, and that I won't do it again." Another shot disappeared down his throat and then Tobin finally turned his gaze up to meet mine. His pale blue eyes were even more bloodshot, and he looked exhausted, but I wasn't going to let him off that easily.

"Good, but don't think for a minute you're forgiven, just like that." I turned and walked to the doorway. "We'll talk properly tomorrow when you've sobered up."

"Looks like you'll be sleeping on the sofa tonight, buddy," I heard Nico tease as I then disappeared out of sight.

"Yep," Tobin replied with a small laugh. "But at least she didn't kick me out, so that's a good start."

***

I hardly slept after my late night wakeup, but I didn't mind the sleeplessness as it gave me time to think and mull things over. I knew it wouldn't be all that hard to forgive Tobin, and wanted our fight to be over, but at the same time, I also wanted to keep my independence. Yes, I was going behind his back and doing things I perhaps shouldn't be, but Nico deserved to have his secrets kept and I wasn't about to ruin both his life and his future by outing him and Calvin. There was also Liev. He deserved the chance to move on, and I vowed to leave him be. I'd find another way to get rid of Calvin that didn't involve a painful outcome for my family and friends. There had to be another way. I decided I had to leave things where they were until a way out of the mess presented itself. It wasn't doing me any good dwelling on the past or putting myself in danger, and it certainly wasn't bringing Dita any justice. The best way to avenge her was for me to live my life and be happy. There was a man who loved me that I loved back, and I was determined to get us back on track again, no matter the sacrifices I might have to make to get us there.

I let Nico and Tobin sleep late, figuring it was best they sleep off as much of the booze they'd put away as possible. Jodie had gotten up and gone to work by the time I decided to get up, and I left the bedroom just long enough to grab some breakfast and put on a fresh pot of coffee. Then, with my brew and bagel in hand, I crept back into the bedroom past the guys fast asleep on the sofas.

It was noon by the time they'd roused, and I'd put the time to use deciding for what I wanted for my future. In my small notebook, I'd prioritised the main people and responsibilities in my life, as well as the aspirations I had for the future. Seeing it in black and white helped me to focus and when Tobin knocked on the door, showered and dressed, I knew he was well and truly the man on the top of that list.

"I want you to marry me, Dahlia," he said as he came over the threshold and closed the door behind him. Tobin then fell to his knees and peered up at me, looking lost. "I can't live without you, and I certainly cannot imagine a future where you're not my wife. I'll do whatever you say to make things right."

"You can start by apologising," I answered, crossing my arms.

"I'm sorry," he admitted. "I accused you of something I had no proof of and then tried to invade your privacy and belittle you. I'll never do it again."

"Good," I told him, letting go of my hurt feelings at last. It felt good to release my grip of it and his words warmed me from the inside out. Tobin knew exactly what he'd done wrong without me having to prompt or push him. We had our future back, and I was suddenly incredibly aware of the words he'd first spoken to me. "Do you really want to marry me?"

"Yes," he answered, and pulled a small black box from the inside pocket of his cut. "I've wanted to since you rode on the back of my bike to the new clubhouse that night. Ever since you stared into my eyes a few days later and accepted me as yours." He opened the box and showed me his chosen engagement ring. It wasn't huge, but I wasn't after anything elaborate anyway and I loved knowing he'd put a lot of thought into the style and cut of it.

After nodding my head yes, he slipped it onto my finger, and I was surprised to find the ring had a good deal of weight to it.

"Yes, Tobin. I'll marry you," I gushed, and fell to my knees, holding him tightly. "I want to spend some time together, just you and me. Take me to Dahlia's so we can be alone, like we were at the beginning. So, we can start over."

"You got it, babe," he agreed, and together we then packed up and got ready to leave Nico's place behind.

My brother was surprisingly sober when we emerged, and he gave us a lift back to Dad's place. He also promised to talk with him about the alone time Tobin and I needed, plus he said he'd cover for me with the night before.

"He doesn't need to know everything," Nico informed me with a wink, and I was glad he had my back. "I'm also putting an end to the other thing," he said cryptically, but we both knew what—or rather who—he meant. I wanted that over more than I could say, but also knew the risks involved in Nico hurting Calvin. He would have to watch his back after ending things with his unstable lover or else suffer his wrath. I knew he was capable of anything, perhaps even hurting Jodie if Nico took his eye off Calvin long enough.

"Be careful," I told him, and after giving my big brother a soft kiss on the cheek, I climbed on the back of Tobin's bike, and we sped away.

Chapter Twenty-Five

We travelled out of the city and reached Dahlia's by nightfall. Tobin was quiet as we checked the house and bar over, making sure nothing untoward had happened to his place in our absence, but he took his time, and I got the feeling he didn't want to talk quite yet. There were things both of us had hidden and I knew there always would be but trusted he would reveal the important things over time, just like I would.

While Tobin was busy, I grabbed Dita's laptop from the office where I had left it after our last visit to the new clubhouse and opened the messenger app, staring at the string of unanswered messages I had sent to Jane Doe over the past few months. Liev hadn't answered a single one, so I figured it was time to stop. Time to put the computer, and the story of Dita's mysterious life, away.

I won't bother you again, but I want you to know that I understand. I know you loved Dita and would've given anything to be with her, but that's over now and you're finally moving on. I can't hold on to her any longer either, so I'm walking away. Nico is putting an end to things with X and he'll make sure I stay safe. You won't hear from me again. Goodbye.

When I walked away, I felt lighter. Freer. As if a

weight truly had been lifted by me, having made the decision to take a step away from the mysterious life of Dita Proctor.

I found Tobin making up a fire in the smaller living area of the old bar and nestled into the old leather sofa, watching as he nurtured the flames until it properly caught before covering the fireplace with the guard. Warmth billowed from the hearth within seconds, and it wasn't long before the chilly edge had properly cleared.

I realised I'd neglected him recently, so decided to talk things through and hopefully put him at ease. It was time.

"I've been obsessed with Dita lately. Searching for answers about her final days. She was a stranger to me, and I'm ashamed not to have known how bad things had gotten between you." I told him when he joined me.

"She cheated first, so I retaliated, thinking it would make me feel better, but it didn't. If anything, it made me worse and after that, it was just a slippery slope from bad to worse."

"Why were you so convinced I'd cheated?" I asked, and Tobin frowned, wringing his hands. He turned to me, those pale blues of his taking my breath away as he stared at my face, but then his expression turned wistful. He was remembering something, and I was glad when he decided to tell me about it rather than keep quiet.

"Because it's exactly what she did. Dita would disappear for a few hours and turn up like nothing was out of the ordinary but couldn't seem to answer me when I wanted to know what she was up to." He then ran a hand through his dark blond hair and left it at the back of his neck, massaging gently as though he had an ache there. I wanted to reach up and rub it for him, but also didn't want to break his concentration, so sat silently, unmoving despite my urge to touch him. "I confronted him once."

"Who?" I asked, surprised to be hearing Tobin's side of the story after such a long time of being wrapped up in Dita's version of events.

"Liev," he answered, and my stomach dropped. If only I'd asked him sooner, it could've saved me hours, days, and weeks of searching for him. Tobin had known all along. I should've trusted him to tell me the truth—all I'd had to do was ask.

"I went to see him yesterday," I revealed, hoping he wouldn't be angry. Tobin didn't even react.

"I know…"

I jumped and turned to face him, my mouth open in shock. "I've got a contact in the Red Reapers. He's the one who told me about Dita's antics there before, and he called me up yesterday to say they'd just had a visit from the youngest Proctor sister, much to my surprise. I acted the way I did because I wanted you to come clean and tell me where you'd been and why, but when you didn't, I saw red."

"Don't remind me," I groaned, but couldn't blame him. Of course, he had to have thought the worst, especially if Dita had been doing the exact same thing. "I just wanted to talk with him. To find out what'd really gone on between them."

"I know what was going on. They loved each other, and I was in the way," Tobin answered me and he shrugged. I was glad he was over it now, but knew it had to have been hard at the time. "I went down there one night, and she was there with him. I laid into the Ukrainian bastard with everything I had and he didn't even flinch. He refused to fight me, and I knew it was because he had nothing to prove.

He'd already won."

"They were already in love and planning to run away together," I finished his train of thought. Tobin seemed surprised that I knew that but didn't question me on it.

"Yeah. That's why I was such a dick last night. I'd managed to convince myself that you going down there was history repeating itself. Like I was somehow destined to follow the same path with you no matter my intentions for us to be a wholly different couple to how Dita and I had been."

"I would never—"

"I know. But I let my fear and past hurt get the better of me. I came to my senses sharpish when you set me straight and knew I had to trust you, Dahl. I do, I promise," he insisted, reaching over to take my hand in his.

I believed him. It was the most honest we'd ever been when it came to opening up about the past and its effect on our current actions. We'd needed our talk long before, and I leaned over, placing my lips against his. Our kiss was soft and slow, but gained quick momentum and before I knew it, I was straddling his lap and grinding myself against his hard-on like a brazen hussy. I released him from his jeans, unbuttoning the straining length with a little difficulty thanks to the tightness it was creating there. When free, I took him in my hands and started moving up and down, harder, and faster. When I reached beneath his shaft with my left hand to cup his balls, Tobin suddenly hissed and I peered down, seeing where my new ring had just scratched the underside of his cock.

"Shit, sorry baby," I cried, moving to pull my hands away, but Tobin stopped me. He pushed them back down onto his ever-ready erection and showed me how he wanted it. Where he wanted me to pull and tug against his soft flesh.

"As long as you're wearing that rock on your finger, I don't care if I get a few scrapes from it," he teased, still moving my hands up and down how he liked it, driving himself closer to the brink of his release. Pulling one hand away, I unwrapped the soft cotton scarf from around my neck and covered him just in time to catch his load, saving either of us the bother of cleaning up any mess, and Tobin laughed as he shuddered and jolted with his orgasm. "Damn, woman. You get me every time."

"Glad to hear it," I replied with a laugh, and climbed up off his lap so he could readjust himself. Once back in his pants, Tobin then grabbed me around the waist and yanked me back onto the sofa, positioning himself over me with a grin. "What?" I asked, feeling a little shy beneath his hot and penetrating stare.

"Just looking at my beautiful fiancée, you got a problem with that?" he answered cheekily. I didn't have a problem with it at all, and answered by unbuttoning my shirt, opening it up to reveal the sexy push-up bra I'd bought on my most recent shopping trip with Gemma. Tobin bit his lip, watching me with a delectable hunger in his eyes, so I kept going. Once the shirt was open, I unbuttoned my jeans and opened the fly to reveal the matching knickers I was glad I'd decided to buy after all.

"You can look all you like, baby. But, if I'm honest, I'd rather you touch as well," I replied with a sly grin.

Tobin was on me before I could even take my next breath. Using passionate and intense kisses, he commanded my attention to be solely on him, while his hands roamed my body, sliding off the rest of my clothes. He was gentle at first, but soon his horniness seemed to be fully recharged, and he was yanking my clothes from my body and throwing them across the room as though he wanted to get them as far away from us as possible. I cried out when his mouth found my core at last. It was so sensitive and ready to be tended to that I found my first release quickly and was glad when he didn't stop there.

When he was satisfied I was truly putty in his strong hands, Tobin flipped me over and drove himself inside me, pounding me hard from behind. My face was buried in the sofa cushions, but I didn't care. All I could think about was him. All I wanted was to please him.

I came suddenly and with force, screaming out for him and pushing myself up and back to meet his thrusts, clenching and squeezing with the inner muscles I could no longer control.

Tobin grunted and stilled, and I could feel the pulsing of his release inside me. I could barely move afterwards, so climbed forwards, and we lay there together, panting, each of us covered in sweat. The glorious aftermath of another of our amazing lovemaking sessions, but this time, there was more to it. We'd come through our first fight stronger than ever before, and I figured the stories were true—makeup sex really was awesome.

***

We spent the next two days together in blissful solitude. We didn't leave the house for even a minute and ordered our food in once we'd eaten up the main staples in the freezer and pantry. I caught Tobin checking his phone with a scowl a few times as he texted back and forth with someone, presumably my father or one of my three brothers, but didn't want to pop our bubble yet, so chose not to ask him about it.

My phone had gone a few times too, but luckily it was only Gemma checking in and giving me updates on where she was at with her coursework, or where John had taken her on their dates. I loved hearing from her so regularly and knew we would remain firm friends no matter what now. I was drawn to her in ways I had never felt before, not sexual but as a kindred soul. Someone who connected with me not just because of our similar interests and attitudes, but because deep down, we were the same.

That evening, I heard a bike pulling in and crunching over the gravelled parking area and knew our bubble was about to be burst whether I wanted it to be or not. Expecting my father, I was surprised when I came into the main living area of the new clubhouse and found my brother Nico there instead. He still looked like he was in one piece, given that he'd supposedly gone back and finished things with Calvin two nights earlier, but I couldn't really ask him how it'd gone with Tobin standing right beside me. Instead, I opted for my usual quietness and greeted my big brother with a kiss on the cheek.

"Sorry guys, Dad says you have to come back by tomorrow night otherwise, in his words, he'll come down here and drag you back himself," Nico told me, and my heart broke a little. So much for my father having accepted Tobin as my protector. Jodie had been right. The torch clearly hadn't been passed after all, and it made me sad to think that perhaps our dreams of living out from under my father's thumb might be foolish.

"Did you tell him we needed some alone time?" I

asked timidly, and Nico nodded.

"Of course, Dahl. But the fact remains that he needs his VP by his side, not disappearing for days with his old lady," he replied, which reminded me how Dad's possessiveness wasn't only about me, but also about his right-hand-man. "He's still on edge when it comes to having you out of his sight, especially because you did it without running it by him first. I handled him, but he wants you two home, that's all I've come here to say." Nico held up his hands.

"So, I can't shoot the messenger?" I replied with a half-smile. I couldn't be angry, really. I knew what our father was like, so couldn't be surprised he'd sent Nico to come and get us. He shook his head and then gave me a hug, holding onto me as though he needed it, so I hugged him back as hard as I could. "I'm gonna go take a shower and then we'll start getting ready," I said as I pulled away.

"No rush," Nico answered. "I'm heading back anyway, just need to have a quick word with your fiancé here before I go."

"Okay. See you tomorrow then," I replied as I pulled away and crept up the stairs. It surprised me how quiet Tobin had been throughout our talk, but I soon heard the two of them chattering and laughing, so knew nothing was up between them. The pair had been best friends for a few years, and I loved hearing them together. He had to need a friend just as much as I did, so I was glad they had one another.

The hot water felt wonderful against my skin as I showered away the remnants of my day. Tiredness washed over me, and I realised just how little sleep Tobin and I had gotten over the past few nights. I was ready for some serious rest and made quick work of drying myself off, opting for my towel robe so I could be lazy and dry off as I fluffed my hair to dry it as much as I could without having to use the hairdryer.

I then heard Nico shout from downstairs and jumped up to give him a wave goodbye from the window. Watching him leave felt strange, like it was wrong. As though I should call him back, but I couldn't understand it. I had Tobin there with me, so I padded out to the hall and shouted down to him.

"I'll be up in a minute, babe. Just have to call your dad," he answered, putting me more at ease, but still, something didn't feel quite right. I decided I'd get dressed in some pyjamas and go down to sit with him, but then I heard the back door close and the sound of Tobin lighting a cigarette by the back porch, so decided going to bed was probably a better option.

Still fluffing my hair with the towel, I bent my head over and began tousling it, and when I was done, I flicked it back up over my head and down my back.

That was when I came face-to-face with pure evil. I gasped and swallowed the lump in my throat, shaking my head. How could he be there? Why hadn't either Tobin or I heard him invade our home?

"I warned you, Dahlia. When I get in a mood, bad things happen," Calvin calmly reminded me, but I could see he was shaking in rage. He looked almost delirious, and I watched him close my bedroom door behind him as he stepped silently inside. His eyes were black in the darkness, but seemed even darker, if that was somehow possible. I didn't doubt he had come to punish me, so didn't stick around for chitchat. I turned and ran for the bathroom, the only other way out being blocked by the man I knew would hurt me the moment he got his hands on me but didn't get far.

"Tobin!" I screeched as Calvin reached me and grabbed a fistful of my hair, hoping to God, he might hear me, but knew it was pointless when my tormentor started laughing in my ear.

"He's busy, pretty girl," he said as he wrenched me closer to him and pressed himself into my back. "Just you and me for a little while, but don't worry. This won't take long." Calvin then threw me down onto the wooden floor with such force I head-butted the ground and my nose exploded in pain. Crying with the shock of the agony, I scrambled forward, still trying to find the bathroom, but couldn't see a thing.

Calvin was on me again before I even found my bearings and he yanked up the back of my robe, exposing my naked backside to him. I shoved my legs closed, hoping to restrict his access to my body, and he simply laughed. He climbed on top of me, his knees on the outside of mine, pushing my legs closed even more. I hoped perhaps he wasn't there to take me in the same way he had Dita but couldn't understand why he'd expose my naked body if he wasn't planning to defile it.

I could then hear the unmistakable sound of him undoing his belt and removing it from the loops of his jeans. I turned back, trying to see through the darkness, but my head was fuzzy after the blow to my nose, leaving my vision nothing but dark blurs.

"Please, don't do this," I begged. "Nico will never forgive you or take you back. Not if you rape me too."

Thwack! His belt came down hard against my arse

cheek without warning and without any mercy. Pain screamed through me and I cried out again, writhing beneath him in an attempt to get away, but Calvin squeezed his legs tighter on either side of my knees, holding me in place without needing to use his hands at all. Thwack…Thwack. He struck me repeatedly, his movements frenzied and full of rage as he whipped me without a care for my agony. Hell-bent on causing me more in a bid to show me how much pain he was feeling in his black heart.

Calvin whipped my legs, back and bottom relentlessly, coaxing my anguish and despair from me without pausing or faltering even once. He was a man who struck me as having hurt so many women in the past, he didn't even care for how hideous he was being. It was as though he needed to punish me, to take his frustration out on my body, no matter that I was innocent of a crime harsh enough to warrant it. I didn't know how many lashes he gave me but prayed for the pain to be over. For all of it to be over.

I wondered if he might never stop, but then realised how when he did, it wouldn't mean the end of my punishment, only the start of whatever the next phase of it might be.

"You think you can convince Nico to finish with me and I wouldn't realise it'd come from you? That I'd believe he'd decided it all of his own accord after all the times he's told me no and always meant yes?" Calvin asked, his voice that eerie kind of calm again. I shook my head, trying again to buck him off me. "After all my warnings, you still had to push me, didn't you? Daddy's little princess always gets what she wants, doesn't she? Well, not this time," he added, and I went into fight mode when he then leaned forward and put his hand around my throat.

I thought he might be about to throttle me, but I was wrong. It was far worse than that. Calvin slipped the belt around my neck and pulled, tightening it with a snap to my tender skin. I struggled for air and gasped hurriedly, desperate for more. My head throbbed and all I could hear was the thudding of the pulse in my ears. I tried to scream, to call for Tobin again, but it was no use. Calvin was slowly strangling me. I could feel myself growing drowsy from the asphyxiation and when he finally released some of the tension, I wanted to feel grateful, but couldn't. I knew what was coming next.

With a grunt, he had my hips tilted up off the floor and he was inside of me. I let out a garbled cry, struggling to believe it could be happening, retreating inside of myself in a bid to block it all out. To block him out.

It was no use. Calvin had all the control, and we both knew it. He was calling all the shots while I could do nothing but lie there, powerless to stop him from raping me while slowly suffocating, thanks to the belt still wrapped tightly around my neck. "Hmm, you're tighter than she was," he groaned, almost appreciatively as he took me, dipping in and out of my trembling body without a care for my pain. "I fucked Dita like this, too. With my belt around her neck, choking her until she passed out while I took what I wanted and then left her to come around in her own time. She'd wake up later, covered in my cum and sore from my beatings, but she never told a soul what I'd done. We both knew I'd do it again. I think, deep down, she enjoyed it. That she riled me on purpose so I'd take her over and over." Calvin told me, but I couldn't reply. I could barely process his words thanks to my fuzzy head, and I slumped down against the cold and hard floor, losing my fight against him one tight breath at a time.

Calvin didn't stop fucking me, going slow at first, as if he were enjoying himself, and then suddenly he was pounding me harder and faster. I'd been so sexual with Tobin over the couple of days before that I figured I was wet enough that he seemed to take me easily, even though I was far from welcoming. Nor did I enjoy the intrusion. I was also surprised that it didn't hurt—not that it felt at all pleasurable being violated by him. He wasn't as big as Tobin though and part of me wanted to laugh and call him a pencil dick, but the tightness around my throat was still blocking my voice as well as constricting my airway, focusing my mind back on the strangulation to my neck rather than the invasion at my waist.

A few more hard plunges, and Calvin suddenly slowed. He didn't lose control of himself or the belt for even a second, though, and I cursed him for being so used to taking women by force. I wondered how many others had fallen prey to him. How often he'd done this same routine in the past. "Will he still want you after you're broken, Dahlia? I doubt it. When I'm done with you, you won't ever let another man touch you again. All you'll be able to remember is the night I ruined you."

"No," I managed to groan, and I tried again to scoot away, but a sharp pull on the belt stopped me in my tracks without Calvin having to so much as say another word. He tightened it further and then I felt him pop the buckle pin into one of the holes, securing it a little more permanently on 'choke' mode.

"Do you like that, princess?" he teased as he

withdrew and flipped me over onto my back. My nose was still throbbing, as was my head, but I could still see him readying himself to fuck me some more and I began writhing, lashing out, and kicking with every ounce of strength I had left in my already sluggish muscles. "It's okay, fight all you want. I like it," he added with an evil smile as he ran his hand over my pussy, stroking my folds before pinching my clit roughly.

I hated how weak I was. How he'd caught and punished me so easily. I cursed him and vowed to have my revenge. I would find a way to murder the sick son of a bitch if it was the last thing I did.

"What the fuck!" I heard from across the room a second later, and then there was suddenly a ton of commotion. It had to be Tobin, I knew it, but I also knew I was in no position to try and help him. Scrambling back, I hit the side of the bed and tried desperately to get the belt undone from around my neck. I couldn't see what I was doing and knew in my panic I was taking longer. My fingers pulled and fiddled with the buckle, taking forever to find the right way, but eventually I managed to pull the long pin from the hole. I then threw the damn thing across the room, sucking in breaths at such a rate I felt I might pass out from the oxygen overload.

All the while, Calvin and Tobin were beating the shit out of each other on the floor beneath the huge window. I pulled the robe around myself, regardless of knowing it was fruitless, and watched in horror as the pair of them fought like two men hell-bent on killing each other. I screamed and shouted as best I could, begging them to stop, but at the same time, I wanted Tobin to do it. I hoped he would win and end it for all of us.

Tears streamed down my face and time seemed to slow as I continued to watch. When Calvin was on the ground and lay there panting for breath, seemingly bested, Tobin finally stood and stared over at me in shock.

"He forced me," was all I could think to tell him, hoping to God he didn't think what he'd seen going on between me and his cousin was consensual, and Tobin rubbed his bloody hands on his jeans in a bid to clean them up.

"I know, Dahl. Of course I know," he answered, much to my relief. "Call the police, babe. This sick fuck needs to be put away."

"No fucking way," Calvin groaned, clearly having heard him. With a sudden second wind, he clambered to his feet and sucker punched Tobin in the gut. As he doubled over, Calvin then shoved him, and I watched in horror as he lost his balance and fell backwards—right through the huge bedroom window.

I screamed with all my might as the glass shattered and gave way as though thinner than paper beneath Tobin's weight. He went right through it and was gone less than a second later. I charged forward, running to the window without even thinking about what Calvin was doing. I had to check on Tobin. To see if he'd fallen to his death or had survived the fall. I hoped and prayed for the latter.

He was lying on the gravel below, the security light illuminating him like some awful spotlight. But he wasn't moving. Not choking on pained breaths or groaning in agony. Tobin was perfectly still. As though dead. I wasn't close enough to check his breathing either, so all I could do was stare down at him and hope he might wake up and charge back in the house to save me a second time.

I was still screaming his name when Calvin grabbed me from behind and thrust me back down onto the hard floor. He'd found more than just his strength again. He was ready to pick back up where we'd left off, but I wasn't going to let him just take it a second time. Delivering a kick to his groin, I took his second of shock to bolt for the door Tobin had thankfully left open.

I was going too fast though, and before I knew it, the ground had slipped beneath my feet, and I was falling face first down the hard wooden steps. I tumbled over and over, bashing into the walls, bannister, and stairs as I fell down them. Every contact was agonising, making me cry out as I toppled downwards. I wondered how could I have been so foolish? Why had I thought I could win? I had been so wrong, and now I was paying the price for it.

Chapter Twenty-Six

When I came to a stop, everything hurt. Even breathing was agonising, and I couldn't move. Looking around, all I could make out were blurs, and I peered up the stairs at the blackened figure of my torturer. Calvin was standing at the top and he began to descend slowly, clapping his hands and laughing to himself.

"I don't know why you'd think you could run. But thanks to you being a fucking klutz, it looks like this is going to be even easier for me to take what I want and leave you to die, Dahlia. Oh, imagine the headlines... 'Lover's quarrel turns to joint murder' or perhaps he'll be accused of raping you and throwing you down the stairs to your death before committing suicide. Maybe I'll go with that option when I'm setting the scene," he told me, and I could do nothing but lie there in my crumpled heap and listen to his vile words.

I was going to die at Calvin's hands. That much was clear. If Tobin wasn't already dead, he soon would be too. I wanted to fight him. To reach out and push my fingers through his eye sockets or grab his balls and not let go until they were nothing but mush, but I could do nothing. My body was broken and wouldn't move, no matter my internal pleas, and I could feel myself going into shock, the pain numbing me inch by inch.

I cried out as Calvin lifted me up into his arms when he reached me, the movement only showing me exactly where I was hurt. My left ankle was screaming at me, as was my right arm. My vision was so blurred I could barely see a thing, and I didn't know why. I had to assume it was the pain still reverberating through my nose from where he'd probably broken it in his initial attack, or perhaps a blow to the head I'd endured during my fall down the stairs.

Holding me in a fireman's carry, I had my head resting on his shoulder, watching the shadows in a daze as he took me into the living room. The place where Tobin and I had made such amazing memories together. Calvin was going to ruin it all by turning our place of hope and wonder into somewhere tainted by evil. A tear escaped me as I mourned the memories I was no longer going to make there. The life I was no longer going to live. And the man who was no longer going to spend it by my side.

Calvin put me down on the sofa, ignoring my tears and garbled pleas for help and mercy as he opened my robe and inspected the flesh at the tops of my thighs. I groaned, trying to move away, but he pushed down on my already roaring ankle to remind me who was the one in control, relishing in my cries.

I felt dry as a bone as he forced his fingers inside of me, the pain searing my core as he thrust them up into my sex. He tried putting his whole fist in, but I was too tight, so he opted instead to let three of his fingers violate me, almost punching their way up into me in a bid to make me hurt somewhere else. Somewhere new. A pain all his own doing.

I panted in shallow, steady breaths, trying to block out what was happening, and let my head fall to one side, staring across the room in a daze.

There was a blur over by the doorway, but I didn't let myself hope it was Tobin come to save me a second time. He had to either be dead or still unconscious out on the driveway. I figured I must be seeing things, but then Calvin suddenly stopped what he was doing and turned away.

I then heard a great thud and a voice suddenly calling my name.

I couldn't place the voice, but knew I'd heard it before. It was soft, like an angel, and I looked up to see my sister standing over me. Dita was stunning. I knew then that she'd come to watch over me in my hour of need. That had to be it.

"You're so beautiful," I told her as she covered me up again and she took me in her arms, cradling me like a child against her chest. I gripped her tightly, feeling surprised how real she felt. "I want us to be together, Dita. Have you come to take me back to heaven with you?" I asked, feeling ready to give into the pain. To let the darkness wash over me and take me away. She shushed me, stroking my hair, and I relaxed into her embrace.

"Liev," I heard her call, but I was already slipping out of consciousness. "Finish it, Liev. End him," she said, and I had to wonder why an angel would command death but didn't ask. I knew why. He had to be her unfinished business. The thing binding her to our world. Mine too, so I was glad he wouldn't survive, even if I also had to leave my family and friends behind to ensure it.

"With pleasure," I heard the deep, heavily accented voice answer. Then there was a loud snapping sound, followed by nothing but the panting of breath. Silence descended and so too did the last shreds of my conscious thought.

I breathed her in, my angel, soaking up the feel of her arms around me and the sound of her humming breathing. Accepting death, I then simply let go.

Epilogue

When I came around, it was four days later, and I was in a hospital bed. My body was indeed broken in many places, as I was informed the moment I awoke and tried in vain to move. The doctor told me I'd suffered multiple fractures and breaks, as well as the bruising to my neck from the strangulation by the belt and, of course, the whipping Calvin had given me with it. He waited until a nurse was present to discuss the rape with me, and I was glad to discover Calvin hadn't left me with any scars or bruises there. I was assured a counsellor would also visit me, but I didn't want to talk about it. I didn't want it to be real.

They also wouldn't let my family see me until I'd spoken with a police officer about what'd happened, but I was too confused about the whole thing to give a proper statement, anyway. She had no choice but to leave me to rest, promising to come back again later when I was feeling better.

Dad came through first, and he could barely look at me as he took a seat beside my hospital bed.

"Is Tobin okay?" I asked before anything else. I had to know and began shaking and crying the second my dad nodded his head yes.

"He's still in a medically induced coma after a considerable blow to the head, but the doctors say he's gonna be fine. Did he fall from the window?" he asked, and I nodded.

"Well, he was pushed," I answered, groaning as a shot of pain stopped me in my attempt to reposition myself on the bed.

"By Calvin?" Dad checked, and I nodded. "What happened, Dahlia?"

"He raped me," I croaked, and my usually so calm and collected father coughed on a sob and buried his face in his hands. "He had been messing with me for months, toying with me because I found out it was him who'd hurt Dita, but I had no idea he was going to turn nasty."

"Then what?"

"Tobin found him hurting me and they fought. I thought he'd won, but then Calvin pushed him out the window and came back for more from me. I ran but fell down the stairs," I answered, but wasn't sure how to continue. Should I incriminate Liev in his part of Calvin's demise? Should I tell him about my hallucination of Dita? I closed my eyes and saw her in my mind's eye again. I inhaled, remembering her smell and the feel of her. So real, and yet it couldn't have been, surely?

Suddenly, realisation struck. She hadn't been a mirage at all. She'd been real. Not an angel sent to take me to heaven with her, but a living and breathing person along with the man she loved and had run away with. Dita wasn't dead. She'd been hiding from her abuser, but more than that, she'd run away from all of us and only returned when she knew I was in real danger. She wasn't dead at all…

I knew I might never truly know her reasons for

having faked her death, but I was going to honour the decision she had made to run from her past. From the club. From our father and brothers. From me. Whether I understood or agreed with her or not, the fact remained that Dita and Liev had saved my life that day and I owed it to them not to reveal their secrets.

"How did Calvin die?" Dad asked, breaking my thoughtfulness.

"I killed him," I answered, and saw the doubt in his eyes. "Tobin had done a number on him and when he tried to take me again, I guess I went into fight-or-flight mode or something, because I went crazy. Snapped his neck somehow and then I fell down and I guess I passed out."

"Good story," he answered, and I could tell he knew there was more to it than I was getting at, but he seemed ready to let me keep my secrets, for the time being at least. "That adds up. Tell the police the same as you told me, okay?"

"Okay," I replied, nodding.

Tobin was woken up the following day and while it was hard, we talked things through and left the hospital together a few days later. I had crutches, and we were told to go home and rest, which was exactly what we did. We stayed at Dad's place, neither of us wanting to head back to the new clubhouse quite so soon after our ordeal, but I was determined to still make it our home one day. To erase the bad memories and make new ones there, together.

The pair of us were inseparable after that, needing the comfort and security the other gave, and slowly we found our way back to being the happy, hopeful couple we'd been before Calvin's attack. I told Tobin everything and let him read Dita's diaries. He had to know all how things had become so dangerous for us, even about Nico and his secret relationship with Calvin. Tobin was shocked to find out the truth but was also too loyal to Nico to so much as threaten him with telling everyone the truth, and so we kept it our secret. We let my big brother have his life back and get himself ready to become a father and husband to two people who deserved to have all of him. We moved on, slowly and yet surely.

Calvin wasn't going to win, and I was pleased when his death was deemed self-defence. I took the blame for murdering my rapist and promised myself I'd never tell anyone otherwise. That I would protect the secret Dita had jeopardised by coming to my rescue.

In fact, once my arm wasn't throbbing anymore, and I felt up to typing, I opened Dita's old laptop and decided to tell her that too. I'd come to realise that Liev wasn't Jane Doe at all. Dita was.

I wanted her to know I'd keep her secrets safe. That she didn't need to run again. That I understood. So, I told her, by the only way I could. Via Jane Doe and her fake profile.

I know what I saw was no apparition or angelic hallucination after all. You were real. You're alive, and you chose to come and save me. I'm so glad you did, Dita. I'm so grateful that you protected me, because now I can honour your memory properly by living a happy life, knowing you're doing the same wherever you and Liev end up. If you want to stay gone, I'll let you, but please know that I love you and will never forget the secrets you shared with me.

I miss you.
I love you.
Goodbye.

The end.

About the author

LM Morgan started her writing career putting together short stories and fan fiction, usually involving her favourite movie characters caught up in steamy situations and wrote her first full-length novel in 2013. A self-confessed computer geek, LM enjoys both the writing and editing side of her journey, and regularly seeks out the next big gadget on her wish list. She spends her days with her husband looking after her two young children and their cocker spaniel Milo, as well as making the most of her free time by going to concerts with her friends, or else listening to rock music at home while writing (a trend many readers may have picked up on in her stories.)

Like many authors, LM has a regular playlist of tracks she enjoys listening to while writing, featuring the likes of Slipknot, Stone Sour, Papa Roach, Five Finger Death Punch, and Shinedown. If you'd like to listen along with her, you can find her Spotify playlist by searching for 'writing dark romance'.

LM also loves hearing from her fans, and you can connect with her via the following:

www.lmauthor.com

If you enjoyed this book, please take a moment to share your thoughts by leaving a review to help promote LM's work.

LM Morgan's novels include:

The Black Rose series:
When Darkness Falls: A Short Prequel to the Black Rose series (Permanently FREE)
Embracing the Darkness: book 1 in the Black Rose series
A Slave to the Darkness: book 2 in the Black Rose series
Forever Darkness: book 3 in the Black Rose series
Destined for Darkness: book 4 in the Black Rose series
A Light in the Darkness: book 5 in the Black Rose series
Don't Pity the Dead, Pity the Immortal: Novella #1
Two Worlds, One War: Novella #2
Taming Ashton: Novella #3

And her contemporary romance novels:
Forever Lost (gangster/crime)
Forever Loved (gangster/crime follow on from Forever Lost)
Rough Love (MC crime/mystery story. Can be read as a stand-alone)
Ensnared – A dark romance (Permanently FREE via LM's webpage)
Tommy's Girl parts one and two (dark psychological thriller)
Dark Nights and White Lights: A collection of short stories, flash fiction and poems

LM also writes YA Science Fiction under the alias LC Morgans, with her new novels:
Humankind: Book 1 in the Invasion Days series
Autonomy: Book 2 in the Invasion Days series
Resonant: Book 3 in the Invasion Days series

Hereafter: Book 4 in the Invasion Day series
Renegades: Book 5 in the Invasion Day series

LM also writes dark vampire fantasy under the alias Eden Wildblood, with her new novels:
The Beginning: Book 1 in the Blood Slave series
Round Two: Book 2 in the Blood Slave series
Made of Scars: Book 3 in the Blood Slave series
Even in Death: Book 4 in the Blood Slave series
Tortured Souls: Book 5 in the Blood Slave series

Printed in Great Britain
by Amazon